SKIES OF FREEDOM

SKIES OF FREEDOM

A Political Novel

Sven R. Larson

RESOURCE *Publications* · Eugene, Oregon

SKIES OF FREEDOM
A Political Novel

Resource Publications
An Imprint of Wipf and Stock Publishers
199 W. 8th Ave., Suite 3
Eugene, OR 97401

www.wipfandstock.com

PAPERBACK ISBN: 978-1-6667-3645-8
HARDCOVER ISBN: 978-1-6667-9473-1
EBOOK ISBN: 978-1-6667-9474-8

JANUARY 24, 2022 9:22 AM

THIS BOOK IS DEDICATED TO

Mr. Emmek Rohax, who used his vast fortune to spread freedom throughout the galaxy,

and

those who died in the fight for the freedom of the Ripoman people.

A warning had been given to the refugees in the camp. One of the watchmen had spotted something in the clearing among the trees, a hundred leaps away from the camp. He had spotted movement—but by what? Soldiers?

Had the military finally tracked them down? Were the soldiers coming to kill them all?

All able-bodied men were on the alert, armed as best they could, quietly awaiting the approach of the enemy. The women sat in silence, their eyes anxiously sweeping the forest, searching the lingering darkness for something, anything, that could be a threat to them. Sitting still, dead silent, they breathed through their noses. They had been told that it helped them stay calm under stress.

The mothers gently held their hands over their babies' mouths, clutching them with their other arm to keep them warm, comfortable.

And quiet.

One of the men, older with a grey beard and a bald head, quietly turned and looked over at the women. The white skin on his face was marked by scars of battles, harsh weather—and grief. His brown eyes were tired from having seen too much pain and suffering.

Evil deeds by evil men.

But his back was still straight. Despite having celebrated 70 birthdays he still walked tall and proud. His fist, when clenched, was still hard and firm. Like his handshake.

And his determination to bring this group of men, women, and children to freedom.

He glanced at the babies. He could tell that the mothers were worried about the babies. About them crying.

The slightest sound, and . . .

But the babies didn't cry. It was almost as if even the babies understood what was at stake. Even they sensed the danger. The fear. The desperate need to be quiet.

Maybe they also sensed the hope. Soon, their ticket to freedom would arrive.

The old man nodded slightly. He gave away a faint smile to the mother closest to him. She smiled back. Only for a second, but she did.

He turned and looked down toward the opening, down where one of the watchmen had spotted movement. The dark of night was slowly giving way to dawn. The wind was still making its way through the forest. If he squinted, he could see the watchman who had alerted them.

A sign. A flash with a handheld light. Two more flashes.

The old man sighed with relief and tapped the shoulder of a younger man, hunkering down next to him. The old man pointed toward the opening. The younger man pulled out his pocket telescope and looked down in the direction the old man was pointing. The watchman was coming up toward the camp. He made a victory sign.

"No soldiers" said the old man and sighed with relief.

The younger man smiled and said, joyfully:

"Looks like . . . they . . . have finally arrived."

He was shorter than the old man and not even half his age. When they set out on this journey, he had been a bit heavy set and not very athletic. But the strenuous conditions of their long trek through the mountains had forced him to lose weight. His dark hair and dark beard had grown longer and wilder.

In the old days, before their journey, he would have cared a great deal how he looked. He would have had a special trimmer for his beard, and an extra coupon card with his hairdresser and carefully chosen clothes that matched in both style and color.

That was then. Out here, on their trail to freedom, all that mattered was to reach that spot, a hundred leaps away—and embark on the final part of their journey to freedom.

"Tell them they can relax" the old man said.

The watchman arrived:

"It wasn't the enemy," he said, still breathing hard from the rapid march up the slope. "It's them. They just landed!"

The moment had arrived. The old man felt a surge of joy from within. He, who had not smiled more than a few seconds in the last moons; who had lost friends to tragedy and peril along the trek; he, who was the Ripoman government's most wanted man . . . he finally had a reason to feel unmitigated joy.

He turned and looked out over the camp.

There were 60 refugees there. They barely fit in the shallow pit where they had set up their primitive camp. Eight young couples with children accounted for 38 of them. Two more couples without children. The rest were individuals from all backgrounds.

They all looked at the old man. He stood on the edge of the pit, looking out over them. He sensed their faith in him. Even as the first rays of sunshine scrambled to climb over the horizon, he still could not make out all their faces in the darkness, but he knew what they said.

Faith. Freedom or death.

They placed their lives in his hands. Their children's lives.

He had a small boulder to his right and some dense shrubbery to the left. Right behind him was one of the oldest, largest trees in the forest. A thick, dark trunk stretched its arms and its crown up toward the sky, fighting all the other trees for daytime sunlight.

The trees rested through the night. Now that the moon was giving up the skies to the sun, it was almost as if the trees woke up again and began striving for that precious sunlight.

"Armo!" a voice whispered right next to him.

He turned to the sound of his name. It was Strebber, the young man with the dark hair and the unruly beard.

"There! Down there!"

He pointed toward the opening in the trees way down at the bottom of the slope. Armo Torndale looked. And smiled again.

"It's her," he almost laughed. "And she is carrying a big bag."

Strebber frowned. Then his face turned into a smile.

"I see," he said. "She is bringing us something."

Torndale nodded.

"Probably food rations."

"That's good."

"Not entirely."

"Why not?"

"It means she knows we will have to remain here for some time."

❈ ❈ ❈

LOPUTON, THE CAPITAL of the People's Democratic Union of Ripoma, sat on the shoreline of the Silver Sea, the enormous ocean that stretched almost halfway across the planet. The Epinaq river split the city in half, with downtown and the federal government buildings clustering to both sides of the river.

The city was partly protected from the ocean weather by two large islands further out from the coast. They took the brunt of the storms that often roared in from the Silver Sea, but from time to time, big storms made it all the way in, drenched the capital city in rain during the summer and buried it in snow in the winter.

State Security had built its headquarters at the northern edge of what was defined as downtown, or the central district of Loputon. It was a large complex, stretching across three city blocks, with two block-size parking facilities attached to it.

Armo Torndale had lived in Loputon most of his professional life. He was originally from down south, from the Riverlands, where the weather was milder, where it almost never snowed and the storms they saw were a breeze compared to what winters could be like in Loputon. His brother still lived down there and always asked Armo when he was planning on moving away from those hideous winters. Armo Torndale replied that he didn't really mind the winters, but that he would probably move back when he retired. After all, he had no family of his own, but his brother had four children and was beginning to see grandkids come into the family. Would be nice to be closer to them when the working years were over.

For the longest time he had not wanted those working years to end. He had loved his job with the national intelligence bureau. It was a purposeful job where he did something good for his country. But that was back when Ripoma was a federal republic. Now, since the People's Democratic Union had replaced the old republic, things had changed. And not for the better. The old agency had merged with the national police service and two other, smaller agencies and become State Security.

But Torndale still went to work every day. He did his job as diligently and dutifully as he could. He had reached a high rank, Group Commander with the investigative division, and was entrusted with some of the most sensitive investigations that the agency encountered. He had many agents under his command and sometimes joked that some days he felt more like a personnel manager than a security investigator.

This day started just like that. He had called in two junior agents to his office.

Personnel matters were boring. He tried to make them more enjoyable in whichever way he could. But he also had to maintain his professional integrity and—especially—make sure they respected, perhaps even feared his rank.

He leaned back in his chair, toyed with a pen and looked at his two subordinates across the desk. He examined them carefully, doing his best not to give away any of his thoughts. For a moment he thought about appearing annoyed or concerned, to give them the idea that this was a serious matter. But he had always had a hard time amusing himself at other people's expense.

His two subordinates waited quietly. They were both sitting with their arms tightly to their bodies, their legs closely together. Mouths shut, eyes cautiously trying to find some expression in the face of their superior, a clue to why they had been called in to his office.

Commander Torndale looked at the woman. She seemed a bit more confident than the man. She was tall, almost as tall as Torndale. Her background in athletics had given her a toned, muscular body that made her look naturally confident.

Normally, she was confident. In fact, her confidence and belief in herself often outsized her rank. For this reason, Torndale found it a little bit difficult from time to time to work with her.

This morning, however, she was not all that confident. Her face gave her away. Her eyes were fixed on the commander. Her eyebrows were raised, not lowered. If they had been lowered, she would have been irritated, annoyed, impatient or even combative. With her eyebrows raised, she signaled that she was cooperative, accommodative, eager to listen to him, whatever he had to say.

The man next to her did not sit as tall as she did. He was leaning forward, if only slightly, his face turned a little bit down. He looked up at Commander Torndale, he too with his eyebrows lifted a bit.

They were both the same age, about 30. Less than half Armo Torndale's age. He was ranks above them and wore a much nicer uniform than they did. His was graphite with dark blue accents. Theirs were light grey with dark grey accents.

They both apparently thought that this was indeed a serious matter. Little did they know it was just a trivial case of temporary personnel reassignment. The formal term was "secondment", a word Armo Torndale thought of using just for fun. Then again . . .

He did not want to keep them waiting any longer. He wanted to get this matter off his desk and move on to something more interesting.

Perhaps he would have thought differently, had he known that this boring administrative matter would mark the beginning of the end of his own career.

He had angled himself at about 45 degrees to the table. He had to turn his head to the right to see them. When he turned to the left, he looked out the big window to the south and the city center. Even though they were on the seventh floor, they still saw the tops of some of the trees in the park outside. Beyond them, the city took shape, first with lower, older houses, then with taller buildings of modern architecture.

Torndale was a tall man, about 6'4". Once upon a time his hair had been blond, but it had given way to the grey that came with age. He had brown eyes and a face with prominent character traits and what looked like a battle scar. He was clean-shaven and his hair was very short.

Torndale could tell that his two subordinates were getting impatient. Soon, one of them would ask a question. He bet it would be the woman.

As much as he liked exercising his authority, especially over junior agents, he also did not like playing games with people. He certainly did not want to play a game just for the sake of playing it.

He swiveled his chair a little bit until he faced them. He leaned forward on his elbows, clasped his hands and gave the two one last quiet look before he said:

"I went over your files this morning to brush myself up on the two of you. I am impressed with your commitment and professionalism."

The woman's face shifted immediately. The attentive attitude gave way to confidence. She lowered her eyebrows and looked at him with eyes that were inquisitive more than cautious.

The man also reacted positively to his words. He nodded slightly and seemed to smile just a little bit. He looked around the desk as if to relieve some stress.

His eyes fell on Torndale's right hand. It had a scar from his knuckles across his wrist into the arm of the uniform shirt.

Armo Torndale noted his curiosity.

"You never saw that before, did you?"

The young man looked up.

"Uh, sorry, sir . . . no, I didn't . . . "

"It's a memory from a field operation."

"I didn't mean to be . . . "

"It's from my time with covert field operations."

He quickly shifted attitude and became more authoritative.

"But let me get to why I wanted to talk to the two of you," he said in a deeper and more formal voice. "As you know, working for the investigative division, we have recently seen a surge in cases involving seditionists. To handle that we have expanded recruitment. And as I am sure you know, the academy has so many new students that they are in desperate need of more instructional staff. All divisions are short on staff . . . operations especially, apprehending all the seditionists we investigate, but we are also stretched thin. Even administration is working overtime. We really can't spare any senior agents at this time. Therefore, Storm Commander Kolmov has decided that we should reassign junior agents instead."

A fly came humming from behind him into the air between him and his two subordinates. He looked at it, waited for the exact right moment, then smashed it between his palms. It fell on his desk. He grabbed it by one of its wings and tossed it into his waste basket.

"I am temporarily reassigning the two of you to the instructional division," he continued. "It was not too long ago you yourselves graduated from the academy, but your performance has been good, so I feel confident that you have what it takes to educate our new recruits. You will report to Doctor Smersch. He is in charge of teaching assignments over there."

He casually pointed in the direction of the north side of the building.

"I spoke to him this morning. You, Mic Olgar . . . "

He looked at the male officer.

"Yes, sir."

"You will be teaching political theory. And you, Eda Strebber, will be assigned to teach a theory class on sedition."

"Thank you, sir," Eda Strebber replied with a grain of confidence in her voice.

"How is your husband?" Armo Torndale asked her.

"Well, thank you."

"Has he recovered from that bike accident?"

"Yes, sir, thank you. He is home from the hospital."

"Good," Torndale said and returned to his notes.

"Sir . . . " Olgar interrupted.

"Yes?"

"I am honored by the trust, of course . . . the trust you have in my . . . in our teaching skills. But doesn't the agency require you to have a doctorate to teach theory classes?"

"Normally, yes. But Doctor Smersch will be the supervisor for your teaching. He will be responsible for the quality of your instructional work. You will report to him as soon as we are done here."

He paused artfully.

"If you do well," he added slowly, "it means faster rank promotion."

That was the sugary part. He leaned back again in his chair and added:

"If, on the other hand, you do a poor job . . . well . . . you will be sorting mail for the rest of your careers."

Another artful pause. A brief smile follows by a very serious face:

"Or worse," he added.

❄ ❄ ❄

THE REFUGEES IN THE CAMP in the forest quietly shared the excitement over the news that "they" had arrived. Most of them still only had an abstract idea of who "they" were, but they trusted Armo Torndale and his deputy, Rhem Strebber.

The new food rations were warmly welcome. The men shared their rations with the women, giving more to those who had children. The food was basic and did not taste much, but nobody complained. They had been going for days on end with only one meal and a small snack per day. The adults had focused on feeding the children, to a point where some of them were beginning to suffer symptoms of malnutrition. For the most part, the symptoms were still mild, and hopefully the low level of nutrition would not leave anyone with permanent scars, but they also knew that they could not go for much longer without eating adequately again.

Armo Torndale knew this more than most. For the past four days he had only eaten half of his rations, splitting the rest between two mothers with children. At his age, it was not a good thing to make a habit of, but he also thought that the children mattered more than he did. They were the future, the ones who would reap the harvest of freedom that they were sowing. They would build an grow a new colony on a distant planet.

It was all going to turn out well, once they had been evacuated from this mountain top.

Torndale had succeeded in leading the group to this point; if he did not make it onboard the spaceship, but the children and their parents did, he could die in peace.

The woman who brought them the food was a Danori. She was the liaison between Torndale and the refugees on the one hand, and the organization for refugee settlement on the other. She assured Torndale that there would very soon be enough to eat for all of them.

"I will bring more," she said.

She was tall and slender, with grey, almost blue-ish skin. She had a tall face with a protruding forehead, a small nose and a thin but sharply visible mouth. Her ears were long and slim, following the contours of the skull almost to the neck. Her eyes were brightly blue, and she had no hair on her head. Her arms were long and thin, as were the five fingers on her hands.

She was dressed in slim, black pants and a dark jacket with a hood. When she had gotten close enough to the pit, she had pulled down the hood, taken off a pair of protective glasses and made eye contact with Armo Torndale. He had acknowledged and they had met about ten leaps from the pit. He very gratefully received the bag with the food rations.

Strebber had never met a Danori before. He stood on the edge of the pit, next to the big rock that looked like a pulpit and looked at her in amazement.

And with poorly contained fear.

Torndale trained his flashlight on Strebber.

"She is here to help us," he said. "Fear not. Make sure everyone gets food."

He handed Strebber the bag. Strebber did not react at first. Then he looked at Torndale in confusion, shook his head, remembered where he was, and why.

"I am sorry," he mumbled. "I just didn't know . . . "

"What a Danori looks like" Torndale smiled. "Now you know."

While Strebber began distributing the food, Torndale went back down to the Danori woman. She was a smidge taller than him. She stood with her hands clasped in front of her, eyes moving between Strebber and Torndale.

Over time, Torndale had learned a great deal about her and her species. They were known for excellent night vision. They had very quick reflexes, ran fast and were highly intelligent.

They were also reliable people, adamant about keeping promises and sticking to agreements. Perhaps their only weakness was their physique:

they were not nearly as strong as humans, which made them reluctant to coming near anyone who was not of their species. On the rare occasions they interacted with humans, they preferred to keep a good distance.

Armo Torndale was an exception. He and the Danori woman had met many times. It was not at the level where he would call her a friend, but he knew her name, her job, some of her educational background, who she represented, what planet she came from and that she had three brothers and a sister.

Torndale saw a faint smile move across her face.

"Thank you," he said.

"I am glad to see you here," she said. "It has been a long journey."

"It has not been easy."

"You look weak. Tired? What is the right word?"

"You surprise me sometimes," Torndale smiled. "You speak our language so well, and yet on occasion you are at loss for words. I guess when I learn your language . . . "

He looked at her. She nodded, clearly amused at the thought of him trying to master her native language.

"I think 'exhausted' is the word you are looking for," he said. "I am drained of energy . . . my will is stronger than my body. I feel inadequate."

"Inadequate? Not enough? Why?"

"There is so much more I could do."

"You put too heavy a burden on yourself," she said and tilted her head slightly. "Interesting. Male characteristics are the same regardless of species. My brothers also do that."

Torndale glanced over his shoulder. Strebber returned with the empty food bag. Torndale gave him a thumbs up and turned to his Danori friend:

"I need to ask. How long will we have to wait here? You mentioned bringing more food."

"Tomorrow. We have to evacuate your group in portions."

"What is the hold-up? I thought the ship had arrived. You are here . . . "

"I arrived with a small shuttle craft. The ship that can take you all onboard is in orbit, but not allowed to enter your solar system."

"Not allowed to? I don't understand."

"Legal reasons," she said matter-of-factly.

"You have no formal relations with our government," Torndale noted. "Yes, informal relations, but . . . you should not need their permission to land. Besides, they don't have the technology to detect you."

"You are correct," she nodded. "We don't need their permission. But we need the approval of our own central directorate, the executive body of The Rohax Freedom Foundation. We are a private organization, privately funded, but our projects, to help build new colonies on new worlds, are in cooperation with our government. We have to comply with their laws. One of them is about non-interference with indigenous societies. The evacuation of refugees is technically interference, but there is an exception clause in the law, which says that where a totalitarian regime reaches a certain level in its oppression, it is permissible to evacuate dedicated refugees in small numbers."

A bird flew by, chirping merrily. The Danori woman looked up.

"It's just a happy little bird," Armo Torndale explained.

She looked at him for a second, apparently not sure whether to believe him or not.

"The exception clause is restrictive," she continued. "We had to make a strong case to the government agency for refugee resettlement that your group falls under the exception clause. We obtained a preliminary approval, which is why I let you know that you could start your journey to get here. I was hoping to have had the official approval two days ago, but it was delayed. The delay is not related to us, just other matters of higher, more urgent priorities. A civil war on a world in a distant sector. Our representatives are about to go into a meeting with officials from the resettlement agency. I have no reason to believe they will deny us the formal go-ahead at this point."

Armo Torndale chuckled. The woman looked confused.

"What is amusing?" she asked, genuinely bewildered.

"You have a bureaucracy that is getting in the way of a good project," Armo Torndale explained. "As you said, we have a lot in common."

❈ ❈ ❈

DOCTOR SMERSCH WAS AN EFFICIENT MAN in every way possible. He was short, clean shaven and built like a long-distance runner. He kept his brown hair in very short trim and wore minimal glasses. The officers of lower ranks at the instructional division, where he was the curricular manager, knew him as the two-word man. When they approached Doctor Smersch with a question, he rarely gave an answer longer than two words.

Higher-ranking officers, of course, got a lot more out of him. But as Group Commander, the same rank as Armo Torndale, he did not have that many superiors.

The two adjutants who had been sent to Doctor Smersch's office by Torndale, had only heard Doctor Smersch speak in entire sentences when he was lecturing. He gladly lectured both students in the agency training program, and junior colleagues.

"Doctor Smersch's office is on the fifth floor," Adjutant Olgar noted as they walked away from Torndale's office.

"Over in the north extension," Adjutant Eda Strebber added.

"Political theory," Olgar said, almost as if the was thinking out loud. "That's an interesting class. I liked how we got to review our nation's value foundation in the context of alternative political theories."

"You liked that?" Eda Strebber asked, seemingly surprised.

"I liked the perspective. Different viewpoints help you better understand the superior one."

"I would have preferred it that they just taught the value foundation and no other political theory," Eda Strebber replied. "One story, easy to tell right from wrong. No room for doubts."

"Oh, I have no doubts about right and wrong," Olgar added quickly. "But I find that it is easier to understand the right when you also get to know the wrong."

"That's why I like the sedition class. Sedition is such a clear concept. Either you commit an act of sedition, or you don't. Either you oppose government, or you don't."

They went down the first flight of stairs.

"But surely, you will explain to them that the definition of sedition has expanded over the years," Olgar suggested. "We use a broader term now, a much broader term, than they did under the federal republic."

"What do you mean?"

"Back then, it was not considered sedition to be opposed to government in general. Sedition was an active attempt to overthrow the existing government."

"Expressing disagreement with your government is the first step toward overthrowing it."

The second flight of stairs was slower. A group of senior officers were walking up. Olgar and Eda Strebber stood in silent honor position as they passed. None of the superior officers took any notice of them.

Doctor Smersch barely said a word. He pointed to his visitors' chairs and had them sit in quiet while he reviewed their files. His face remained completely neutral as he examined their work history, their evaluations from superiors and their loyalty rankings from the Office of Internal Review.

He nodded absentmindedly as he skimmed through the last section of each file.

"Mhm . . . " he mumbled and put both files on his desk.

He looked up, studied Eda Strebber's face, then Olgar's face, then he looked down again at the two files and took a deep breath. Slowly leaning back in his chair, he examined a spot on the wall behind the two adjutants.

"So," he said in a slightly raspy voice. "Armo thinks you can teach."

They sat quietly, waiting for his next line. They knew better than to try to have a conversation with Doctor Smersch. Not only was he a Group Commander like Torndale, but he also held a doctorate from the national military academy. It was considered even more prestigious than a doctorate from a civilian university.

Doctor Smersch outranked them, both formally and academically. In addition to that, his almost universal unwillingness to engage in conversations with anyone made him an intimidating character. Adjutants and other lower-rank officers felt more comfortable talking to any other Group Commander, especially Commander Torndale, than to Doctor, Commander Smersch.

In fact, it wasn't even a matter of talking to Doctor Smersch. It was a matter of absolute attention and compliance, and nothing else.

Which was exactly how Doctor Smersch preferred things to be. It made his job easier.

"You are both teaching theory classes," he said slowly. "Some think theory classes don't matter. I do."

He made an artful pause.

"I think they matter a great deal," he continued. "Theory classes teach our cadets the importance of our nation's value foundation. A good understanding and appreciation of our nation's value foundation is the backbone of our agents' loyalty, both to the agency and to our government."

He paused again. Eda Strebber was nodding approvingly. Olgar was also nodding, but not as emphatically. Doctor Smersch found that curious.

"Adjutant Olgar," he said.

"Yes, sir!"

"The class that you will be teaching, on political theory, is instrumental in building loyalty among our cadets."

"Of course, sir."

"You cannot leave them with any doubt about the superiority of our nation's value foundation."

Olgar glanced for a split second at Eda Strebber. She sat straight and confident in her chair. She looked straight ahead, but he noted a smirk on her face.

"Absolutely, sir," Olgar said, trying to sound eager and committed.

Doctor Smersch examined him for a moment.

"You seem a little doubtful, Adjutant Olgar," Doctor Smersch noted.

"No, sir . . . I . . . it's just that I haven't been instructing before, and . . . I'm just a little bit nervous."

Doctor Smersch relaxed.

"Well, if that's all, then I can certain understand."

"Thank you, sir."

"Prepare carefully. And ask me if you have any questions."

"I definitely will do that, sir."

"Adjutant Strebber."

"Yes, sir."

"You are teaching sedition. This class did not exist when I was in the academy. It was created when we transitioned from the federal republic to the people's democratic union. You both took this class, but it has evolved further since then. In fact, this class is quintessential to building loyalty among the students. It is a class that explains to students why any opposition to our government is also an act of sedition. It also explains the difference between sedition and insurrection. These are the two key terms in identifying individuals who have or may harbor any intent to overthrow our government."

"Yes, sir," Eda Strebber agreed forcefully.

"When you instruct, you will be using a lot of cases that the students are supposed to learn from. They are supposed to learn the theory behind the sedition and insurrection charges, and they are supposed to learn it by applying the theory to actual cases."

"I understand completely, sir."

"Good. Now, normally these students take political theory before they take sedition, but our recruitment of new cadets has been so successful that we need to be more flexible, in order to get all through the academy.

Therefore, you will have some students who take your classes concurrently. It is important that the two of you coordinate. The students must understand how the theory of sedition is derived from our nation's value foundation."

He reached for a stack of syllabi in his drawer.

"Here are your syllabi. Read them carefully."

"Yes, sir," the two adjutants replied in unison.

"Good. My junior adjutant will hand you the relevant textbooks. Any questions? No? That will be all."

It was lunch time when they left Doctor Smersch's office. They went to the junior officers' cantina in the basement, a rather utilitarian facility with light green walls, narrow windows in a row just below the ceiling, and furniture made mostly of metal and plastic. The floor was fully water resistant with drainages along the two outer walls.

"I have always wondered what those drainages are for," Olgar said absentmindedly.

Eda Strebber followed his eyes.

"Oh," she said, "you don't know?"

"No."

"When they first built this new headquarters, just after the foundation of the People's Democratic Union, they used this room as a holding facility for seditionists."

"But why would they need such large drainages? And this floor? You could hose it."

Eda Strebber looked him in the eyes. She was a stately woman with a straight back and piercing eyes. She made a strong impression on anyone, even senior officers.

"What do you think they hosed off the floor?" she asked in a hushed voice as they lined up for their food rations.

Olgar frowned at first, then looked startled for a second before he nodded and glanced again at the drainages.

"I see," he almost whispered.

"Once they started bringing seditionists here, and in similar facilities around the country," Eda Strebber explained, "their numbers dwindled quite rapidly. Fewer and fewer people were interested in opposing government. I guess people realized that once you were arrested for it, you would never return again."

The standard food rations for the day were poultry-based and included a hardboiled egg from the redwing river bird. As they sat down, Olgar told Eda Strebber about how during his childhood he had spent a lot of time at his grandparents' house on the Superior Plains up north. The redwing river bird was abundant in the river valley. His grandfather had kept domesticated redwings for their eggs, which were large and tasty. The redwing itself was an ill-tempered bird that would protest loudly whenever someone came near it, but other than that it was easy to keep.

"I grew up in Orwell," Eda Strebber replied. "District 1984."

"That's a nice place."

"I'm not sure I would agree," Eda Strebber laughed, but with a slightly condescending undertone. "Small town, mostly backward people with a backward value system. No understanding of progressive, democratic thinking."

She spoke forcefully, as if to broaden the audience beyond their conversation. Olgar glanced over his shoulder and spotted two cappers, second rank. That explained Eda Strebber's grasp for attention. She was ambitious and made no secret of it. They had worked together for four years in different parts of State Security. Olgar was familiar with her professionalism, but also with her desire to climb the ladder at the agency.

He decided to change the subject of their conversation.

"Shall we take a look at our textbooks?" he suggested. "I believe the first chapter is identical. It is about the value foundation for the People's Democratic Union."

Both books were fresh from the printer. The chapter on the value foundation was dense and heavily footnoted. Olgar looked at its first two sentences and smiled.

"On the fourteenth day of the year sixteen sixty-five, Grand Chancellor Sorto swept away the old federal republic and sent it into the dusty corners of our shameful past. That day marked the birth of the People's Democratic Union of Ripoma, which brought true democracy to our people."

"A day for all of us to be proud of," Eda Strebber quickly replied, again glancing over at the cappers.

"Forever and ever," Olgar agreed emphatically.

❊ ❊ ❊

Armo Torndale took some time to rest. The Danori woman had left and returned to her spaceship. He laid down, closed his eyes and dozed off for a few moments. When he woke up, the sun was just about at midday.

He raised his head and looked out over the group. Some were resting, some went quietly about their morning routines. A couple of women nursed their babies. A few were eating, sharing a muted but lighthearted conversation.

Everyone was low key, but they seemed to have faith that their long, arduous journey would finally bring them to freedom.

Strebber was sitting next to Torndale.

"Good morning," Strebber said. "I am glad you got some sleep."

"I was up most of the night. Have you slept?"

"A little bit."

"Get some more sleep. You are going to need it."

"I will," Strebber promised.

Torndale reached for his water bottle. It was half empty. He finished it and laid down on his back. His eyes followed the nearest tree trunks to their crowns. It was easy to tell that the summer was coming to an end: the leaves were still mostly dense and dark green, but a small number of them had begun shifting in yellow.

He had promised his group that they would be on their way to freedom before the season of transition began. But it was not until his Danori friend had visited, that he actually felt confident that it would still happen. This their latest delay would only be a minor bump in the road.

As if reading his thoughts, Strebber moved a little bit closer and asked:

"What do you think, honestly? Do you think it will be much longer?"

"No," Torndale replied without a doubt. "Our Danori friend has the preliminary go-ahead, and she expects to have the final approval within a day or so. They are already here, so I am sure it is only a minor delay."

Strebber was sitting with his legs pulled up and his elbows resting on his knees. He had a piece of wood in his hands that he slowly turned and looked at from different angles. It seemed like a deliberate distraction from something.

"Are you worried?" Torndale asked.

Strebber nodded.

"I'm worried we will be found," he said in a hushed voice. "That all this will be for nothing."

"I share your worry," Torndale admitted. "But this is a very good hiding spot."

"But aren't they looking for us?"

"You mean State Security?"

"Yes."

"They would like to, but they don't have the manpower. Or the resolve."

Strebber looked at him. He was bewildered.

"My wife always said that State Security would hunt down the last seditionist to the end of the world if they . . . if you had to."

Torndale nodded.

"Eda was always a hardliner," he remembered. "Yes, State Security is run by hardliners now. They want to live up to that ambition, but they are stretched thin. Besides, they aren't the military. Most officers in State Security are too lazy to come up here in the mountains. They are career officers and very protective of their jobs. They don't want adventures that could get someone under their command injured or killed."

He paused.

"Not to mention themselves," he added almost sarcastically. "And with officers like that, is it any wonder that the field agents aren't very risk prone either? They all have a cozy life compared to the general public. They get extra rations of almost everything, access to exclusive shopping that the general public can't get to. They are assigned government-provided housing in safe areas. Their children always get good grades in school, because . . . what teacher is going to give a bad grade to the kid of a government employee? It is not easy to get those privileged positions, so once you do you do not want to lose it."

"But how would they lose it? I mean, if they die in the line of duty, don't their families get survivor's pension?"

"Yes, but you can also lose it if you make a mistake. If you fail to capture someone, for example. I worked for the agency both under the federal republic and the new union. Before Sorto declared the new people's union, we operated as a regular security agency. All the employees, well, almost all of them, where in it because they believed in our mission. Self sacrifice was honored. And you have to keep in mind that there were no privileges back then to having a government job."

"I've heard that," Strebber remembered.

"We had price stability, the shops were open for everyone, you made a good living in the private sector, often better than in government. People came to work with the agency because they believed in its mission."

He paused for a moment. Someone came by and left him a note. Armo Torndale read it, nodded to the man and got up.

"There is a mother back there who needs some medical attention," he said. "Do you have a first aid kit?"

The young woman had taken a wrong step while picking berries nearby. She had scraped her calf on a piece of rock and was bleeding. She was sitting on a blanket while an older woman attended to her. The older woman, a former nurse, reassured the young woman that the wound was not serious. The first-aid kid had all the help she needed.

Torndale helped wash the wound but handed the kit over to the former nurse. While she applied the bandage, Torndale talked to the young woman. She was weak and clearly in need of more nutrition.

"Are you not getting enough to eat?" Torndale asked.

"I share some of my rations with Nuri," the young woman replied and pointed to the older woman. "She is an old friend of my mother's. She has no family."

Torndale looked at Nuri. Her face was worn and torn, like his own. Her silver-colored hair was unruly, tied down only partly with an old rubber band. She had a mole on her cheek that did not look good.

Nuri was kneeling, methodically applying the bandage to the young woman's leg. When Torndale looked closer, he noted that Nuri's hands had fine-line lateral markings just below the knuckles, like somebody had cut her with a knife. Her fingers were stiff, and she took her time applying the bandage. She had to turn her entire body to move her arms, so that her hands and fingers could reach around the young woman's leg.

As if noticing Torndale's eyes, Nuri said:

"I used to be much better at this."

"You are doing a fine job, Nuri" the young woman reassured her.

Strebber was standing to the right of Armo Torndale. He, too, examined Nuri's hands. Torndale heard him draw a deep breath as if to quell an urge to ask an uncomfortable question.

When Nuri had completed the bandage she struggled to get up on her feet again. Armo Torndale offered a hand. She looked up and gratefully accepted his assistance. He helped her move to a place where someone had built a makeshift seat from rocks, tree branches and large leaves from the tallest trees in the forest.

Nuri struggled to walk the few short steps, and when she got to the seat she sat down, closed her eyes and took a deep breath.

"Arthritis?" Torndale asked.

"No," she said, slowly relaxing.

She glanced up at him.

"You saw my hands," she said.

"Yes."

"I have more scars than that."

"Those scars . . . was that the EFF?"

She nodded.

"The Equality Frontline Fighters came to the clinic where I was working," she said.

"I know all about them," Armo Torndale assured her

"I know you do," Nuri replied. "With your background."

"We were not allowed to open formal investigations into the EFF, but we monitored them. Those of us who weren't entirely politicized feared that they would go so far out of hand that it could threaten the very stability of the country. It never did, thankfully."

Nuri shook her head.

"Not allowed to investigate," she said quietly. "With all that they did."

"They came to your clinic because you refused to do abortions?"

"It was that, but we also accepted private insurance plans."

"Yes," Torndale said and looked over at Strebber. "The EFF claimed that private insurance was the privilege of the rich."

"And yet, almost everyone had it," Nuri recalled. "The EFF stormed in one morning when we were just opening up. There must have been fifteen of them, all dressed in black and fully masked, of course. They took over the reception desk and forced their way into the treatment area. They were armed with knives and insect spray and other things. They forced everyone out in the common area back there, I think there were six of us in total. We were forced to sit down on the floor. They gathered around us, some of them kicked and hit us to force us to bow our heads. Their leader, I recognized his voice . . . their leader told us that this was our chance to commit to equality in health care. We had heard of these things happening to other clinics, but we never thought it would happen to us. Their leader asked who was in charge of the clinic. Doctor Venuda replied that she was in charge. They pulled her up . . . harshly as if to intentionally harm her . . . and pushed her up against the wall. The leader pulled out an iron rod, perhaps six inches long. He placed it against her throat and pushed until she could not breathe. He demanded that she stop taking the insurance plans of the privileged and the rich, and that instead she open her clinic to the poor."

Strebber wanted to say something, but Torndale waived his hand at him to wait.

"We all tried to reassure them," Nuri continued, "We tried to reassure them that we would happily open our clinic to anyone. It would have been crazy because we wouldn't sustain, but what could we do? Doctor Venuda begged for her life, with panic in her eyes. In the very last second, the leader of that group let her go. She collapsed on the floor. They kicked her again. One of our nurse assistants tried to make them stop. They pulled her up, dragged her into another room . . . and beat her savagely. The rest of us had to identify ourselves and tell them exactly what we did at the clinic. Then the leader asked: "So who provides abortions here?" I answered that our clinic does not provide abortions. They pulled me up and forced me up in front of the leader. He asked . . . and at that time I knew whose voice I was hearing . . . he asked why we weren't doing abortions. I said we weren't set up for it, but he asked if we were against women's rights. I replied, sternly of course, that as a woman, how could I be against women's rights? He got in my face and demanded to know if I was for or against abortions. Personally, I told him, I do not believe that abortion is right."

She paused. Her voice was breaking up. Torndale and Strebber stood as if frozen in time, waiting for the last few words from the woman.

It took a moment. She closed her eyes, swallowed and explained:

"That's where the beating started. They cut across my hands with a scalpel. They said that if I didn't want to provide reproductive health to women, I was not worthy of working as a nurse. So they had the right to cut my hands."

Her voice broke down. Tears filled her cheeks. She cried, quietly, with all the dignity she could summon. Armo Torndale stepped up to her, held her and leaned down to kiss her forehead. He looked her in the eyes, without saying anything. She looked up at him.

They shared the moment until Nuri sighed, wiped her tears and whispered:

"Thank you."

As Torndale and Strebber made their way to the front side of their camp, Strebber could not help but note how moved he himself had been moved by Nuri's story.

"There are thousands of them," Armo Torndale noted. "Thousands of victims with similar stories. What was it you wanted to say before?"

"Before? Oh, right . . . one of the watchmen found a strange object among the trees, not far from here. Let me show you."

❊ ❊ ❊

Olgar was surprised to see that he had been assigned to teach his class in the largest lecture hall the academy had. The only room larger than it was the assembly hall, but the academy never taught classes there.

He had been told that he would only have 30 students in his class. He asked the course administrator in charge of the classroom schedule.

"Yes," said the administrator. "That was the plan. But now you have sixty students."

"What happened?"

The course administrator looked down at her notes and said, in a hushed voice:

"You are taking Adjutant Escher's students as well."

Olgar's first instinct was to ask why, but then he remembered he had not seen Escher in a while. The administrator's voice suggested that he better not ask any more questions.

"Alright," he said, trying to sound as upbeat as he could. "I'm fine with that. But it does give me a bit more work with correcting exams, and all. Can I get some assistance with that?"

"I'll see what I can do," the administrator mumbled, "but no promises."

The lecture hall was bright and roomy with large windows and a tall ceiling. The seats, good enough for a hundred people, were spread out over ten staggered rows. In the front was a pulpit, a large desk with a chair and two large whiteboards. A projector screen was bolted to rails that allowed the lecturer to pull it in from the side, in front of the two whiteboards.

Olgar looked at the students. A muted conversation among them died down as soon as they realized he had entered the door. The sixty of them had spread out almost perfectly evenly across the 100 seats.

They all stood up and saluted him when he walked in.

"Good morning," Olgar said and walked up to the desk in front of the white screen.

"Good morning, adjutant!" the students hailed in unison.

He put his notes, his textbook copy and his communicator on the desk and looked up.

"Sit down," he told them. "We will suspend the formal salutation for the rest of this class. I am Adjutant Olgar, I will be your teacher for this class. Obviously, I have been through the same educational program as you are in now. It has changed a little bit, but it is largely the same. I am currently with the investigative division, on secondment to the academy."

He spent a couple of minutes taking attendance and explaining a couple of practical matters regarding the class. He did it not because he needed to, but because it allowed him to warm up a little bit before he started teaching. It had been a long couple of days preparing, and he was still nowhere near certain that he had gotten everything right.

Nevertheless, here he was. All he could do was dive right into it.

He turned to the nearest whiteboard and wrote with capital letters: DEMOCRACY.

"This word," he said and turned to the students, "is at the core of the value foundation of our people's democratic union. Our nation. When you are fully trained and have graduated from here, it will be your job to defend this value foundation. It will be your duty to track down and apprehend its enemies."

He let those words sink in for a moment before he continued:

"Since this is a class in political theory, the first thing you need to concern yourselves with is to understand what 'democracy' means. And to do so, you first need to forget that it is a word. Because, as your textbook explains with such eloquence, 'democracy' is a term. It is a term that carries within itself an entire value proposition. You will be learning how you as State Security agents can and should apply that meaning in your daily work."

He pulled in the projector screen to a center position. It was right in front of the students when he turned on the projector and pulled up a list of bullet points.

"These bullet points list three questions that help us understand the superiority of our nation's value foundation over any other alternative."

He paused, looked around and smiled.

"You," he said and pointed to a random student. "Read the first bullet point, the first question, out loud."

The student, a young man with dark hair and glasses, looked like he was not sure exactly what to do. Olgar watched him for a moment, then asked:

"Does the first question make you uncomfortable?"

The student did not answer, but he revealed his feeling by giving away an uncomfortable smile.

"I understand," Olgar said. "Don't worry. I think the first question makes you all uncomfortable. So let me read it out loud: 'Should we question our national value foundation?'"

He turned to the students.

"There it is," he said. "What is the answer?"

He turned to a student in the first row.

"Cadet Lennerz," Olgar read his name tag and walked up to the student.

He stopped right in front of him, looked down on him and waited.

"Yes, adjutant," Mr. Lennerz said, revealing discomfort with Olgar's question.

"Why should we question our national value foundation?" Olgar asked.

"We should not, sir," Mr. Lennerz answered.

"Good answer!" Olgar commended him and walked back to his pulpit. "We should not question our national value foundation. You were all a bit uncomfortable when I presented this question, and for good reasons. You have had it engraved into your minds that we do not question our government, because doing so is an act of sedition. Naturally, this question makes you uncomfortable. Cadet Lennerz gave the right answer, but it is only the beginning."

He pointed to the projector screen with a light beam.

"The second bullet point is a proposition. It says: 'Democracy is the rule of the majority'. This bullet point actually answers the question we just asked. Because every alternative to our value foundation means that the majority does not rule. And if the majority does not rule, we do not assign the same value to every individual person."

He looked out over the students. They were all paying close attention. A few looked at the page in their textbooks where this explanation of democracy was found. Some nodded as they followed Olgar's explanation, others took notes.

"In the old federal republic," Olgar continued, "there were features in place to protect minority opinions. The old federal assembly was sometimes unable to pass laws because a minority of assembly members could express dissent and stop the legislative process. Of five hundred assembly members, as few as one could stall the legislative process and prevent a bill from becoming law."

"How did they do that?" one student asked.

"There were various measures in place, one was called 'endless talk'. They could run out the clock on legislation by simply continuing to talk from the podium. Another was a rule that said you had to have two thirds majority to pass certain types of laws, such as a government budget. There were other techniques, too. We did away with those obstructionist techniques when Grand Chancellor Sorto ushered in the new people's democratic union. Today, the majority rules unobstructed. Again, why?"

He tossed the question to the students. A woman up in the back section of the lecture hall raised her hand with some eagerness.

"Yes, Cadet . . . Irmo?"

"Because it is only under majority rule that every person has the same value," she replied with the voice of a student who was seeking the instructor's approval.

"And that's the answer that deserves to be repeated," Olgar replied. "And that is, again, why we don't question our value foundation. But there is one more reason . . . " and he pointed to the bullet point on the projector screen, " . . . namely the universality of rights. Under democracy, under our nation's value foundation, every person in the People's Democratic Union of Ripoma has the exact same rights. We have the right to full nutrition, quality housing, to health care, clothing, transportation, and education. Everyone has the right to economic security, recreation and to an annual quality vacation. Every Ripoman has these rights, regardless of what they do, who they are, whether they work or not. Every Ripoman's rights are being fully provided for by government."

He paused, consulted his notes and nodded. This was the part he was most excited about discussing with the students.

"Now," he said and scanned the room to see if everyone was listening. They were.

"Why, under democracy, does government provide for your rights?"

The students seemed a bit confused.

"The obvious answer," Olgar continued, "is that when you have a right, who else, other than government, would give you what you need and have the right to? It is, plain and simple, government's duty to provide for those rights. I mean, how can you have a right without someone providing for that right?"

Some students nodded. He saw a few smiles of relief. But he also noted one student who seemed to have a question on her mind:

"Cadet Fernek," Olgar addressed her. "You have a question?"

The short, young woman with auburn hair and green eyes cleared her throat and took a deep breath:

"Yes . . . and it is only for historic context . . . "

"Go ahead."

"In the old federal republic, did not the constitution prescribe rights that nobody provided for?"

Olgar had been warned to look for these students. Someone who had read up on the old federal republic could be an avid student who simply wanted a thorough understanding of the value foundation of the people's democratic union. But it could also be a student who had started to stray from the official doctrine of their government.

Olgar personally was fascinated with these contextual questions. Not everyone was, and perhaps not every instructor would have allowed it. Eda Strebber certainly would not have allowed it . . . But Olgar wanted the question to be asked, to be put out there for all the other students to consider.

"Interesting question, Cadet Fernek. Can you give us examples of those rights that people had, but nobody was obligated to provide for?"

"I believe one of them was the right to freedom of speech."

The entire room fell so silent that Olgar could have sworn he heard the footsteps of a spider in a corner somewhere.

"Well," he said and shrugged his shoulders. "You have the right to free speech today."

"But today," Cadet Fernek continued, "that right is provided for by government."

"Of course."

"I was just curious . . . if you wouldn't mind elaborating on the difference."

"The difference between what?"

"Freedom of speech that nobody provides for, and freedom of speech that government provides for."

Olgar looked at her. She looked at him with attention and focus.

He gave away a smile. She smiled back. He wanted to answer her question, but he also knew that it could lead to a dangerous conversation that may have undue influence on some students. They could even start questioning the nation's value foundation, and Olgar certainly was not going to allow that to happen. He may appreciate a broad discussion about political theory, but he was also a trained, loyal agent with State Security.

"I am sorry, Cadet Fernek," he said. "I appreciate the question, but I will have to save it for next time. We have some other material we need to cover today."

When the class was over and the students left, Olgar collected his notes while trying to keep an eye on the inquisitive Miss Fernek. She picked up her things while chatting with another student, but she glanced at him a couple of times.

On her way out she talked with her friend. When she passed Olgar she looked over at him and smiled.

"Cadet Fernek," he said.

She stopped and turned all her attention to him.

"Yes, sir."

"Bye, see you," her friend said.

She nodded to her friend and stayed focused on Olgar.

"I am sorry I didn't have time to answer your question in class," he said.

"Oh, that's OK!"

"But if you want to . . . you can stop by my office instead. That way we get to talk a bit more about it without the time constraints of a class."

Her face lit up.

"Yes, I would like that," she said. "Thank you."

She did not catch up with her friend until they got back to their student housing unit.

"Naia, what did he want to talk to you about?" her friend asked.

"He offered me to come to his office and discuss my question in more detail," Naia Fernek explained enthusiastically.

Her friend examined her face.

"What?" Naia asked.

"You're going to see him because you want to know more about whatever you asked about, right?"

"Of course."

"So it has nothing to do with anything else?"

Naia looked at her with a business-like attitude.

"What's that supposed to mean?" she said and disappeared into her room.

She had a lot of work to do to prepare for the sedition class that Eda Strebber was teaching. She also had to write a memo on part of the literature for the psychology class, where they studied interrogation techniques. But more than anything, she needed to eat something.

She was not overly happy with their food rations. They always seemed to fall just short of what was promised them, and the taste was not very exciting either. She remembered fresh fruit and berries from her childhood.

Speaking of which. She had not spoken to her mom in a while. She glanced at the clock. The town up on the northern shore where her mom and grandmother lived was one bell behind in time.

She had a small meal first while going over her class notes. She filled in some blanks from memory and added a couple of comments about the discussion from class.

Olgar's face appeared to her. She smiled as she remembered him talking. She tried to remember exactly what he had said about democracy.

She heard his voice in her head . . . she leaned back, closed her eyes . . .

Then she snapped out of it. Was she having a crush on her teacher?

No, of course not!

To take her mind off the class, and off Olgar, she decided to call her mom.

It took a little bit for the call to patch through. Apparently, the phone connections were busier than normal. Although lately, it had seemed like they were this busy most of the time.

"Hello."

"Mom!"

"Naia! My love, how are you?"

"I'm good, mom! How are you? So good to hear your voice!"

"Yes, you, too. We are good up there. Grandma is better. She got over that cold pretty quickly."

"That's good to hear. Is she there? I'd love to talk to her."

"She is outside right now. How are you, my dear?"

"I'm good. I'm enjoying my classes. Oh, I have to tell you! I started a new class today, in political theory. It's really interesting. We talk about democracy, and rights, you know, and how rights have shifted from the federal republic to now. It was fascinating."

"Sounds great, honey. Oh, hang on . . . mom! Mind the step! There . . . good. Sorry, honey, grandma was just coming in from the porch."

"That's okay. Mom, this class is so good. It's the most interesting class I have taken so far! You know how I've always liked history."

"Uh-huh . . . "

'"Right, so in this class I get the opportunity to talk about the really substantial differences between the federal rep . . . "

"Hang on, honey . . . yes, mom, why don't you sit over there. I'll bring you some lemonade. Go on, honey."

"Oh, that's . . . that's okay. I was just saying how much I like this new class I'm taking."

"Good, honey. How is the weather? Mom! Do you want red lemonade? Okay! Is the weather good down there, honey?"

"Yes, it's been good."

"I'm so glad to hear that you are doing good. I'm pouring some lemonade for grandma here."

"Can I talk to her?"

"Oh, sure. Mom, Naia wants to talk to you. Yes, I'm bringing the lemonade. Here, honey, here's grandma."

"Hello. Naia?"

"Hi, grandma! How are you?"

"Oh, you know. My age . . . but I'm fine. How about you?"

"I'm good!"

"Are you doing well with your studies there at the security agency?"

"At State Security? Yes, I'm doing really well. I just started two new classes, one in political theory and one on seditionism."

"Sounds interesting. And what do they teach you about sedition?"

"We have just gotten started, but I've been reading ahead, and it is really fascinating."

"Can you tell and old lady like me what it means to be a seditionist?"

"It means you oppose government."

"Is it that simple?"

"Well, that's the short version of it. But yeah, basically."

"Then we must hope government is always right."

"Why?"

"Because otherwise, someone would have to point out that government is wrong. And who would do that if you could be charged as a seditionist if you did?"

"Grandma," Naia giggled. "You've always been silly. But I love you!"

"I love you, too, dear. Here is your mother back."

"Naia?"

"Hi, mom."

"I want you to do me a favor."

"Okay . . . "

"We are a bit short on bar soap and other hygiene articles up here. I want you to get some extra down there and ship them up to us. Can you do that?"

"I don't know, mom . . . I have consumer coupons, you know, rations, like everyone else. My ration is no different. It's the same for everyone."

"Oh, I'm sure you can find some down there. Let me know when you ship them."

"Okay . . . "

"Gotta go. Love you, honey!"

"Okay . . . love you, too, mom . . . bye . . . "

❄ ❄ ❄

AT FIRST, ARMO TORNDALE did not recognize the strange object that one of the watchmen had found. It was small, about the length of a hand from wrist to the top of the tallest finger, and about half the hand's width. It was cylindrical in shape and grey with two blue lines running from top to bottom, on opposite sides.

The colors of State Security.

"It looks like it has a lid," Strebber noted.

"Uh-huh," Torndale said absentmindedly.

He turned to the watchman.

"Where did you find it?"

"Over there," the watchman said and pointed to a densely wooded area.

He brought them over and showed them exactly where he had spotted the object.

"It was just lying there," he said and pointed into the grass.

Torndale examined the ground. He found a small dent, in the shape that matched the small cylinder in his hand.

"Did it stick up like this?"

"Yes, actually, it did."

"As if it was dropped from above," Armo Torndale thought out loud.

He looked up. The trees had rich, densely leaved crowns and thick branches. It was almost impossible to spot the sky from where they were standing.

"How could anything fall from up there?" the watchman asked.

"It couldn't," Torndale agreed. "But the big question is what it fell off."

He held the object between his thumb and his index finger and looked at it from different angles. It looked the same, of course, safe for the two blue stripes.

The top almost looked like it had been screwed on.

"Can you remove the top?" Strebber asked.

"Hmm," Torndale mumbled, lost in his thoughts, trying to figure out where he had seen this object before. "What?"

"The top. It looks like you can just screw it off."

"I think I know where I have seen this before . . . " Torndale kept mumbling, "but I can't put my finger on it . . . "

"Why don't we open it and see what's inside?" Strebber insisted.

Torndale turned to him. He examined the young man carefully as if he was trying to figure out what the hurry was all about. Then he smiled:

"I'm sorry, I was lost in my own thoughts. I know I have seen this object before. I just couldn't remember where. But your insistence that we open it was helpful."

He turned to face both Strebber and the watchman. He held up the cylinder as if it was a trophy.

"You know what this is? It's a messenger tube. These are used by a special branch of State Security. It is bolted onto the bottom of a flying robot, a drone, that flies into the area where a message is to be delivered, and then drops it. Simple as that. You fly it by remote control. It's a brand new, state-of-the-art piece of technology. Good for delivering messages to your own units, and it's hard to intercept. It's an expensive little machine. But . . . " and he pointed up to the treetops, " . . . it could not have been dropped by a drone flying above the trees."

"Uh, the tube," Strebber tried. "Can we . . . "

"The treetops are simply too dense with branches and leaves," Torndale kept talking. "The angle . . . look again at the angle of how it landed . . . the angle suggests that it fell from a drone flying right here, somewhere not far above . . . well, our heads. Right here, among the trees. The remote pilot has to be very good to navigate in this terrain. Whoever flew it is not far away from here at all . . . There is a little camera in the front. The radio signal won't travel very far."

Strebber looked worried.

"But that means they know we are here," he said.

"State Security knows about us," Torndale replied. "They have been aware of our trek ever since we left the city. They just haven't had the resources or the will power to try to stop us. You see, one of the most pervasive character traits of a totalitarian state is that its functionaries become loyal to their privileges, not the cause. At the entry level, when they start working for the totalitarian state, they enjoy the very methods that a totalitarian regime uses to, shall we say, govern its people. Random arrests, invasive home searches and so on. As the servants of the regime climb the ranks, they enjoy more privileges, like better pay, more food rations, they get permits to move to bigger, better homes. Permits that regular citizens can only dream of. As they climb the ranks, their privileges are gradually extended to family and relatives. They become more interested in preserving their privileges than anything else."

He paused, shook his head and sighed. Again, Strebber tried:

"I wonder what's in the tube."

"Me, too!" Torndale agreed enthusiastically. "The entire lives of State Security agents revolve around the position they have built for themselves. And that's how the totalitarian state buys the loyalty of its enforcers. Those functionaries will do more and more to preserve their status quo and less and less to risk it. Of course, they will always obey an order, and if the order is to go out into dangerous lands, in hard terrain under unforgiving weather conditions, then yes, they will do so. But if the field commander of the group that is sent out is more concerned with coming back home so he can continue to provide protection and privileges for his family, and less concerned about the ideological purpose of the totalitarian regime, then his efforts in finding the people he has been sent out to track down, well, they will not be his most earnest efforts. Especially if he knows that the group of people he is tracking is led by a former State Security officer trained in both intelligence and special operations."

Strebber looked even more worried.

"Armo . . . are you . . . are you saying that . . . State Security has been monitoring us all along . . . but they didn't dare to take us on because . . . because they know you are here?"

"I wouldn't say they didn't dare," Torndale replied.

"Can we open the tube and find out?" asked the camp watchman.

"Sure," Torndale agreed and kept talking. "It just hasn't been worth the while for them. They had a team tracking us through the woodlands and the lower mountain range, but there were only six of them. We have forty men who can handle firearms. We don't have forty firearms, but they didn't know that. And at the very least we had enough to deter them. An attack on us would have been a losing proposition for that group of State Security agents."

"You knew they were there? And you didn't tell us?"

"No need to create more stress than the trek itself inflicted on us. They turned around when we passed the Devil's Watchtower."

"Did they start sending up drones instead?" the watchman asked.

"No," Torndale replied firmly. "This drone was not sent by State Security."

Strebber and the watchman exchanged a look. They both looked very confused.

"What are you saying?" Strebber asked.

Torndale smiled.

"If it is who I think it is, there is a friendly message inside this tube."

He held it up again as if it were a trophy. Strebber and the watchman were beginning to look impatient:

"So . . . " Strebber said. "Can we open it?"

❊ ❊ ❊

OLGAR HAD TWO REASONS FOR ASKING Naia Fernek to come to his office. He wanted to know more about why she had asked the question about freedom of speech. She had asked it either because she was genuinely curious, or because she was having doubts about the value foundation itself. It was his duty to identify students who may not be completely committed to the value foundation of their people's democratic union.

But he also had another motive. A more personal one. And he did his best to deny to himself that he had such a motive.

It was difficult. Naia Fernek was young, probably the youngest in the group, and very attractive. She was relatively short, with straight, auburn hair, bangs over bright, curious green eyes, she had shapely lips and cheek bones and a chin that completed an incredibly beautiful face.

And no man could miss her ample female attributes.

As she walked into his office, Olgar found himself taking a deep breath. She noted it, stopped and looked a bit confused. She was carrying her textbook and a notepad in her arms, and the standard issue book bag over her shoulder.

"I'm sorry, sir," she said, noting Olgar's reaction. "Is something wrong?"

"No . . . " Olgar rushed to assure her. "No, nothing at all. Have a seat."

Naia sat down and placed her textbook on the desk. She leaned back in the chair and looked at him with attention and what seemed to be a little worry.

Olgar looked her in the eyes and for a moment could not come up with anything to say. He found himself thinking that he had not met such a beautiful young woman in a very long time. He tried not to let his eyes wander, but for a split second he noticed the curvature of her uniform shirt.

"Sir . . . " said Naia.

He raised his eyes, met hers and got ahold of himself:

"Yes . . . yes, of course. Thank you for coming in, Cadet Fernek."

He consulted a note on his desk:

"It's Naia Fernek, correct?"

"Yes, sir."

He pondered for a moment to use her first name. He felt an urge to get to know her better, to break the barriers of rank and form between them. He looked up and once again felt a sting of attraction when their eyes met.

But it would be incredibly unprofessional. Socializing with a student was highly inappropriate, so much in fact that he could risk his job.

He quelled his urge.

"Yes," he said, placed his underarms on the desk, clasped his hands and leaned forward slightly. "The reason why I wanted you to come in here is the question you asked in class. As I explained, there was not enough time to address it then, but I found it important enough that I wanted to hear more about your motives for asking it."

"My motives, sir?"

"Yes," he confirmed.

Naia looked a bit confused. She raised her eyebrows. Her beautifully shaped lips formed an O. Her forehead wrinkled for a moment. Even when she was confused, her beauty overwhelmed him.

Olgar had to summon a great deal of strength to remain professional and neutral.

"Well . . . " she said, sounding a bit worried. "Sir . . . When I was preparing for the class . . . I got thinking about a book that my grandfather gave me when I was in high school."

Her face shifted. She no longer looked confused but more as if she was actually concerned that her question had brought up something she was not supposed to bring up.

Olgar noted her worry. He wanted to put it to rest.

"That's interesting," he said in as positive a tone as he could summon. "Not many students at your level exhibit such interest in going beyond the curriculum and the syllabi."

She relaxed. Her smile returned, she nodded slightly.

"What book did you read?"

"The Foundations of the Federal Republic. It was written by a philosopher . . . "

"Yes, a man named Quennec," Olgar nodded.

"Right." Naia agreed

She relaxed and smiled. And a gorgeous smile it was.

Olgar knew that he needed to find out just what Miss Fernek's thoughts were on the contrast between rights under the federal republic and rights under the people's democratic union. He knew he had to establish that, and to what extent her reading up on the philosophy of the federal republic had compromised her loyalty to the value foundation of the union.

But he was also just a man. When he looked into her smile, he found himself caught completely off guard.

"Well," he said and smiled back. "I trust you enjoyed that book."

"I did, actually," Cadet Fernek said with some enthusiasm in her voice. "And what I found most interesting is that Quennec says outright that you can have rights without someone providing for those rights. I mean, it's such a different concept from ours, I just thought it was fascinating to read about it."

Right there, Olgar had all the reasons he needed to open an internal inquiry into Cadet Fernek. Her enthusiasm for studying the philosophical foundation of the old federal republic, and to do so independently, without being assigned such studies by an instructor or supervising officer, was considered a red flag for disloyalty, possibly even the first sign of sedition.

Protocol prescribed that he ask her a series of questions from a standardized form. He knew those questions by heart. He could easily fire them off one by one in an authoritative tone. He could scare the living daylights out of this young woman if he wanted to. Or he could ask the questions in a subtle manner, giving her the impression that he was just curious, conversational.

Either way, he would gather the information he needed to write a formal note about their conversation. And to possibly derail this young woman's career before it even got started.

But when he looked into her lively eyes, when he saw her face, like sculpted to make a man's heart melt, and when he heard the unmitigated joy in her voice as she talked about what she had learned from that book, he just could not bring himself to question her.

He did not want to turn this into an interrogation. He wanted to continue their conversation.

"What do you find fascinating about it?" he asked.

She looked genuinely happy that he was interested. As she continued talking, he noticed that she had dropped the formalities that were otherwise universally applied in all conversations at the agency. There was no "sir", no pause to await the approval of the outranking officer.

"Well, as I understand it," she said enthusiastically, "Quennec believes that a person's right to free speech is granted simply by the fact that nobody prevents him or her from speaking. I've been trying to understand how that works in practice."

"Does it work in practice?" Olgar asked.

"That's what I've been asking," Cadet Fernek agreed. "I was too young when the federal republic ended, so I don't have any real memories of it."

"What about your parents?"

Her smile disappeared. She lowered her eyes. Olgar felt a sting in his heart.

"I'm sorry," he said. "Was that an inappropriate question?"

Again, he transgressed the lines of protocol. No question from a senior officer was inappropriate. No reaction from a junior officer, let alone a cadet like Miss Fernek, was the reason to hold back. Rank was always right.

Olgar noticed a tear in her eye. He wanted to reach out and wipe it off her cheek. But before he could offer a napkin, she shook her head and wiped her eye with the back of her hand.

"No, it's alright," she said in a hushed voice, sprinkled with sadness that contrasted sharply against her enthusiasm from just a moment ago.

"Are they . . . not with you?"

"My dad died a long time ago . . . my mom moved to the northern shore two years ago to care for my grandmother."

"Do you have any other family?"

She shook her head again.

"Well, a brother, but he and I have no contact."

Her eyes were fixed on the textbook in front of her.

Olgar was overwhelmed by a desire to embrace this young woman, emotionally, physically. He had to pinch himself hard between his index finger and his thumb to keep himself in line.

"I am so sorry to hear that," he said.

"Thanks," she said. "I'm sorry for being emotional."

"No need to be sorry," he said and smiled.

She nodded gratefully. Their eyes met. She gave away a smile again.

"Thank you," she said quietly.

"You are welcome."

They looked at one another for a second. Olgar wagered for a moment. He shouldn't do this, but . . .

"Look, I . . . I would actually like to hear more about your thoughts on this . . . this book . . . Quennec and rights . . . Would you have time to stop by later today or tomorrow?"

She looked relieved, even happy at the question. She nodded emphatically.

"Yeah, uhm . . . " and she scrambled to check her calendar. "I . . . I have kind of a full schedule today, but I . . . I guess I could rearrange something . . . " and she spoke faster, as if she was a bit nervous, "I could skip my choir tonight . . . "

"You sing choir?"

"I do . . . "

"I wouldn't want you to skip that. How about tomorrow?"

"Is the third bell a good time?"

"That works for me."

When she had left his office, Olgar sat still, took a couple of deep breaths and sensed the lingering scent of her perfume. He closed his eyes and remembered her smile.

He had completely lost his professionalism. He knew it, and he cursed himself for it.

But he was also a man. A lonely man with a woman-shaped hole in his heart.

❀ ❀ ❀

THERE WAS A SMALL PIECE of paper in the small cylinder that Armo Torndale held in his hand. The paper was rolled up and had a rubber band around it.

"It's a message," the watchman noted. "But is it for us?"

"It is," Torndale confirmed. "As I said, the drone came in here below the treetops, where someone had to navigate it carefully. The range of the radio frequency that the remote pilot would need is too short for anyone to do it beyond the mountains. The pilot has to be within an hour's walk of where we are now. Two, maybe."

He rolled off the rubber band. Strebber examined his face.

"You know who sent this," he said.

"I do," Torndale nodded.

He rolled up the piece of paper and smiled.

"Exactly," he said. "They made it."

"Who made it?"

He put the piece of paper back in the cylinder and screwed on the top.

"When our group left," he said, "as I mentioned, we were tracked by a group from State Security. They weren't overly aggressive about tracking us, but they marked their presence and they kept me on the alert. It was their way of telling us that we should not be too sure that we would get here. They didn't know, of course, where we were going, but they wanted us to know they were watching us. They thought they had the upper hand, that they were the strategic masterminds."

He put the cylinder in his shirt pocket.

"They weren't," he said with a self-congratulatory tone in his voice.

Strebber looked at Torndale with squinting eyes, tilted his head slightly and pointed at him with his right index finger. He smiled.

"Are you saying . . . that we drew attention to us . . . so that someone else . . . someone else could get out of . . . could leave behind us without being noticed?"

"My dear Strebber," Torndale nodded. "You got it in one. State Security is stretched thin. They have a lot of people on their payroll, but because the bulk of them are lazy administrators who push papers and data files between them, they aren't very efficient. They sit in meetings and attend meaningless political seminars where they make another pledge of allegiance to the value foundation. Those who are tasked with actual field work are in the lower tiers of the agency hierarchy. They aren't very well paid compared to the bureaucrats, and people try to leave those functions as quickly as they can. If they can't advance, they go look for other government jobs, preferably one where they can bring their privileges and benefits with them. And that is not too hard. Having worked for State Security is a merit, of course. But the operational units are stretched thin. The agents are almost always unwilling to take risks."

They turned and started walking back to the camp.

"I knew they would dispatch one unit to go after us. They had to, and some in the agency certainly wanted us to get caught or at least numerically decimated. And we had a very important . . . item . . . that we wanted to bring with us on this trek, but I could not take the risk that State Security would actually close in on us and maybe manage to get hold of this item. I thought it unlikely, but I could not rule it out. So, I made our departure a little bit more conspicuous than it needed to be, just to make sure that they would come after us. Once I knew they were on our trail, another small group could leave in almost guaranteed peace and quiet."

"And that unit brought with it . . . this item?" the watchman asked.

"Yeah, what item are you talking about?" Strebber wanted to know.

"I cannot tell you," Armo Torndale said. "Not yet. But I will show you when they get here."

"Do you trust this group? I mean no disrespect, but . . . "

"No, it's a fair question to ask," Armo Torndale reassured Strebber. "Yes, I do trust this small group. Its leader is one of the most dedicated young agents we ever had in the agency. Her name is Naia Fernek. I was impressed with her from the first day I met her. She has with her five other young agents, about her age. They are all defectors from State Security. Seditionists, by the definition of our laws."

When they got back to the camp there was some uneasiness among the group. Another of the camp watchmen approached them.

"There is a rumor going around that State Security has found us," he said. "That you found one of their crashed flying robots. Is this true?"

He was genuinely worried.

"Rumors are devious foes," Armo Torndale said. "Who is worried?"

"A lot of people."

Torndale looked at him. He looked out over the camp and saw multiple pairs of eyes trained on him.

"I would like to address everyone. That would be the easy way to quell this rumor. But we cannot make too much noise. I will talk to as many as I can. But please help me. Let people know that the rumor is false, that what we found was a message from friends, and that I will talk with every single person who is worried, and explain exactly what is happening. But make sure to tell everyone that State Security has not found us and that I am confident that so long as we stay quiet and wait in patience for our departure, State Security will never find us."

ADJUTANT EDA STREBBER had been assigned the same lecture hall for her sedition class as Olgar had for his class in political theory. She, too, had more students now that one of the other instructors had quietly disappeared. But many students also crowded to her class because it was considered prestigious among the students. Many of them believed that the sooner you took the class, the better you looked in the eyes of the agency.

They were right, of course. Any student who did not do well in Sedition was on a watch list. There was no higher duty for State Security than to root out seditionists among the population. When the people's democratic union was first declared, the pursuit of seditionists had led to a wave of arrests and charges, with tens of thousands of people thrown in jail on the mere suspicion. The mass arrests had reached such proportions that they had begun affecting the ability of key industries and services to function.

Most of the arrests targeted people with advanced academic degrees: engineers, medical doctors, architects, accountants, business managers, lawyers. They were often more involved in politics, perhaps because their professions brought them into frequent contact with government and gave them plenty of opportunities to see government in practice. Since the laws under the new People's Democratic Union defined every expression of disagreement with government as sedition, many people who had been used to free speech under the federal republic suddenly found themselves being on the receiving end of government power.

With jails and prison camps filling up with professionals who had been taken out of key functions in society, the economy was being disrupted and drained of badly needed experts. Grand Chancellor Sorto's administration had tried to compensate by opening the borders for generous immigration, but for some reason that the government could never quite figure out, foreign nationals were not as interested as in the past of moving to Ripoma.

The situation had led to a debate within the inner circles of the government about where to draw the line in terms of enforcement against seditionists. Hardliners claimed that if only government maintained its tough stance, eventually seditionism would die out and everything could go back to normal. Or, at least, the new normal that the People's Democratic Union had established. On the other side of the line, pragmatists claimed that the hardline crackdown was disrupting the economy to the point where people might be attracted by seditionism out of frustration and despair.

So far, the hardliners had prevailed, but the debate had spread deep into the layers of staff at State Security. The dividing line between hardliners and pragmatists was not as pronounced as it had been for some time within the Sorto administration, but it was there.

Eda Strebber considered herself to be a hardliner. She had participated in some arrests of highly educated professionals in key social and economic positions, and she was more than happy to share those experiences with her students.

"My first hands-on experience with seditionism was at the S4 call center. Who knows what S4 stands for?"

She paused and looked out over the crowd. The lecture hall was filled to the last seat. One hundred eyes eagerly watched her, and she could tell most of them were scrambling to remember what S4 stood for.

Suddenly, a hand shot up in the crowd.

"Yes," Eda Strebber said and nodded at the student.

"See something, say something," the student replied.

"Good," Eda Strebber commended the student. "That is exactly right. See something, say something. The S4 call center was set up when we reorganized the existing federal law enforcement and intelligence services into one big agency, State Security. That is when we started the S4 call center. It was a success right from the start. When Sorto's party had won both the national assembly election and the presidential election, we knew we had to reduce the threat from seditionists and eventually eliminate that threat once and for all."

She paused, looked around the room and smiled.

"I did my part," she said with pride in her voice, "working long hours at the S4 call center, and we got a lot of calls from day one. It was almost uninterrupted. At first, it was party functionaries within Sorto's party who called to report political opponents. And that is logical, isn't it? That is what sedition means: to oppose and try to overthrow a legitimate government. You can try to overthrow it in different ways. You can try to do it violently, which of course we respond to, vigorously. You can also passively resist government by not cooperating with government agencies that want information of some kind. That is of course also sedition. Or you can run as an opponent in an election."

Another pause to make sure the students were paying attention.

"Or," she continued a bit more slowly, "you can express a dissenting view in some public forum, or you can share your dissent, your criticism of government, with coworkers, friends or family members. It all falls under the legal realm of sedition."

She paused for a moment. That was a lot to take in for these students, although she assumed that they had all studied up on the class material ahead of time.

She turned a page in her notes and was just about to continue when a hand was raised among the students on the side close to the windows. It was a young woman with long auburn hair and green eyes.

"Yes," said Eda Strebber. "And you are?"

"Cadet Fernek, ma'm."

"Cadet Fernek. Thank you. What is your question?"

"I was just trying to keep account of the definitions of sedition," Naia Fernek said, looking at her notes. "Violent action against government, passive resistance by means of non-cooperation, and being a candidate in an election. Did I get that right?"

"Yes, almost. Being a candidate in an election is not enough for sedition. Suppose you want to run for a seat that is held by an incumbent, for example in your city commune, or even in the national assembly. If the incumbent approves of your candidacy, you are not a seditionist."

Another student raised his hand:

"But why would an incumbent approve of another candidate?"

Eda Strebber smiled:

"Yes, that would not make sense, would it? In other words, anyone deciding to run against an incumbent is practically a seditionist."

She turned to Cadet Fernek:

"Then there is the case of an open seat. For example, let's say an incumbent on the board of your local city commune decides to retire. When the incumbent announces the retirement, he or she includes a public call for candidates to announce themselves. Suppose that you, Cadet Fernek, announce your candidacy. Suppose that I also announce my candidacy. If the incumbent approves me as the candidate, then you have to withdraw your candidacy, or else you would be committing an act of sedition."

"And just to be clear," Cadet Fernek replied, "this is not how it worked under the federal republic, correct?"

"Correct," Eda Strebber confirmed.

She was quiet for a moment and looked Naia Fernek sternly in the eyes. That made Naia nervous. Eda Strebber noticed it and nodded to herself. Good. She had Cadet Fernek on the defense.

"Why do you make that reference?" she asked. "To the old republic. Why?"

"I am just trying to learn the differences."

"Yes, but why?" Eda Strebber wanted to know.

Naia looked at her with caution in her eyes.

"I am just interested in history," she said humbly.

Eda Strebber examined her for a moment. She noticed that Cadet Fernek was getting a bit worried.

"Okay, Cadet Fernek," Eda Strebber said in a formal tone. "Thanks for letting us know your interest in history. The proper forms for studying history are under a specifically approved project. If your interest is that strong, you should petition Doctor Smersch for an approved study project in history. But without such an approval, I would suggest that you don't have the time in your schedule. Okay?"

Eda Strebber gave Naia a formal, cordial look accompanied by a cold smile.

"Yes, ma'm," Cadet Fernek replied. "Of course, thank you. I appreciate your instructions."

When Eda Strebber entered the cantina to have lunch, she almost collided with Olgar.

"I didn't see you," she said.

"Oh, my fault," he smiled. "I was just chatting with Zidernik, from the S4 center, you remember him?"

"Yes, of course. How is he doing?"

"He is doing well. He just started with electronic surveillance."

"Good for him. By the way, it's funny you should mention S4. I was just talking to my students about it this morning. I was giving them an introduction to the concept of sedition."

"The time we spent at S4," Olgar remembered. "It was a valuable experience."

"Yes, it was."

"We worked some long hours there."

"We did," Eda Strebber agreed and looked for a table. "How about we sit over there?"

The cantina was getting crowded.

"They have some extra staff called in today," Olgar noted.

"Operations personnel, I think," Eda Strebber suggested.

"It's a major sweep of the northern suburbs," said an officer at the next table. "We just got done."

"Did you catch any fish?" Olgar asked.

"Plenty," the officer smiled. "Including a group of high school kids who were studying insurrectionist history."

"Speaking of history," said Eda Strebber. "There was this student in my class, a Cadet Fernek, who asked some unusual questions. I believe she is in your political theory class?"

Olgar's face lit up in a bright smile.

"Oh yes," he said lightheartedly. "She is very interested in history. Bright young student. In fact, she is probably one of the smartest in my class."

"Is that so?"

"Yes," Olgar continued enthusiastically. "Shows deep interest in the subject, even outside the classroom. I have had two meetings with her in my office."

"Oh, really?"

Olgar nodded and took a bite of his bread stick.

"She is curious and smart," he said with a smile, looking at his bread-stick. "You don't see that every day."

"Yes, and kind of cute, too," Eda Strebber mumbled.

"She is," Olgar chuckled.

Then he fell silent. He glanced at Eda Strebber. She was looking at him with no facial expressions. She took a sip of citrus water, put the cup down and nodded, still with her eyes fixed on him and without giving away any emotions:

"I mean . . . " Olgar said.

"Oh, no worries," Eda Strebber reassured him.

He noted the cold tone in her voice. He realized what he had just said and how she was interpreting it. He pondered for a moment to elaborate, to explain or at least to do some damage control. But he could not immediately come up with any natural way to do it.

He focused on his food. They ate in silence for a moment.

"I think we are getting some cold weather," said Eda Strebber.

"Yes, I think you're right," Olgar agreed.

"My husband got tickets for the opera tonight."

"How nice," Olgar said in a professional tone. "What's playing?"

"The Voice of Tomorrow."

"I have heard it is magnificent," Olgar rushed to say.

"Yes," Eda Strebber agreed, leaning back and looking at him with focused eyes.

"Well," Olgar replied, and finished his meal. "I have some class prep to do. Thanks for the company. Enjoy the opera."

He got up, collected his tray and dashed off.

" I will," Eda Strebber replied to the empty chair across the table.

She turned and watched Olgar dispose of his dishes, navigate the crowd and leave the cantina.

"I heard that," said the officer at the next table.

"I'm glad you did, sir," Eda Strebber replied and turned to him. "May I have your internal contact code?"

IT RAINED ON THE CAMP OVERNIGHT. It was a hard rain, long and chilly, right in the middle of the darkest hours from dusk to dawn. The refugees had rain shelters, but they had been through a lot in recent weeks and some of them were beginning to fall apart. It was also difficult to keep the water from accumulating in the shallow pit. They had to stay there, at the camp site, as much as possible to minimize the risk that they be detected, but they also had not taken into account that they would be staying at the camp this long. They simply had not taken enough time to dig rainwater drainage.

And then there were the small food rations. It was hard labor digging drainage canals in this tough terrain. Not many had the energy to do it.

"It is getting tough for many," Strebber noted.

He just got back to Armo Torndale after a tour of the camp.

"Families with children that are having a hard time staying warm," he continued, while sitting down and removing his waterproof hat. "Two babies that are catching a cold."

He leaned back, wiped his face with his hand and sighed.

"We are close to running out of root nuts, sunflower juice and . . . I forget . . . one more . . . "

"Silver milk," Torndale filled in.

"That's right," Strebber nodded and closed his eyes.

He sat quiet for a moment, then opened his eyes again and looked at Armo Torndale.

"We can't do this much longer," he said bluntly.

"I know," Torndale nodded wearily. "Our Danori friend should be back in the morning."

"Should?"

Torndale shrugged his shoulders.

"What else can I do?" he asked.

Strebber looked at him and thought for a moment. Then he bowed his head, sighed and nodded slowly.

"I know . . . It's just so . . . frustrating . . . "

"We've come so far," Torndale noted.

"We have. So close . . . "

"The Danori always keep their part of a deal. They always have, ever since I got to know them. I have faith in them returning as planned."

"I hope they bring food. And medicine. We need penicillin. Among other things."

A woman approached them. She was thin, her hair striped by rain, her skin worn by wind and stress. Her eyes looked pale and her lips were thin and dry.

Torndale immediately invited her in.

"Come, sit down," he said.

She took a seat with some distance from him. She avoided eye contact, which Torndale thought was a bit strange.

"How can I help you?" he asked.

She did not answer right away. It was as if she was looking for the right words, or hesitating because she knew he would not like what she had to say. She held up her hands and examined them.

"I know you have been working hard for us," she said in a voice that cracked with sorrow and—something else.

Bitterness?

Torndale waited.

"And I am very grateful for all that you do," she continued slowly. "But I am not sure how much longer I . . . we . . . can hold out here."

Strebber wanted to say something, but Torndale shook his head at him. Strebber was a great companion with good leadership skills, but he also had a tendency of speaking when he should be listening.

"I am starving," she continued, pushing herself to remain calm. "I give half my rations to my children. My husband does what he can with gathering berries . . . "

"I know your husband," Torndale confirmed. "He works very hard."

" . . . and we try to share with everyone," she continued as if she had not heard him. "But we are getting to a point where neither of us, and none of our closest camp mates, can hold it together much longer."

She took a couple of deep breaths to calm herself down.

"I can live with the lack of hygiene. We can wash our children . . . We do our basic needs as designated, downslope, at the hidden area . . . But when we don't have anything more to eat . . . There comes a point where it is not worth the struggle anymore."

She let her arms hang down along her sides. She closed her eyes for a moment, then looked at Torndale.

"Some people are beginning to question if we should stay here."

Torndale waited.

"I am one of them," the woman confirmed.

She looked him in the eyes.

"I will not let my children die on this mountain," she added in a slightly aggressive tone.

"Nor will I," Armo Torndale replied calmly.

"Then give us more to eat," she shot back in a hushed but pressed voice.

"In a few hours it will be dawn. At that time, the Danori liaison will return. She will bring two things: an evacuation ship and more food."

"More food?"

"Yes."

"But that means we are going to stay here! For how long are we supposed to sit here in this . . . this dirt hole on the top of this mountain?"

Her tone was getting more aggressive. Again, Strebber wanted to say something, but Torndale intervened:

"The Danori are here," he reminded her calmly. "They have an evacuation plan. We will know the details of it in the morning. But they will evacuate us. They did not fly a thousand light years out here to our little planet, just to leave us sitting here."

The woman looked at him.

"And you don't know how and when we will leave?"

"I don't have the exact details yet. What I do know is that the Danori liaison will be here at dawn. If we can't leave right away she will bring more food. It may be that the evacuation will begin but be slower than we had hoped for. Either way, it will begin. I'm sorry I don't have more information than that, at least now now."

The woman sighed.

"We gave up everything we had," she said in a bitter tone. "My husband was the foreman of a road maintenance crew. A good government job. It gave us protected status. Compared to many others, many of our friends and family, we had a good life. We had been assigned a nice house. Our food rations had increased. When my mother needed hip surgery, I was even able to get her priority on the hospital waiting list. It would have taken her a year and a half to get in otherwise. I got her bumped up, past many others, so she could get in within two moons. Our children had been assigned the best school in our town. Most of the students there had parents who also worked for government. We were on a prioritized list for college so the kids could get past most other kids in the admissions process. We even had an automobile, and we had travel permits for thirty of our thirty-six provinces. Only during the winter, but still. We could travel. A lot of people have to apply for permits every time, and many are denied travel permits."

She looked out at the camp.

"And look at us now," she said, sounding even more bitter.

Torndale waited. She looked out over the campus and muttered something that sounded like 'look at this'. She leaned back again, closed her eyes and cried. She clasped her hands.

Torndale kept waiting.

Then, eventually, she opened her eyes and looked at him.

"Do you have anything to say?"

Her tone was not aggressive, but still bitter.

"No," he replied. "But I do have a question."

"What?"

"If you had accomplished all this . . . If your husband had a good, privileged government job . . . why did you give it all up to come with us on this journey?"

THE EPINAQ RIVER WAS WIDE AND MIGHTY. Its massive stream of water moved quietly, majestically, down toward the ocean. There were always boats making their way up or down the stream. Day or night, ferries, freighters, tugboats and fishing vessels broke the water surface in both directions. The boats were often surrounded by grey longfish, who jumped up, splashed their fins against each other in the air, and dived down again. It was as if they were greeting the boats, welcoming them to the peace and quiet that was the Epinaq river.

Olgar had a small apartment. It was just a bedroom, a living room, a kitchen and a bathroom. All the windows faced the river. A small balcony made the living room feel a bit bigger.

He stood on the balcony, looking out over the river.

Naia Fernek stood right next to him.

He pointed to the left, to the mighty bridge. It was lit up, with lights along the roadway, the massive railings and on top of the two towers on each side. Only half the lights were lit, but it was still an impressive view.

"That's the Rivermouth bridge," he explained. "It is more than a century old."

"I did not know that," said Naia.

"It's tall enough that even the big freighters can pass underneath it. See that fishing boat over there?"

He pointed to a red and white vessel making its way up the river. It had a small crew compartment in the back, a crane and a big net rolled up on a roll in the front.

"My grandfather owned a fishing boat like that one," Olgar said. "It was his own business."

"He owned it?" Naia asked, a bit surprised.

"Yes. This was during the federal republic, of course."

"Oh, of course. Was it common for people to own their own businesses back then?"

"Yes. Everything, from retail stores to manufacturing plants . . . taxi vehicles, fishing boats . . . people owned all kinds of businesses."

"How did your grandfather do with his business?"

"He did well, for the most part. He had a small crew who worked with him on the boat."

"That's what is called inequality, isn't it?" Naia asked. "When someone works for someone else."

"Today we call it that. Back then it was just called employment."

They were silent for a moment. He turned to her.

"What about your family?"

"My grandparents . . . on my dad's side . . . they were teachers. My maternal grandmother was a nurse, my grandfather was a salesman of some sort. He sold home appliances, I think."

They looked out over the river.

"I like the breeze from the river," Naia noted.

"I often sleep with my window open, just to get that breeze into my bedroom."

She looked up at him. He met her eyes. She smiled. He felt that sting in his belly, a sting that only her smile could bring him.

He turned to her. Their eyes locked. He raised his hand, touched her cheek, stroked some hair away from her eye.

Her smile got even brighter.

"Naia," he whispered. "I . . . you . . . you are . . . beautiful . . . "

"You too," she whispered, almost inaudibly.

He knew he should not do it. He remembered Eda Strebber's reaction over lunch. He remembered it all. Every moment.

And yet, he could not resist. He could not hold himself back.

He leaned forward a little bit. She came closer. He touched her cheek again. She gently placed her palms on his chest.

Their lips met.

He wrapped his arms around her. She embraced him. They kissed. Olgar felt a passion rising through his body that he had not felt in years. He was intoxicated by the smell of Naia's perfume, her hair, her scent . . . he drowned in her beautiful green eyes.

She pushed herself onto him. He felt her large breasts, her legs against his . . . A surge of desire . . .

"Would you like to spend the night?" he whispered.

"Yes," she said. "Yes!"

The night was long, hot and passionate. They rode the storm of love in a wild, romantic union. Wave after wave of erotic energy pulsated through the room, through their bodies. He loved her like he had never loved a woman, ever. She received him, embraced him, pulled him in like she had never wanted a man before. He opened the floodgates of passion, long locked away in loneliness. She consumed it all, hungering for lust, desire and the trusting, naked love she had never felt in her life, but so often dreamed of, so deeply yearned for.

They were lost in time and space. Nothing mattered, nothing was, nothing could be . . . except them and their intense night together.

When their love making subsided; when sleep overcame them; the room cooled off. The breeze from the river brought a shift of seasons, from the last lingering fragrance of late summer to the first, faint winds of early fall.

He woke up, holding her in his arms. He was lying on his back. She was sleeping with her head resting on his chest. He listened to her, breathing quietly in her sleep.

He gently caressed her back. She moaned a little, even smiled in her sleep.

He looked up into the ceiling. He was happy. Happier than he had been in many years.

And he was worried. He knew he had crossed a line, a hard line that officers with State Security were not supposed to cross.

He was many years older than her. He was ranks above her. And he was her instructor.

He closed his eyes for a moment. Eda Strebber had already picked up on his passion, his love, for Naia. She could easily do something with that, against him. If she wanted to.

But why would she want to do that? They were friends, fellow officers. They had worked together, at S4, at operations, at the investigative division. He had backed her up, she had backed him up. He had always been supportive of her.

She had no reason to do him any harm.

THE BITTER WOMAN LOOKED AT Armo Torndale as if she had never thought about the question before.

"Why did you give up your privileged life?" he repeated, in as kind a voice as he could.

Slowly, her face changed. The hostility and the bitterness subsided. Her shoulders relaxed, she buried her face in her hands.

"I'm sorry," she whispered.

"Don't be," Torndale replied. "This is hard for everyone of us. We are all sacrificing something. Rhem here," and he pointed to Strebber, "he left his wife."

Strebber nodded, clearly taken by the reminder.

"Why?" the woman asked.

"She works for State Security," Strebber said quietly. "Or . . . worked."

The woman wanted to ask more, but Strebber's face showed a great deal of emotional pain, so she turned to Torndale instead.

"This is hard for all of us," she acknowledged.

She lowered her hands and let her tears flow down her cheeks.

"Please remind me again why we are here," she begged.

"You know why," Torndale reminded her.

She nodded.

"One of our kids got bullied in school," she said slowly. "Because someone had found out that my brother-in-law . . . my sister's husband . . . had been prosecuted as a seditionist."

"What did he do?" Strebber asked.

"Nothing, really. He was working as a logistics coordinator for the national railway company. Coordinating freight. This was when the power shortages started. They cut down on the number of trains . . . because they run on electricity."

"Did they load more freight onto fewer trains?" Strebber asked.

"Yes," the woman said.

"The renewable power generators could never replace the old plants," Torndale added. "Rolling brownouts."

"My brother-in-law was concerned that the increased load would be more than the bridges outside of town were built for," said the woman. "And he was ordered to put more freight on fewer trains."

"He was criticizing the government-owned railroad company," Torndale noted.

"Yes."

"That's bizarre," Strebber muttered.

"It is," Torndale agreed. "But that is how the sedition law works. It defines sedition widely, and State Security has decided to interpret it to the extreme. Your brother-in-law fell victim to that extreme interpretation."

"My wife . . . " Strebber said reluctantly.

"She was one of those hardliners," said Torndale. "One of those who pushed for an even more extreme interpretation."

Strebber nodded. He was not happy about the conversation, but he wanted it out there. Maybe it helped him grieve his marriage.

"What I don't get," he said, "is why the top bureaucrats at State Security would want to take the sedition law to its extreme."

"There are two answers," Torndale explained. "One is that the top bureaucrats want as broad a definition as possible, so that they can expand their ranks, get more agents and more resources. The other answer is that once you have arrested and prosecuted . . . or should I say persecuted . . . everyone who actually is a seditionist, in other words anyone who actually wants to overthrow government, then in order to maintain the pressure on the opposition to government, you expand the definition. You see to it that more acts of opposition are considered acts of sedition."

"And the two go well together, I suppose," Strebber noted. "The desire to grow the bureaucracy and the desire to expand the definition of sedition."

"Precisely," Torndale confirmed. "Eventually, anyone expressing a viewpoint that even in some minor way can be interpreted as a disagreement with government, eventually falls under sedition. Which," and he turned to the woman, "is why your brother-in-law was arrested. And I am sorry he was. It should never have happened. But it did. Do you know what happened to him?"

"He was in jail for half a year," she said. "No trial, nothing. Then he was released but had, of course, lost his job."

She looked at Torndale again, with a more relaxed look on her face.

"Thank you," she said. "Thanks for listening. I'm sorry for my negativity."

"Don't be," he said. "And the Danori will be here in the morning. I promise."

The woman thanked him again and left. Torndale and Strebber sat quietly for a moment. Torndale had a small sip of juice. Strebber looked at him. His eyes were sad from the memories of his wife.

"Sorry about bringing up Eda," Torndale said.

"It's alright. We have all made sacrifices for this. But . . . . I can't let go of this . . . what if the Danori don't return in the morning?"

"They will."

"But what if?"

Torndale thought for a moment. Then he said, very reluctantly:

"Then God help us all."

They were interrupted by a camp watchman. He looked a bit excited.

"There is a small group of people making their way up the west side of the mountain."

"That's opposite from the landing spot," Strebber noted and turned to Torndale. "That's the way we came up."

"Could it be State Security?" the watchman asked.

"So they sent someone after us up here anyway," Strebber sighed.

"No, it's not them," Torndale explained.

Strebber and the watchman looked confused.

"How do you know that?" Strebber wanted to know.

Torndale hauled out the cylinder they had found.

"Remember this one? The message in it? It is the small group that left after us."

He got up and grabbed a small flashlight. Strebber and the watchman looked at him as if they waited for something.

"What are you waiting for?" Torndale asked. "We need to go and meet them."

The climb up the west side of the mountain was steep, but it was the only way to climb the mountain without sophisticated climbing gear. It was a major challenge in the dark and the rain. They had to walk very carefully, place every step with the utmost precision, and not lose pace.

Armo Torndale crawled out on the edge of a rock from where he could see a part of the path. In daytime, of course. At this time of day he had to rely on his hand telescope. He had stolen it from State Security, of course. It was equipped with a first of its kind heat-signature function. It did not always work as it was supposed to, but this time it seemed to function just fine.

"There are only four of them," he said. "There were supposed to be five."

The four individuals were struggling to make it up the last stretch. They looked exhausted, to the point where they could trip and fall any time.

"They need our help," Torndale said. "Let's go meet them."

They walked cautiously down a path in the grass. On their right side were rocks and shrubbery, beyond them the tall, centuries-old trees stood densely, forming an almost impenetrable section of the forest. On their left side the slope steepened rapidly, opening toward a deep valley with scattered bushes and rocks giving way to a vertical cliffside. The other side of the valley, the other steep-sloping mountain side, was not far away, though they could not see it for the dark.

The path was normally easy to walk, but the rain had made the dirt slippery. Torndale, a strong and physically fit man despite his age, walked like a martial artist, his knees slightly bent, his arms close to his body with muted movements to avoid losing his balance, his hips doing the work to compensate for shifts in the uneven ground. He moved almost like a feline.

Behind him, Strebber tried to keep up. He did not have the long experience with physical exercise that Armo Torndale had, and his weight loss during their trek was due more to limited eating than to being constantly on the move. He tried his best to keep up with the older man, and he tried desperately to not think about the deep chasm that opened up to his left.

The watchman was young and at least as fit as Armo Torndale. He noticed Strebber struggling with the terrain and kept a close eye on him. But he was not sure what he could do if Strebber slipped and fell, especially if he fell to the left.

When they reached a flat section of the path, Torndale stopped and raised his flashlight. The rain had stopped.

"There they are," he said and pointed ahead.

They heard movements. People climbing up the hill, making no effort to stay quiet. They were not talking, just moving.

Moving forward as if their lives depended on it.

Which they did.

"They are struggling hard," Torndale said. "Three . . . four . . . Sounds like they're all very tired."

He flashed his light. The noise from the climbers stopped.

"Armo," a voice called out.

"Yes."

He moved forward. Suddenly, out of the thick forest on the other side of the little plain spot where they had stopped, he saw a figure coming. It was a short woman, dressed in black. She was carrying a backpack and had a two-hand firearm in her hands. She fought for every step she took, moving mechanically as if she was at the end of the rope. Her green eyes looked at him, but there was almost no life left in them. Her auburn hair was full of dirt and soaked by the rain.

"Naia," Torndale shouted and rushed toward her.

She dropped her firearm on the ground, staggered into his arms and collapsed.

"You made it," he whispered.

She did not reply. She breathed more easily, but he felt her entire body melt into his arms. He fell on his knees, holding the young woman close.

"Come, sit," he said and helped her sit down on the ground. "Come here, my hero."

He held her tight. He could not remember when he last hugged someone like this.

"Oh, my hero," he whispered.

"Water . . . " she begged.

He hauled out his water bottle. She took it and emptied it in almost one swallow.

The others from her group also dropped to the ground. Strebber and the watchman tried their best to help them.

Naia Fernek slowly relaxed. Her breathing slowed down, but she did not let go of Torndale's hug. She crept as closely into his arms as she could. She leaned her head against his chest. He held her, kissed her on the top of her head and whispered how glad he was to see her.

The watchman handed her a small snack bar. It was not bigger than a pinky finger, but at least it was some nutrition.

"Thank you," Naia whispered, and even tried to smile.

"We have to get you to the camp," Torndale said. "We should not wait down here, and . . . I am expecting our evacuation to begin very soon."

Naia looked at him.

"How far is the walk?"

"Fifteen minutes, maybe less."

"I can't make it."

Torndale smiled.

"Then I will carry you," he said.

"You can't do that, not all the way . . . "

"Or would you prefer that I leave you here?"

She examined his face for a second. Then a weak but warm smile came over her.

"I am too tired to appreciate your sense of humor," she said.

Torndale stood up. He handed Naia's backpack to Strebber.

"Is this the essential backpack?" he asked Naia.

"Yes," she confirmed.

"I got it," Strebber promised. "We will take it straight to the secure section."

"Where is my rifle?" Naia asked.

The watchman held it up to confirm that he had it. Naia nodded gratefully.

Torndale reached out with his hand to her.

"Come on, my hero," he said. "Get up. I will carry you on my back."

"Are you strong enough . . . "

"Of course I am," he smiled.

"But it's a long way up there . . . "

"Naia," he said and leaned down. "I will carry you to the end of the world if I have to."

❈ ❈ ❈

THE SUN ROSE OVER THE MOUNTAINS in the west, waking the Ripoman capital to another day. It was a chilly morning full of crisp autumn air. The general curfew, created to protect the people of the capital from crime, ended two bells before daybreak. Almost immediately, the streets filled up with people on their way somewhere: to work, to school, to the stores to get their food and clothing rations and hopefully find those items that often seemed to be in short supply.

When the first rays of sunshine reflected in the windows of the State Security headquarters, Armo Torndale had already been hard at work for some time. His office was full of people. It was not big, so six people easily made it look crowded. Armo Torndale was sitting behind the desk. He had two regular visitor's chairs and had arranged three fold-out chairs in a half circle around them. He watched five adjutants cram themselves in and sit down as best they could.

Torndale offered them hot purple tea.

"I'm afraid I am out of tea biscuits for the moment," he said.

The adjutants chuckled and expressed gratitude for the tea.

"Olgar, close the door," Torndale said, leaned forward and shifted to an authoritative voice he usually reserved for serious matters. "This meeting was called on short notice, so I understand if you are all a bit confused. I am sure you all know about the staff shortage. It is not limited to us at investigations. The operations division is overwhelmed with all sedition cases they have to execute. We here at investigations have done a good job, sending more cases of sedition activities to operations for them to pursue. The problem is, again, that they are short on staff. They have a substantial backlog and are asking for help. Storm Commander Kolmov forwarded their request to me, with an order to put together a group for temporary secondment to operations."

He looked specifically at the two junior adjutants in the room, Olgar and Menzer.

"I know you all have your regular assignments, with Olgar and Menzer currently on loan to the instructions division, so you have your classes you need to attend to. To minimize the disruptions in your teaching, I have only promised operations that we are going to help them out for two days, today and tomorrow."

He noticed a glimpse of disappointment in the faces in the room.

"I know tomorrow is a holiday," he continued, "but the security of the state is always our priority."

"Yes, of course, absolutely," the present company mumbled.

"Good. Now, since we are not regular operations, they have given me a list of low-risk cases to execute. Since the list is long, I don't want us to waste any time. Meet me in Garage Two halfway to next bell, with full protective gear. We will sign out firearms and vehicles at the garage. Any questions?"

"Do we get a list of the cases?" one adjutant asked.

"You will get the information before each case. Any other questions?"

All five shook their heads.

"Alright. Go prepare yourselves."

Olgar and Menzer exited Armo Torndale's office behind everyone else. They chatted about teaching while walking down the hallway. As they reached the first elevator, Menzer said:

"I have to pick up something real quick. I'll see you at the garage."

Olgar nodded and turned to walk to his office. For the second time in a couple of days he almost collided with Eda Strebber.

"Oh, sorry," he excused himself and took a small step back.

"Good morning," she said. "You are here early."

"Yes, we had a meeting."

"About what?"

"I can't really talk about it" Olgar said quietly. "Need to know. You know how it works."

"Yes, of course," she smiled coldly. "Lunch?"

"Uh, no . . . I'll be out all day. Sorry, it's a tight schedule. I have to rush."

A long workday later, as they were driving back from the incarceration center, Armo Torndale leaned back in the command chair of their operations vehicle. He glanced at their schedule and noticed satisfyingly that they had covered four of their seven assignments. They had also arrested ten of the fourteen seditionists they were supposed to arrest.

"Three more assignments tomorrow," he said to the team. "And four more to apprehend."

"Sounds like a lighter workload, sir," Olgar noted.

He was sitting on the side bench right behind the driver.

"Yes," Torndale confirmed. "Hopefully we will get some holiday out of the holiday."

Just as they turned to enter Garage Two, the radio beeped.

"Operations Four Two Eight," Torndale replied.

"Group Commander Torndale" the radio dispatcher replied. "Contact Extension Xray Eighteen for a message."

"Copy and out," Torndale replied and turned off the microphone. "Perfect. I was hoping to go home."

He sent the rest of the group home and went to the garage manager to make an internal phone call. The message was brief yet puzzling:

"Report to GC Smersch for a personnel meeting."

What could that be about? Why would Group Commander Smersch, or Doctor Smersch as he himself preferred to be addressed, want a meeting with him? They did not even work in the same division of State Security. Torndale and Smersch had nothing to do with each other.

Except, of course, for Olgar, Menzer and Eda Strebber. The meeting must be about one of them, and since Menzer and Olgar had been with him all day, he had his suspicions what the meeting could be about.

"I wonder what that Strebber lady has been up to," he muttered as he made his way up through the long, winding corridors of the State Security headquarters.

He nodded in confirmation of his own analysis when he saw Eda Strebber sitting in Doctor Smersch's office. He wondered just how serious the situation was when he also noticed that Storm Commander Kolmov was there. If the chief of personnel at the investigative division was at the meeting, this was definitely a serious matter.

At the same time, Kolmov had not called the meeting. Doctor Smersch had done that.

"Armo," said Doctor Smersch, interrupting Torndale's thoughts on what the meeting was all about. "Good of you to come. Have a seat."

"Commander Kolmov," Torndale saluted the storm commander. "Vigo," he nodded to Doctor Smersch, "Eda," recognizing Adjutant Strebber. "What can I do for you all?"

Commander Kolmov was an old, fat man with small eyes and a big mouth. He was close to retirement and known around the investigative division for being lazy and uninterested in anything except the end-of-work bell.

Since Doctor Smersch had called the meeting, it must have something to do with Eda Strebber's teaching. But that did not make sense, either. Torndale noted that she looked far too relaxed. She sat straight in her chair, with a confident expression on her face—not the tight lips and tense cheeks that a person would have if he or she was accused of something serious.

In fact, Eda Strebber looked almost too confident.

What was really going on here?

※ ※ ※

When Naia Fernek and her team had been brought to the camp and could rest, Armo Torndale made the one discovery he did not want to make.

"You have no food?" he said.

Naia was leaning against a piece of rock with a thin mattress behind her back. She was sitting on a blanket and covered by a crude rain shelter. She sipped citrus water from a cup Armo Torndale had given her.

She was still weak. He was hunkering down next to her, noticing that she had lost a lot of weight.

Naia shook her head.

"We have not eaten for two days. Our rations are depleted."

Armo Torndale hung his head.

"Why?" she asked. "Are you short on food?"

He nodded.

"We have cut down on parents' rations to prioritize kids," he said wearily.

Naia looked down at the cup in her hand.

"And now you have four more mouths to feed," she noted. "I'm sorry."

"I thought you had enough when you left. I even planned your rations so you would bring some extra . . . "

"And we had the extra rations," Naia said in a voice that was breaking up. "I'm sorry I let you down."

Tears ran down her cheeks. Torndale sat down, moved closer to her and took her hand.

"Naia, you did not let anyone down. Especially not me."

"I did," she said and wiped her cheeks. "I didn't hold it together. You just said so yourself."

"I didn't mean it that way. I was just surprised . . . I thought I had planned this well . . . "

Naia cried.

"I'm so exhausted," she said. "I haven't eaten in two days . . . I'm just exhausted . . . and I didn't even hold it together . . . "

"You did, my dear," Torndale said and put his hand on her shoulder. "Naia, you got here, with the package I asked you to bring."

"But no food . . . "

She wept quietly. Torndale turned, reached for his food ration and pulled out a small piece of bread and a slice of silver-milk cheese. He gave it to Naia.

"What's that?" she whispered and wiped her tears again.

"Have this," he said quietly.

"That's your food ration."

"I want you to have it. You need it more than I do."

She looked at him, as if she was searching for something to say.

"Don't say anything," he insisted. "Just have this."

"Thank you," she whispered.

He had never seen bread and cheese disappear that quickly. She swallowed it with the rest of the water.

"The Danori will be here at sunrise," Torndale said. "They will bring food rations. It won't be everything we need, but it will make things better. And they never break a promise."

Naia nodded.

"I'm sorry I'm so emotional," she said, looking down at her dirty clothes.

"You have all the right to be. What you did was heroic. I really mean that. Not many men or women without special training would have pulled off what you did."

She looked up at him and gave away a smile.

"Tell me," Torndale said slowly. "What happened to Enizom?"

His mention of the missing member of her group made Naia close her eyes for a moment. She leaned her head back, sighed and shook her head.

"It was my fault," she said.

"Don't take the blame. Just tell me what happened."

"We set out as you had instructed us to do. Everything went as planned up through the foothills. At one point we even spotted the agents that were tracking you guys. We slowed down and move slightly to the north, so we got a little bit away from them. Just like you had instructed us to do. It worked really well. We even found some terrain that made it easier to climb into the mountains. We also found a spring lake where we replenished our water supply."

She paused, glanced out in the dark and took a deep breath.

"Everything was fine, until . . . six days ago. Or was it eight? I've lost track of time . . . We were setting in for the day. We only traveled at night . . . "

"Excellent," Torndale commended her. "That is a basic rule, but many people forget it."

"As we were setting in, I took inventory of our stuff, like I always did before we camped. And I noticed that there were two nutrition bars missing. Enizom and Hoda thought it was no big deal . . . "

"Actually, it is."

"That's what I thought," she said, looking at him gratefully for his support. "So I asked everyone if they had taken more than their ration. I said it's OK if you did, but just report it and let's not do it again. Hoda admitted that she had taken one, but Enizom refused to admit to anything. I didn't pursue it further, and the next night Hoda apologized again to me and said she was struggling to keep up with the pace, and she didn't want to slow us down. But then the next morning when I took inventory, three bars were missing. I confronted Enizom and he got really defensive about it. I explained that we might not make it all the way if he kept eating more than his ration. Then . . . it was like his mood changed on the spot, and he said . . . I don't remember exactly . . . but he said that it would be better if we didn't make it all the way up."

"What?!"

Naia nodded.

"Was he an infiltrator?" Torndale asked.

"We asked him," Naia continued in a hushed voice. "And he gave it away. He said that we were betraying the people and . . . he pulled out a gun."

"Did you shoot him?"

"Hoda did."

Torndale thought about what she had just told him.

"I was so careful picking what people to trust. Enizom was one of the best agents I trained. I thought I knew him."

"The rest of the group was good," Naia reassured him. "The only problem was that when Hoda shot Enizom, both bullets went through the food supply that he was carrying. Most of the packages were destroyed."

"Well, if you look at it from a strict survival point of view . . . if he was dead, his rations would have been a surplus for the rest of you."

Naia lowered her eyes.

"That's where I failed," she said and looked down at her boots. "I allowed him to carry most of our food supply."

Torndale looked at her in surprise.

"I know," she said without meeting his eyes. "He volunteered, he said he was stronger than the rest of us. And maybe he was. I forgot your instructions . . . "

"Yes," Torndale agreed. "And it could have ended up even worse than it did. He could have taken off with your food supply and made contact with the agents that were tracking us."

"I think they had turned around by that time."

"So you think he was out to sabotage your ascent up here?"

"Or find the camp and . . . "

"Good thing you called him out so early."

Naia looked at him for a second.

"Yeah, I guess you can say that," she agreed, though weakly. "Yeah, he could have done some real harm."

They sat quiet for a moment.

"At least you made it here," Torndale said. "I am very glad you did."

"We got the package delivered," Naia agreed.

"And I have missed your company."

She looked at him. He smiled. She smiled back.

"I've missed your company, too," she said. "Thanks for all your support."

Strebber peaked in.

"Sorry to interrupt," he said. "The sun is just rising."

"Then the Danori should be here any time," Torndale noted in a hushed voice that was uncharacteristic of him.

Naia picked up on it.

"You sound like you don't think they will show up," she said.

Torndale looked down at the ground. He shook his head.

"Honestly," he said in a hushed voice, "if something goes wrong there . . . if the Danori liaison does not show up . . . I don't know if we can keep it together here any longer."

"You don't have to worry," said Strebber. "She's coming up the hill right now."

❈ ❈ ❈

"I CALLED THIS MEETING after consulting Storm Commander Kolmov," Doctor Smersch explained.

Torndale recognized him and turned to the highest ranking officer in the room:

"Commander Kolmov, I assume this is about a personnel matter concerning one of my subordinates."

"Partly," Kolmov nodded. "But there's more. Proceed, Smersch."

"Thank you, sir. Yes, Armo, it's about one of the adjutants under your command, who is on secondment to the educational division."

He paused artfully, as if he wanted Torndale to ask who the adjutant was. But Torndale was not going to give him the pleasure. Eda Strebber was present, and she looked too confident to be the subject of their conversation.

"Go on," Torndale said plainly.

Doctor Smersch looked a bit disappointed, but he forged ahead as planned.

"It's about Adjutant Mic Olgar," he said.

Torndale nodded.

"I figured as much."

"You did?" Doctor Smersch asked. "So you do know why we are here?"

"No. I just assumed that since Adjutant Strebber is here, and Adjutant Olgar is not, and Adjutant Strebber seems to be too comfortable to be the reason for this meeting, I simply deduced that this has to be about Olgar or Menzer. And . . . " he glanced at Eda Strebber, " . . . somehow I don't think Adjutant Strebber would be here if this was about Menzer."

Eda Strebber blushed. Torndale's psychological trick had worked. He had a nagging feeling that Eda Strebber was somehow behind this in the first place. He could not put his finger on it, but it probably had something to do with the fact that she always seemed to want to compete with Olgar.

Doctor Smersch did not look happy with Torndale's conclusion. Commander Kolmov, on the other hand, chuckled and nodded approvingly, as if he was impressed with Torndale's deductive prowess.

Doctor Smersch noted Kolmov's face. It appeared to irritate him, but he could of course not let that irritation reveal itself.

He took a deep breath, frowned for a second and consulted his notes:

"Let's get to the main point, then. If you don't mind, sir."

"Proceed," Commander Kolmov agreed.

"Thank you, sir," Doctor Smersch said and turned to Torndale. "We have reasons to believe that Adjutant Olgar is straying from the ideological purity of our government."

That was a bombshell, no doubt. And Doctor Smersch dropped it just like that.

"Well," Torndale said and frowned for a moment. "That's certainly a serious accusation. I suppose you have solid back-up for it."

Doctor Smersch nodded with something that almost looked like a smirk on his face.

"Oh, we do," he confirmed. "And I'm afraid it's a sordid story, one that you should have caught wind of, Armo."

Torndale looked at him with a completely neutral face. He did not flinch, did not move a muscle in his face. Doctor Smersch did not like it. He scrambled to continue, nodding to Eda Strebber.

"Adjutant Strebber will give us the details," he said.

This was definitely unusual. Doctor Smersch handed over the meeting to the most junior officer in the room, to let her explain a complaint regarding another officer. Any such complaint should be handled by the commanding officer, or whoever was highest ranking in the meeting. Torndale was Olgar's permanent commanding officer, and Doctor Smersch temporarily had that position, so either one of them should be responsible for presenting any complaint.

Not an officer at Olgar's own rank. And certainly not the most junior officer in the room.

Torndale got the distinct feeling that the allegation about ideological impurity was a façade for something else. A pretext. It was a serious allegation: if this went downhill, Olgar could be accused of sedition. To be a seditionist within the ranks of State Security was the same as asking to be whisked off to the harshest labor camp in the country. If not immediate execution.

No, there had to be something else behind all this.

Whatever it was, Torndale congratulated himself quietly for having figured out that Eda Strebber was instrumental in this case. It helped him zero in on what was going on under the surface.

Eda Strebber looked at Torndale as if she was looking at someone of equal or lower rank. Torndale did not say anything—he avoided taking the provocative bait—but he made a mental note of putting her in place when he got the opportunity.

And just like that, she dropped the next bombshell:

"Olgar has been ideologically compromised by having an affair with one of his students."

Her tone was blunt, plain and void of excitement. Torndale looked at her in silence. She remained confident.

"And you have proof of all this?" Torndale asked quietly.

"Yes," Eda Strebber replied, almost condescending in her tone.

Torndale kept his eyes fixed on her. He watched her intensely. She looked him in the eyes, and he could tell that she was getting nervous. Apparently, she was not getting the reaction from her superior officer that she had been expecting.

Or been promised by others in the room.

When Torndale did not react as expected, Eda Strebber's eyes flickered a bit. She cleared her throat and looked at Doctor Smersch for approval.

Torndale thought that was curious. She did not look at Commander Kolmov, the highest ranking officer in the room.

Torndale thought for a moment, then replied, plainly:

"Yes, that is a serious allegation."

"Yes, it is indeed . . . " Eda Strebber said quickly, but Torndale interrupted her.

He raised his hand and shook his head. She stopped her mouth in its tracks, ground to a complete halt in her sentence and suddenly looked like she had realized that she was disrespecting a superior officer.

"I'm sorry, sir . . . " she mumbled and looked down at her notes.

"Don't interrupt me," Armo Torndale said slowly, sternly and quietly.

"Yes, sir, of course."

"As I said, this is a serious allegation, in both its parts. About Olgar having an affair with a student and about him being ideologically compromised. It is inappropriate to have romantic affairs with anyone at work, be it instructor and student or any other relationship. It compromises the integrity of one's work, dilutes one's loyalties. You open yourself to corrupting influence."

He paused and shifted position in his chair. It was uncomfortable and not what he wanted to sit on after having been running about the city all day.

"Armo," said Commander Kolmov.

"Yes, sir."

"Have you not had any suspicions about Olgar?"

"Of this sort? No, sir."

"I find that hard to believe," Doctor Smersch blurted out.

Torndale ignored him.

"Commander Kolmov," he said. "You are the chief of personnel at the investigative division. You have long experience handling sensitive personnel issues."

The commander nodded wearily.

"You know better than anyone that when someone is accused in this way, it takes quite a bit of evidence to establish the veracity of those accusations. Now, I am not questioning these accusations per se . . . "

"And yet you haven't seen any problems yourself," Doctor Smersch interrupted him. "I find that interesting."

Torndale looked at him for a moment.

"You do, don't you," he said quietly.

Doctor Smersch was about to say something, but Commander Kolmov made a gesture to him to keep quiet. Kolmov was old, fat and lazy. He was close to retirement and had lost all interest in pursuing his duty with anything more than minimum effort. But he was also the second highest in command at the investigative division, and he outranked both Torndale and Doctor Smersch.

"Armo," he said. "I have to ask you . . . why haven't you seen any indications of improper behavior from Olgar?"

"Sir, with all due respect," Torndale said and looked Commander Kolmov straight in the eyes. "One reason could be that the allegation of ideological impurity simply isn't true."

"Are you suggesting . . . " Doctor Smersch started but was interrupted by Commander Kolmov:

"Shut up, Vigo," he said in a voice that was sprinkled with irritation.

Doctor Smersch shut his mouth with lightning speed, clasped his hands and drew a big chunk of air through his nose to calm himself down.

Torndale waited with anticipation.

"Armo has a point," Commander Kolmov continued. "Allegations of this level must be substantiated. The burden of doing that is on your shoulders, Vigo. You delegated that work to the adjutant here . . . " and he did not even look at Eda Strebber, " . . . so the two of you should probably get to it. Don't you think?"

"Yes, sir," Doctor Smersch mumbled. "Yes, sir, of course, sir. It was Adjutant Strebber who discovered Adjutant Olgar's improper relationship. Adjutant?"

Eda Strebber hesitated for a moment. She was clearly taken by Commander Kolmov's putting Doctor Smersch in his place. She nodded nervously, looked at them all for a moment and cleared her throat.

"Yes, sir . . . Yes. Some of my students are concurrently taking Olgar's class. A couple of them have expressed concern to me regarding Olgar's teaching. They say . . . uh . . . that he teaches them about different political theories in a way that does not elevate our nation's value foundation above its alternatives. He does not . . . uh . . . does not seem to . . . uh . . . be able to explain how . . . uh . . . our people's democratic union is morally superior to the federal republic."

Torndale noted how she was struggling to maintain her argument. He noted how, every time she paused and uttered an "uh", she avoided eye contact. Her voice also temporarily lost its force.

Classic signs of a liar.

"Thank you, Adjutant Strebber," said Doctor Smersch. "Very good explanation. My question, as head of instruction here at the academy, is . . . what do I do with Adjutant Olgar? Commander Kolmov?"

He turned to Commander Kolmov. The storm commander sighed and adjusted his seating position. He pulled out a smoke stick from the inside pocket of his uniform jacket, rolled it between his fingers and seemed to ponder his words for a bit. They all waited.

"Well," he said eventually. "What do you think about all this, Armo?"

"Sir," Torndale said. "If all of this is true, it is of course of a nature that calls into question Olgar's continued affiliation with State Security. However, so far I have only heard Adjutant Strebber's accusations, and while I am not questioning them per se, I do believe that accusations of this nature must be verifiable before we proceed with any disciplinary action."

Commander Kolmov nodded.

"Yes," he said wearily. "That is obviously the case. But in the meantime, it is reasonable to limit Olgar's engagement in more sensitive activities than teaching."

"What do you mean, sir?"

"He is currently participating in a two-day operational assignment under your command."

He put down the smoke stick on the desk in front of him. He spoke in a slow, tired voice, leaning against the side of his armchair. It was clear that his deteriorating health was taking a toll on him. His stamina was well below that of the average officer, even behind that of other officers of his age and rank.

"And in that capacity," the commander continued in a strikingly conversational tone, "he is privy to sensitive information regarding the apprehension of seditionists. He knows who the seditionists are, even before they are arrested. It would seem appropriate that you remove him from your team, even if that team only has one more day of operations to execute."

He picked up the smoke stick again, smelled it and smiled briefly.

"After all," he added, "it's only one day, so it shouldn't do too much harm to anyone."

Torndale did not like the idea, but he was being given an order by a higher-ranking officer.

"Yes, sir. If that is what you think is best, I will remove him from my team. But I would like to get some more information about these accusations."

He looked specifically at Doctor Smersch, who nodded, as if to acknowledge that he was pushing the limits here, and maybe even exceeding them.

"Yes, Armo . . . Yes. Well, Adjutant Strebber can tell us more about that."

"Thank you, sir," she said. "Yes, Olgar is having this romantic relationship with a student named Naia Fernek. She is a first-year cadet. She is also in my class, so I have had some time to get to know her."

"How did you discover their relationship?" Torndale asked.

"Olgar inadvertently told me. And I have another officer's affidavit that he overheard the conversation. I have also seen them together a couple of times. They are clearly romantically involved."

"Okay, so that's the romantic relationship. What about the part about him being ideologically compromised by this relationship?"

"I believe I can answer that," Doctor Smersch intervened, coming to Eda Strebber's rescue while reading from his notes. "According to Adjutant Strebber's formal note on Cadet Fernek, she is showing an unusual interest in the history of the federal republic. She questions the values of the people's democratic union and she constantly wants to know the purposes behind our work."

He looked up.

"And Olgar seems to be encouraging that," he added. "We have a recording from one of Olgar's lectures, where Miss Fernek asks questions beyond what one can expect within the realm of student curiosity."

He paused, leaned back in his chair and looked Torndale straight in the eyes.

"Armo, this student may be harboring seditionist values," he said. "And if she does, she has most certainly compromised Adjutant Olgar. And you are his commanding officer. It is your duty to deal with this."

Torndale looked at Doctor Smersch for a moment. He glanced over at Commander Kolmov, who looked like he was ready to take a nap.

"Actually, Vigo," Torndale said slowly. "Olgar is on secondment to your division. You are temporarily his commanding officer. That means you have operational command over him. And . . . as I am sure you remember from when you and I . . . shall we say worked together back in operations . . . "

He paused to enjoy how his words sank in and made Doctor Smersch almost shiver in his chair.

"That was a long time ago," Doctor Smersch muttered.

"As I am sure you remember from a long time ago," Torndale continued with an amused tone in his voice, "operational command supersedes both rank and assigned command."

Doctor Smersch looked down at his notes. Commander Kolmov seemed to be waking up from his half-slumber.

"That's an interesting point, Armo," he chuckled. "Thanks for reminding all of us."

He smelled his smoke stick, put it back in his inner pocket and sighed.

"But for now . . . I think it's imperative that you withdraw Olgar from your operational assignment."

"Yes, sir," Armo Torndale said, trying to stay neutral. "I will do so immediately. And I need to find a replacement."

Eda Strebber looked at him with inquisitive eyes.

"Adjutant Strebber is available," Doctor Smersch pointed out.

Torndale ignored him. He paid close attention to Eda Strebber's body language. Her entire appearance suggested that she wanted the assignment, and badly so.

He did not want her on the group. He was convinced that all the accusations about seditionist behavior from the student's side were over-stated, or maybe even false altogether. A curious young student, eager to learn, will always ask questions. He was also not convinced that Eda Strebber's account of students complaining about Olgar's teaching had any truth to it. In fact, he strongly suspected that she was lying about it.

Now she was sitting here, eagerly awaiting to replace Olgar on his team. He knew she was ambitious. She took all extra assignments she could get her hands on. He had noticed how she flattered upper ranks and sometimes behaved dismissively toward others of her own rank.

Was all this nothing more than an attempt by her to get a prestigious extra assignment that would look good on her resume? Was she simply jealous that Olgar got picked, and not her?

Or was there something deeper going on here? These accusations of disloyalty toward the value foundation in Olgar's teaching had a clear political undertone to it. Torndale had been around long enough to know that an organization sometimes put its employees through loyalty tests. It was perfectly normal.

But this was going beyond the normal. It was not a professional loyalty test. It was beginning to smell of a political crusade against Adjutant Olgar.

And perhaps against himself. Torndale would certainly not hold it beyond Doctor Smersch to pull off such a stunt.

He did not want to play along with their games. He decided to take a different route.

"Commander Kolmov," he said. "If it is indeed true that Cadet Fernek has seditionist leanings, would it not be good for us to find that out as soon as possible?"

"It certainly would," Commander Kolmov agreed.

"I have worked with investigations for a long time, sir. As you know, I headed up our ideological project after we transitioned from the federal republic to the people's democratic union. I led the effort to internally educate our officers on the new value foundation that we had just adopted at the time."

"And you did a fine job," the commander told him.

"Thank you, sir, I appreciate that. I was thinking . . . I do have quite a bit of experience in investigating seditionist activities. Perhaps I should take Cadet Fernek under my command so I can get to know her a bit more?"

Doctor Smersch frowned.

"What exactly are you suggesting?" he asked pointedly.

"That I fill Olgar's spot with Cadet Fernek."

"That's a creative idea," Commander Kolmov chuckled. "Well, you will certainly get some eye candy to enjoy while you're out there."

"Isn't she too young to participate in operations?" Doctor Smersch asked.

"Perhaps," Commander Kolmov replied, sucking on his unlit smoke stick. "But I like Armo's approach here. Getting to know someone is the best way to find out who they really are."

"Thank you, sir," Torndale said. "With your approval I will contact Cadet Fernek tonight. But first, I better get hold of Olgar."

"You might only have to make one phone call to both of them," Commander Kolmov laughed.

They all smiled with him, but Armo Torndale noted that Eda Strebber was furious that she had not been picked. On their way out from the meeting he took her aside and made sure they were alone. She tried to look at him assertively.

"Adjutant Strebber," he said in a hushed voice.

She took a deep breath and lowered her eyes a bit.

"Yes, sir."

"Your behavior in there was absolutely unacceptable."

At first, she looked at him almost defiantly. But when his eyes narrowed and his facial muscles tightened, she lowered her head a little bit and nodded.

"Yes, sir," she said mechanically. "I am sorry, sir."

"I never thought I'd see such disrespect of a superior officer, your own group commander at that."

"Yes, sir," she repeated in a neutral voice.

"I am going to make a formal note of this on your record."

"Sir?"

She looked him in the eyes, again defying protocol for talking to—or being talked to by—a senior officer.

Torndale was unmoved.

"You should have thought about that before you started mouthing off in there. I appreciate that you report inappropriate behavior by a fellow officer, but what you did in there . . . "

He paused. She maintained her attitude, on the verge of defiance. He was a bit surprised to see it, but he realized that it could only mean one thing. This was a political stunt, a power play by Doctor Smersch, and she had his full back-up.

Torndale did not care about Doctor Smersch. He had enough dirt on Smersch to terminate his career if he wanted to. But he did not want to annoy Commander Kolmov. Sure, the storm commander was lazy and did as little as possible to still pretend that he was working. But he was nevertheless one of the highest ranking officers at the investigative division, and he could cause trouble even for someone like Torndale.

He toned down his lecture to Eda Strebber.

"From now on," he said in as clear a voice as he could, "I will expect the utmost professionalism from you. Is that clear?"

"Yes, sir," she said, sticking to her mechanical voice.

"Your job as far as Olgar goes, is done. Go home and get some rest."

She extended a courtesy and dashed away to sign out for the day. Torndale strolled back to his office. He wanted to go home. He wanted to go spend the holiday down in the Riverlands with his brother and his nephews and nieces with their families, but instead he had to get hold of Olgar.

And have a conversation with him that he did not look forward to.

"WE WILL START EVACUATING IMMEDIATELY."

The Danori woman's words were like divine choir music in Armo Torndale's ears.

He looked at her and felt a surge of joy and relief.

"Thank you," he said, almost coming to tears.

She looked at him with some confusion.

"You seem surprised," she noted. "I promised you that we would start evacuating today."

"I know," he said. "I am just happy we are coming to the end of this."

"Good," she said matter-of-factly. "The circumstances are a bit restrictive. We have the large evacuation ship waiting at the edge of the solar system. We cannot let it cross the outermost planetary orbit."

"Why not?"

"For legal reasons," she said in a tone that made Torndale chuckle.

She gave him a look and exhibited something that looked like a smile.

"Our bureaucratic apparatus continues to amuse you."

"Yes," Torndale admitted. "But let's talk about that some other time. So if your evacuation vessel cannot enter the solar system . . . what does that mean for our departure?"

"We have a shuttle craft that can take twelve passengers at a time. Given the distance to fly with it, and the time needed to refill propulsion, we need one day for each load. You have sixty people here, twelve per day means five days to get you all ferried out."

"Actually, there are sixty-four of us."

The Danori woman frowned. There was no mistaking that facial expression.

"You told me there were sixty," she pointed out sharply.

"I forgot the four that were on their way behind us . . . "

"Armo," she snapped at him. "I negotiated the terms of your evacuation based on the number you gave me. You cannot change your end of the deal now. That is an unacceptable breach of our contract."

She looked like she was ready to just walk away.

"I am very sorry," Torndale said. "I . . . let me explain . . . "

"No, met me explain to you," she said, still in a stern voice. "I have stretched the authority of our organization to the limit to make this happen. I have jurisdiction over five shuttle runs. That is all."

"Okay, and I will take full responsibility for my error," Torndale said, near the brink of what he had energy for. "If you can only take sixty people, I will volunteer to remain behind. I will find three others who will stay behind with me."

He turned and looked over his shoulder, back at the camp, trying to come up with names of three more people who could agree to his deal.

"Armo," said the Danori woman in a softer tone. "You would do that?"

"Do what?" he asked wearily and turned back to her.

"You would sacrifice yourself to fulfill your end of our agreement?"

"Of course I would," he sighed. "I damn well nearly gave my life leading these people up here anyway. I was ready to die for them every step of the way."

He rubbed his eyes with his index finger and his thumb.

"I'm sorry," he said. "I have not slept in two days. I have barely eaten, my stomach is a mess, and . . . "

He suddenly felt a touch on his shoulder. He looked up. The Danori woman had reached out with her right hand.

There was a warmth in her eyes that he had never seen before.

"If you are willing to die for the freedom of your fellow refugees," she said, gently and with a dollop of respect in her voice, "then I will make an effort to see if we can fit more than twelve people into each flight. We can only take twelve on this flight. I make no promise, but I will make an effort to get all sixty-four of you onboard."

He smiled at her.

"I would give you a hug if I did not stink so bad," he said.

"We have hygienic facilities on the evacuation ship," she replied dryly. "Get your first twelve evacuees ready. Have them report to our ship immediately."

While Strebber distributed the new food supply, Torndale called up three families with children.

"You have to leave now," he said.

He did not have to ask them twice. He saw the joy and gratitude in their eyes as they collected their very few belongings.

"I will go with you to the ship," Torndale said.

The parents of the three families were as excited as their children.

"It is really happening," one of the dads said to Torndale, his eyes glowing with joy.

"It is," Torndale replied, happily but wearily.

Just as they set off down the hill, Armo Torndale felt someone grabbing his left arm.

It was Naia. He turned and saw worry in her eyes.

"Are you leaving?" she asked.

"I'm just escorting them down to the ship. I'll be back in a little bit."

"Can I come with you?"

"Of course!"

She had gained some strength and was eating a nutrition bar. She had a water bottle tucked into the side pocket of her pants.

"You look better," Torndale noted.

"Thanks," she said while chewing. "I feel better."

The downhill slope was mostly clear shrubbery and rocks. Tall trees towered over them and some of their roots surfaced in unpredictable places, forming traps for the unsuspecting. But nothing kept the group from moving forward. Not hunger, not thirst, not the pain and hardship from the long trek and the agonizing wait.

As they reached the bottom of the hill, a clearing emerged slightly to the left. Suddenly, they saw the shuttle craft. It was shaped like a tube with flat sides. It was silvery in color and stood on a landing gear that looked like an inflated air cushion. It was about the length of a city bus and had a large side door folded down with a short staircase rolled out.

"It's beautiful," one of the women said, almost bursting into tears.

The Danori woman stood outside the ship waiting for them. At her side was a man in what looked like a uniform with officer's markings on the left chest and the arms.

The group moved forward, though a bit more slowly, almost as if they wanted to savor the moment.

"Are those . . . Danori?" asked one of the men.

"They are," Torndale confirmed.

"What are they like?"

"A bit distant, but friendly and very reliable."

The man looked at him as if he was overwhelmed by the moment. Armo Torndale gave him an encouraging pat on the shoulder.

"Welcome," said the Danori woman. "May I introduce commander Renco, second officer of the Rohax, the evacuation vessel."

"Is this the ship?" one of the men asked.

"This is the shuttle craft that will take you to the big starship," Torndale explained.

"Please climb onboard," said the Danori woman.

The man looked at Torndale.

"You are not coming with us?"

"We need to get all you families out first," Torndale said. "There will be more flights."

"Are there . . . facilities and food onboard the ship?" asked one of the women.

"I assume you ask about personal hygiene and food and water," said the Danori woman.

"Yes," said the woman, gasping at the sight of the aliens.

"The Rohax is an evacuation vessel" explained Commander Renco. "We have facilities to harbor refugees for a sustained period of time."

"Please," Torndale said. "Get onboard. We don't have much time."

Cautiously, the three families boarded the shuttle craft. Torndale stood at the bottom of the short staircase and watched them take seats. He heard two of the women start crying.

"This is beautiful," said one of them.

"I can't believe this is happening!" cried another.

Commander Renco slowly climbed the stairs. The Danori woman turned to Armo Torndale.

"Same time tomorrow morning," she confirmed.

"We will be here," Torndale promised. "Oh, and I almost forgot. Naia, the bag."

Naia handed the Danori woman the bag with the precious cargo that she and her team had brought with them.

"What is this?"

"Your government is negotiating in secrecy with our government about interstellar contact," Torndale said.

"Correct. That is how I first got to know you."

"I think you will find that the information in this bag . . . the package inside this bag . . . will shed a new light on . . . the honesty, or lack of honesty, of our government . . . in those negotiations."

The Danori woman looked at the bag for a moment.

"We shall examine it," she said diplomatically.

Armo Torndale and Naia watched the shuttle craft lift off. He reached out and put his arm around her shoulders. She came closer.

"It is finally happening," he said.

"Thanks to you," she noted.

He turned and met her eyes.

"Thanks to us."

"It was your plan. Your determination."

As the shuttle craft vanished out of sight, he let go of her shoulders and started walking back toward the camp.

"It's not over yet," he pointed out.

"Are you leaving on the last flight?" Naia asked him.

Torndale glanced at her and kept walking.

"Are you leaving last?" Naia wanted to know.

"Probably," he said evasively.

"You deserve to leave earlier."

"I won't leave earlier."

Naia jumped in front of him and looked him in the eyes.

"What are you saying?" she demanded. "Are you leaving last, or not?"

"It's not been decided yet," Torndale said, trying to avoid her.

She forced him to stop.

"You are not leaving earlier, and you are probably leaving with the last ship," she said. "Strebber said something about us being too many to evacuate. I thought he meant on one flight."

He noticed her lower lip shaking. She was verging on tears.

"Armo, tell me what is going on here. I can't take any more of this stress."

❊ ❊ ❊

"Yes?"

"Adjutant Olgar? This is Commander Torndale."

"Hello, sir. What . . . uhm . . . what can I do for you at this late hour?"

"Is Naia Fernek at your house right now?"

Silence.

"Olgar!"

"Sir . . . I . . . "

"Come clean with me right now."

"Yes . . . yes, sir . . . she . . . uh . . . she is here . . . "

"Good. So it is true, then."

"Sir?"

"Adjutant Mic Olgar, you realize that you have broken formal regulations and protocol by getting into a romantic relationship with another officer. A cadet, at that, who is your student."

"Yes, sir . . . "

Armo Torndale sat quiet at his desk for a moment. He listened to Olgar's breathing getting more intense.

"Sir . . . " Olgar said, very nervously.

"I was just at a meeting where I was told of this relationship. Storm Commander Kolmov was present."

"The staff commander . . . " Olgar gasped.

"Yes."

Silence.

"Sir . . . is there . . . can I do anything . . . "

"Commander Kolmov wanted you fired on the spot," Torndale lied.

"Okay . . . sir . . . "

"I convinced him not to do it."

"Thank you, sir . . . "

"That doesn't mean you aren't going to be terminated."

"Is . . . is there anything, sir, that . . . that I can do . . . ?"

"To save your career?"

"Yes, sir . . . "

"It's very simple. Kick that young cadet out of your apartment and out of your private life. Right now."

"Yes, sir."

"And never talk to her again outside of strictly professional settings."

"Absolutely, sir."

"Is that clear?"

"Yes, sir. Uh . . . does that mean . . . there will be no . . . staff inquiry?"

"If she is out of your life tonight."

"Absolutely, sir. Right away."

"Good."

"Thank you, sir."

"Two more things. You are off the operations team."

"Oh . . . okay, sir . . . "

"And tell Cadet Fernek to call me when she gets back to her place."

When Olgar got off the phone he almost collapsed into the backrest of the couch. His arms slouched alongside his body. He leaned his head back and closed his eyes.

"Was it that bad?" Naia asked.

She was sitting sideways next to him, her legs pulled up and crossed in front of her. She reached out with one hand and touched his arm.

Olgar nodded without looking at her.

"Commander Torndale," he said weakly.

He rubbed his face with his palms. Naia clasped her hands between her knees.

"He knows about us," Olgar almost whispered.

"And?"

He looked at her.

"And what?"

"Is that a problem?" she asked, slightly worried.

"Of course it's a problem!" Olgar blurted out. "You can't have romantic relationships with coworkers. Let alone if they are your student! I can get fired over this."

He paused, took a deep breath and looked away from her.

"We have to stop seeing each other," he said plainly.

Naia pulled back. She pulled her knees up, wrapped her arms around her legs and looked at Olgar in disbelief.

"You . . . you knew that before we . . . before you got involved with me?" she asked in a voice that told Olgar she felt betrayed.

He looked at her. Her eyes were filling with tears. Her lips were tight, her eyebrows lowered.

"You knew all along . . . " she whispered, tears pouring out of her eyes, down her cheeks.

"Naia," he said quietly and reached out to touch her cheek.

She firmly pushed his hand away. Her face was filled with anger. Bitterness.

"You knew this was wrong," she almost shouted. "You knew!"

"I did," he admitted. "But I could not resist you. You are so . . . so gorgeous . . . "

"Bullshit!" she screamed and jumped up from the couch. "Is that all I am to you?!"

"No . . . "

"A pair of big boobs!"

"No, Naia . . . well . . . "

"Well what!?"

"I find you extremely attractive . . . " he said almost childishly, leaning forward with his elbows placed on his knees.

She stared at him in disbelief. He looked up at her and tried to smile. She shook her head, tears running down her cheeks. She paced back and forth for a moment, as if trying to relieve herself of her stress. She breathed heavily, stopped halfway across the room from Olgar and crossed her arms. She looked out the window, then at him. Tears flooding, she was hyperventilating and her feet moved back and forth.

He looked at her. He saw the same beautiful young woman he had met that first day of class. He looked into her amazing green eyes, he saw her auburn hair that framed the most divinely sculpted face he had ever seen.

He felt that same sting of love in his stomach that he felt the first time she came into his office.

He was shaken out of his romantic mood by Naia's bone-crushing words:

"You betrayed me! Mic, you garbage! You betrayed me!"

Her words cut like knives through his ears. He blinked and looked again. The sorrow in her eyes gave way to anger. Resentment. Her face darkened. Her eyes narrowed. Her nostrils pumped air into her lungs while her lips were so tight it almost looked like she did not have a mouth.

"Do you have any idea how much this hurts!!" she screamed at him.

There was unmitigated anger in her face.

"Do you?!" she yelled.

She turned, paced back and forth again while hugging herself with her arms. She cried uncontrollably.

Olgar watched her, baffled and shocked. He had no idea what to do.

"Naia, sit down . . . " he tried.

"Shut up!" she screamed and dashed out to the hallway.

She started putting her clothes on.

"I'm just a toy to you," she cried. "I'm just something you think you can play around with."

He got up and walked halfway over to the hallway. He stopped well before he got there. He was not sure how she would react if he came closer.

"No, Naia . . . "

"I was such an idiot believing you" she said rapidly while tying her shoes. "I've never had a man before. I told myself I should trust this man. I thought I could trust this man."

She put her coat on and picked up her bag. As she slung it over her shoulder, she turned to him and looked him dead in the eyes.

"I'll talk to the class coordinator about dropping your class. I don't ever want to see you again."

"Commander Torndale wants you to call him when you get home."

"Don't ever call me!" she said while turning to the door.

"Call Commander Torndale when you get home."

"What?"

She stopped with her hand on the door.

"Commander Torndale wants you to call him at his office when you get home."

"Why?"

Olgar shrugged his shoulders.

"I guess he wants to know that you actually left my apartment."

"I'll call him alright," Naia Fernek promised, stepped out and slammed the door shut behind her.

※ ※ ※

THE MORNING SUNLIGHT broke through the forest. Armo Torndale and Naia Fernek stood only a few yards into the woods from the clearing where the shuttlecraft had taken off. The morning birds were beginning to sing, and in the distance a rock hound called for its mate.

Naia stood right in front of Torndale. He was head and shoulders taller than her. She looked up at him, her eyes exuding determination.

Determination to get the truth out of him.

He also sensed desperation. As if she read his mind, she said:

"I fear you are planning on sending me off on one of those flights, while you stay behind because there are too many people at the camp."

Torndale looked down on his shoes for a moment. She waited. She stood with her hands on her hips, her tired legs barely holding her up.

"Look, Naia," he said. "You are young, you have a fantastic future ahead of you . . . in that new colony they are building . . . "

She shook her head. She took a step forward and pointed him in the chest.

"Don't assume to be speaking for me" she whispered, breathing to keep her tears back. "I am not . . . I am not leaving without you."

She turned away from him, wiped her tears and tried to look strong. He stepped a little bit to the side so he could see her face. She turned away from him again, wiping more tears.

"I didn't mean it that way," he said in the kindest voice possible.

"What did you mean?" she asked, trying to regain her balance.

"I only meant that . . . well . . . I guess I meant that . . . why would a young woman like you choose to stay behind with an old guy like me?"

Her tears dried up. She turned toward him again. There was genuine curiosity in her eyes.

"You don't . . . you don't get it, do you . . . ?"

"Get what?"

She threw herself into his arms.

"Oh, you stupid old man," she said.

They hugged for what seemed like an eternity.

"I never really had a father," she whispered eventually. "I'm not sure if that's who you are . . . but I don't care."

"I guess I am a stupid old man," he said and chuckled. "I don't care what I am . . . what we are . . . companions?"

She giggled inside his arms. He kissed her on the top of her head. She slowly released herself from their hug.

They shared a smile.

"Companions," she agreed.

Torndale pointed up the hill:

"Want to go back and celebrate the first flight?"

As they slowly made their way up, Naia brought up the one subject they did not want to talk about:

"What do we do if we stay behind?"

"There is no other country to go to. No other place in the world where freedom reigns anymore. Ripoma was it."

He thought for a moment.

"I guess we can find a way to disappear into some obscure corner of society. Perhaps live quietly, privately, without bothering anyone."

"I could see that," she agreed.

"You don't sound too happy."

"It's not the happiest way to live, is it?"

"No, but sometimes the choice is not ours."

She nodded.

"I get that. It's just a bitter thing to realize. That everything you believed in . . . it turns out to be something else, something that is the very opposite of what you believed in."

"Did you believe in the policies that Sorto put to work in the new people's democratic union?"

"I was too young at the time. I had no clue about those things. But I believed in his value foundation when I was in high school. And when I applied to the State Security academy."

"The value foundation that says everyone gets everything" Torndale noted with a grain of sarcasm in his voice.

"You are always refreshingly blunt when you talk about that value foundation," Naia noted amusedly. "But yeah, that is essentially what it states. That past injustices must be corrected for, that some who have enjoyed privileges had to be made to suffer until all economic and social differences between people had been eradicated. And that's an appealing thought, especially if you are young and you think that some people have a better life because others have a worse life."

"You are made to believe that every gain that someone makes is unjust because you have been taught that his only way to become rich is by making someone else poor."

"Yes," Naia agreed. "That is what we believed. We believed that anyone who had more, deserved to be punished. I remember thinking . . . when I applied for State Security . . . that it would be morally right of me to arrest the privileged, to bring them to justice for having come by their possessions in some unjust way."

"And that is the danger of it," Torndale noted. "You are led to believe that someone who has more than the average man, has committed an injustice in order to come by it."

"You mean it is never proven, just assumed, that it is an injustice?"

"Exactly."

Naia looked up at him as they walked up the hill.

"I remember the moment I started thinking about this," she said. "It was that time you brought me onboard with your operations team. To replace Mic Olgar. We were arresting an old lady who could barely walk."

"I remember her. Her name was Veesaus. She lived in a big house, all alone."

"And that was one of the charges against her, wasn't it?" Naia remembered. "That she had not surrendered her privilege to the state."

"Yes. That was one of the reasons. There was another reason. Remember?"

Naia thought for a moment. They reached the camp and stopped for a moment.

"I do remember," she said. "It was painful."

Garage Two at the State Security headquarters was not really a garage. It was a large, open-air parking lot, surrounded by tall, thick walls and filled with vehicles of all kinds. They were all painted in silver and blue, the colors of State Security, fitted with sirens and dark green emergency lights. There were passenger cars, vans with up to 15 seats, anti-riot vehicles and so-called cage vans, which had a solid, steel-plated cage in the back with no windows. It was accessible only from the back and had two locks on it. A small camera allowed the front passenger of the van to monitor the prisoners during transport.

Whenever State Security wanted to intimidate people or simply make its presence known, it always drove up in silver-and-blue. When it wanted to go about its business unnoticed, its agents retrieved vehicles from Garage One, which was located underneath the headquarters. There, they had vehicles of all sorts: utility trucks, plain civilian cars and vans, metro transit buses, delivery trucks, taxi cabs, even vehicles painted in the colors of local police. They had a vast wardrobe of clothes to go with whatever disguise they preferred.

Many agents looked for a pretext to check out a vehicle from Garage One just to play a little theater among the public. It was also a nice way for them to create provocations, to stir up anti-government protests and then arrest those protesters for sedition.

As Armo Torndale and his team were preparing for their second and last day of arrests, he told Naia Fernek about what the agency was like just after the Great Transition.

"When the federal republic was swept away," he said as they put on their bullet proof vests, uniform jackets, gun belts and com radios, "the operations division was issued minimum arrest quotas. President Sorto had just become Grand Chancellor Sorto, and he issued orders to our agency to arrest as many seditionists as possible. I was in intelligence back then, which turned into investigations, but I was temporarily assigned to operations to help out. My group . . . there were six of us . . . had to arrest a minimum of eight seditionists per day."

"How did you find them?" Naia asked. "Did you have a list of them, like . . . like we do now?"

"Sometimes. Sometimes we didn't. So we used provocation methods. But there were a couple of times when we had to fill our quotas more creatively."

"Creatively?"

"We were parked on a street corner one afternoon, in full uniform and everything, just taking a break. This young man comes up to us and asked for directions to some address. I asked him what business he had at that address, and he said it didn't matter, he just wanted to find his way there, because he was from out of town. I asked again what business he had in town, and he got irritated and said it was none of our business. We arrested him for sedition. That filled our arrest quota for the day."

Naia looked at him, quietly. She did not say anything, but he saw something in her eyes as she put on her helmet.

He had a pretty good idea of what she was thinking.

"Alright," he said. "Let's roll."

Before they made their first arrest of the day, they had to revisit the home of one of the seditionists they had arrested the day before. The operations division had requested further evidence to be collected.

"There is really no point in doing it," Torndale muttered as they parked and climbed out of the van. "It's probably already been ransacked."

"Ransacked, sir?" Naia Fernek asked.

"You'll see. Kelm, stay with the vehicle. Let's go."

They climbed the stairs of the apartment building to the third floor. A long hallway stretched right and left, with multiple doors on each side. All doors were closed except for one door at the end of the hallway to the left. It was wide open.

"Told you," Torndale noted, as if talking to himself.

The apartment was in complete disorder. Bookshelves and cabinets had been looted clean, the kitchen emptied out of anything portable. In the bedroom, the drawers in the big chest had been pulled out and thrown about. They were almost completely empty.

Even the bathroom had been robbed of everything. Someone had tried to tear the showerhead off but failed and left it broken.

Torndale gathered his agents in the living room.

"Anyone found any evidence?" he asked, in a tone that strongly suggested the question was purely rhetorical.

"No, sir," one of the other agents mumbled.

"Let's go."

Before they climbed back into their van, Naia caught Torndale's attention.

"Sir . . . may I ask a question?"

"Sure."

"Why were we sent back there when our agents had already been there collecting evidence?"

Torndale told her to get in and promised to explain as they drove off. A radio call interrupted him, asking them to change the order of their first two arrests.

"That's actually better for us," Torndale noted. "This one is just around the corner."

He was sitting in the front passenger seat. Adjutant Kelm was driving. The other four agents sat on sideways mounted benches in the mid section of the van, with the arrest cage in the back.

Torndale turned and looked at the four agents in the mid section.

"It was not our agents who plundered that apartment," he said. "It was the neighbors. Our agents would not leave the place ramshackled."

Their first and second arrests went smoothly. They apprehended three seditionists, delivered them to the State Security detention facility and went on their way to execute the last arrest. It was on the far side of Oldtown.

"I like this part of town," Torndale said as they turned into a small side street and left the big skyscraper-filled central business district.

"I lived here when I was a kid," said Kelm, the driver. "The next block over, actually."

"These are nice houses," Torndale noted. "What was it like growing up here?"

"Quiet. You were close to everything. My parents enrolled me in a school just . . . "

He cut himself off mid sentence. Torndale glanced at him.

"It's alright," he said. "We all know the school system was different back then."

"Yes, sir," Kelm said quietly.

Torndale wanted to know more, but they made a left turn and were just around the corner from their destination.

"Alright," he said. "Stop here for a moment."

He turned to the agents in the back.

"Let me repeat what this one is about. It's an old lady, she is not in very good health. She walks with crutches. She lives alone, so this is a low-risk operation, but as always, vigilance is advisable. It's a big house, much bigger than the standardized accommodations formula for what one person can expect to have. Therefore, she has been given notice by the city housing board to forfeit her home and move to an assigned apartment, or to convert her house into a multi-residential unit. She has refused both options, so the city prosecutor charged her under Chapter Three, Section One of the Equality Act. Who can recite that section for me? Cadet Fernek?"

Naia looked a bit nervous for a second, but quickly pulled herself together.

"Yes, sir. Any person who is deemed to have possessions of any kind in excess of standardized equality formulas, who refuses to surrender excess possessions, is guilty of failure to surrender privilege."

"Almost perfect," Torndale commended her. "Anyone else?"

"Is guilty of failure to surrender privilege or, in serious cases, aggression toward under-privileged persons," one of the other agents filled in.

"There you go," Torndale nodded. "Well done, both of you. But this woman is also charged with insurrection and sedition. Let's go make the arrest."

The mid-day bell rang just as they pulled up in front of the old lady's house. It was characteristic of the neighborhood, with a large front porch, a balcony over it on the second floor, large windows from floor to ceiling, and a well-kept front yard with flowers, berry bushes and two old trees. The house was painted in a muted brown color with white around the windows. On the porch stood a rocking chair, a two-seat sofa and two low tables. On one of them was a book, on the other a pitcher of what looked like berry lemonade.

The front double-door was of wood. Each section had a tall window and beautifully carved pictures. The pictures were different, and Torndale suddenly realized that they depicted two figures looking at each other. The one to the left was an old man. He held a book in one hand and a pen in the other. He was writing something in the book. The other half of the door depicted a woman. She was also old, about the same age as the man, with her hands reaching out toward the man. She was telling him something.

"The first humans," Torndale said to himself as they entered the gate to the property. "From the Book of Creation."

"What, sir?" asked the agent just behind him.

"Oh, nothing. Cadet Fernek, you stand guard here at the gate. Rifle in hand, shout orders loudly if anyone enters the property. Don't hesitate to fire warning shots if they refuse your command."

"Yes, sir."

"Ahri, take position up on the porch. You are Miss Fernek's back-up."

"Yes, sir."

Torndale mounted the stairs and put his hand on the door handle. He did not have to open it. The old lady approached from the inside and opened the door for them.

She was short, had thick white hair and piercing eyes. Her somewhat crooked nose ended just above a pair of cherry red lips that almost formed a smile. Her back was bent, her legs a bit uneven, as if she had suffered a bad accident at some point in her life. She was wearing an old, light, hand-crafted sweater, a pair of worn-out pants and a pair of shoes that were too old to offer any support for her anymore.

She held herself up with the help of one crutch while slowly pulling the door open. Torndale gently helped push the door open. The old lady reached for her second crutch, pulled back a step and looked quietly at him as he took a step inside.

"Mrs. Veesaus?" Torndale asked.

"That's me," she replied, almost jovially.

"Ma'm, may we come inside, please?"

She took one more step back then stepped to the side and offered them to enter.

"You do as you please," she said.

They stepped in through the short hallway into the expansive living room. The ceiling was tall, the windows large, the floor made of dark wood. The furniture was old but carefully crafted and solid. A couch, right next to the largest window, looked like a man could sleep comfortably in it. Next to it, a leather-clad armchair had been combined with a footrest and a small side table. Two books lay on top of the side table, together with an empty tea mug. A small blanket had been tossed on the footrest.

It was apparently the lady's favorite place to sit.

Torndale looked around as he walked toward the armchair. A wide door opened to the kitchen, where the light was on and he could hear the humming of a cooling cabinet.

He turned and looked at the lady.

"Search the house," he ordered his agents. "Ma'm, you have a cooling cabinet, I hear."

"I do," she confirmed. "I bought it myself."

"Not everyone can afford a cooling cabinet," he noted. "A small refrigerator, but an entire cooling cabinet . . . "

The lady sighed.

"You are here to arrest me, aren't you?"

"What makes you think that?"

"Because you come in here, a whole group of you, wearing uniforms and machine guns. If you were just here on one of your normal intimidation visits, you would be wearing plain clothes. And there would only be two of you."

"You seem to have experience with visits from State Security," Torndale noted.

Mrs. Veesaus smiled, shook her head and said in a mild tone:

"You know better than I do that everyone gets those visits from time to time. I wish you would stop playing this game and just go about your totalitarian business. It would be so much more honest."

He was surprised by her bluntness. She noticed.

"That's right," she said. "I'm old, my health is fading. I don't have much time left to live. The younger people may be afraid of you, because they still think they have something to lose. And maybe they do. But I don't. If I die today, I can proudly say that I have lived my life honorably."

The other agents reported back that the rest of the house was empty.

"Ma'm," Torndale said as kindly as he could. "We have to take you into custody."

"Of course you do," she said with an equal amount of kindness in her voice. "An old lady like me is a grave threat to the totalitarian state."

One of Torndale's agents reacted to her choice of adjective. Torndale gestured at him to let it go.

"Ma'm," he said. "You are charged under Chapter Three, Section One of the Equality Act, for failure to surrender privilege. Living in this large a house on your own is privilege, and you have refused to give it up. You are also charged with insurrection for having posted messages in a public forum with criticism of the state-run health care system. Last but not least, some of those statements are of such a nature that you have also been charged with sedition. This, of course, is a crime that falls under the jurisdiction of State Security."

Mrs. Veesaus remained almost jovial about the whole thing.

"Should I just go as I am, or can I bring my blanket?" she asked and pointed to the blanket on the footrest.

"I will bring your blanket for you," Torndale promised.

As they slowly turned to walk out the door, Mrs. Veesaus asked:

"May I inquire as to the nature of the sedition charges?"

"Normally," Torndale said and picked up the blanket, "that would be a matter for an investigative officer to explain to you, after your arrest and your due processing by the detention facility. But since you are being gentle and cooperative, I will explain to you."

"Please lock my front door," she said and handed one of the other agents her door key.

"Your messages in the public forum contained phrases that demanded a return to the privately funded and operated health care system under the federal republic," Armo Torndale explained. "Those phrases, the way you formulated yourself, constitutes acts of sedition."

"The health care system is terrible," she said. "I am old enough to remember the system we had before. It was much better."

"Mind the steps, ma'm," Torndale said and helped her slowly descend the stairs.

Naia Fernek watched them cautiously as they approached. Torndale signaled to her her to stand down. She lowered her rifle and took a step to the side, watching him and Mrs. Veesaus slowly make their way toward the gate.

"I cannot get the health care I need," Mrs Veesaus explained. "I don't even need surgery or anything like that. I have a heart problem, a valve problem, and there is this medicine for it. But I cannot get a prescription, because I am not allowed to make an appointment at the local health clinic."

"They probably have many others they prioritize," Armo Torndale pointed out.

"And I am not allowed to make an appointment anywhere else," Mrs Veesaus continued. "I have to get in at the health clinic that I am assigned to. But they won't let me. Back in the old days, before this big change, anyone could get in with the doctor of their choice."

"Ma'm," Armo Torndale warned her. "That, right there, is an act of sedition."

"Oh, does it matter? You have already charged me with sedition, and I am sure you will have me convicted, too. I will be sent to some camp somewhere, along with all the others who had something to say. What difference does it make if I speak my mind now?"

They reached the gate. Naia Fernek opened it and made sure Torndale and Mrs Veesaus could exit.

Torndale unlocked the cage at the back of the van. Mrs. Veesaus turned to Naia.

"You know, young lady," she said, looking Naia straight in the eyes. "When I was your age, you could criticize government all day long, and nobody cared. In fact, it was considered a virtue to speak your mind."

"We have sedition laws, ma'm," Naia replied mechanically.

"Obviously," Mrs Veesaus replied with a gentle smile. "Because our government is so good for the people that it has to make it a crime to criticize it."

They helped Mrs Veesaus up into the cage and locked the door. Everyone was quiet. After a moment, Torndale broke the silence:

"There is a good chance that if we don't search her house now, the neighbors will plunder it before we have time to get back. Therefore, we are going to do a good search of it now, for more evidence. Ahri and Kelm, stay here and guard the van."

"What are we searching for, sir?" Naia asked as they re-entered Mrs. Veesaus's house.

"Anything that can substantiate the sedition charges," Torndale explained. "You two, search the ground floor. Search everything, bookcases, cabinets, drawers, closets . . . everything. But be careful and respectful. Do not destroy things, do not make a mess. We are here to find evidence, not to give State Security a bad name. Remember: everything you do ultimately reflects on the image of Grand Chancellor Sorto. Cadet Fernek, you and I are searching the upstairs."

The stairway was long and wide and took them straight up to a hallway on the second floor. The walls were painted in a light green color with white accents. To the left the hallway continued further back in the house. To the right was a small hallway with three rooms in file. At its end was what appeared to be a bathroom.

"This house is big," Naia noted.

"And there is a third floor, too," Torndale noted. "Let's start here, in this room."

They quickly worked their way through the three rooms to the left of the stairway. Torndale worked methodically, demonstrating to Naia Fernek how a search ought to be done. He reminded her again of how their misbehavior would reflect poorly on both their agency and the government.

"We are not here to hurt people," he said as they stepped out of the third room. "We are here to enforce the law. And the value foundation of our people's democratic union."

"We haven't found anything," Naia noted.

Torndale looked around.

"Looks like there is one more room," he said and pointed to the hallway on the other side of the stairs.

He was right. At the end of that hallway was a large room with windows to the backyard. It was the size of all the other three rooms together. Its walls were covered with top-to-bottom bookcases. There were shorter bookcases all over the room, tall enough to reach Torndale to the hips. They were arranged to form narrow pathways, inviting a visitor to criss cross the room and explore what was on the shelves.

On top of the shorter bookcases were droves of photos, personal journals and even scrapbooks. There were photos of Mrs. Veesaus alone, and with a man, apparently her husband. There were pictures of a man and a woman, younger but strikingly look-alike Mr. and Mrs. Veesaus.

"Their children," Armo Torndale commented.

"And their grandchildren," Naia noted, pointing to another set of photos.

A series of pictures showed Mr and Mrs Veesaus in an environment that looked like one of the poorest parts of the world. The people they were among had only rags for clothes, looked like they were starving badly and in poor health.

Naia picked up one of the photos and turned it over.

"Our sixth aid visit to Kowraam," she read. "Aid visit? She must have been involved with a charity."

"Apparently," Torndale noted, holding up another photo. "Here she is meeting with the vice president of Kowraam. What's that note on the back?"

He pulled it out from a clip that attached it to the photo.

"It is a letter to Mr. and Mrs. Veesaus from the Kowraami vice president."

He read the letter in silence.

"What does it say?" Naia asked.

Torndale closed his eyes for a second. He shook his head, took a deep breath and looked out the window.

"Sir?" Naia asked.

"Here," he whispered and gave her the letter.

"Dear Mrs. Veesaus," Naia read. "On behalf of the Kowraami government, I wish to express my deepest gratitude for the generous charity that you and your husband have provided to our nation. We can directly link the survival of at least ten thousand ill and starving children to the aid you have provided. I am pleased to announce that you and your husband will be given honorary citizenship of Kowraam, with the certificates being presented by our president . . . upon his visit to your capital . . . next month."

She looked up at Torndale. He looked down on the floor. His forehead was wrinkled. His lips tight. His hands firmly planted on his hips.

"This letter . . . " Naia said, but Torndale interrupted her.

"Give it to me," he said quietly and reached out his hand without looking at her.

"Sir . . . "

"Give it to me."

She complied. He folded it and put it in the inside pocket of his uniform jacket.

Just as Naia was about to say something, they heard steps from the stairs.

"They must be done down there," Torndale said. "Let's go."

Before they left the room, he stopped, turned to Naia and whispered:

"Never tell anyone about this letter," he said with the voice and facial expression of a commanding officer. "Ever. Understand?"

She looked like she had not expected that reaction from him. She looked surprised, perhaps even a bit scared.

"Yes, sir" she whispered back.

He looked at her for a second. She stared at him, unsure what to make of his attitude but eager to comply. He saw uncertainty, confusion and a little bit of fear in her eyes. He felt a sting of guilt. He realized he had been too harsh on her, but more than that, he had failed to uphold the ethical standards he had set for his own behavior.

He wanted to say something, but one of the other agents approached them to report that they were done with the ground floor. The next part of his conversation with Naia would have to wait.

THE MOOD AT THE CAMP on the mountaintop had changed dramatically. Not only was there more food for everyone, but they also knew that there was an end to their long, dangerous journey. Their struggle to stay alive and keep their spirits up at the camp—it would be worth it.

A small group of young adults gathered around Armo Torndale as soon as he returned to the camp. They were notably happy, almost upbeat.

"Tell us," one of them said, "tell us about the new colony we are going to."

Torndale looked over at Naia. She smiled, nodded and pointed to the hygienic area. She was going to wash herself and try to put on something that was not quite as dirty as the clothes she had been wearing for a couple of days now.

"Okay," Torndale agreed.

He sat himself down at the rock that he called "the podium", with the interested audience gathering around him. There were only four of them, but it suddenly seemed like a lot of people. He did not realize just how tired he was until he looked at their curious faces. Right now, any group of people bigger than two felt overwhelming.

But he did not want to send them away. On the contrary, he deeply appreciated their enthusiasm, and wanted to do his best for them. It helped that they were quiet, respectful and generous. They all offered water, lemonade and a share of their food ration. He had some water and lemonade but kindly refused to take the food.

"You are going to need it, still, for a day or two," he pointed out.

"Tell us about the new colony," one of them repeated. "Please."

"Well, the Danori . . . the humanoid race that we are working with . . . they are always on the lookout for new planets to colonize. They believe in spreading life throughout the galaxy, as best they can. The woman I am working with is the liaison for a private, charitable organization that helps refugees. They specialize in evacuating small groups of people from planets that have been overrun by tyranny. Most of time, tyranny is not the reason why they evacuate people, but from what she has told me it happens two or three times every year that they make contact with refugees from tyranny. Those are the ones they like to do the most."

"So they are not a government agency?" said one of the younglings.

"Exactly. It's all private, with private funding, mostly from a very wealthy man, apparently. But they cooperate with the Danori government, which has strategic interests in colonizing this part of the galaxy. They need colonies in some strategic locations because it helps them build and maintain service ports for their commercial and military spaceships."

"Are we actually going to build a colony from the ground up?"

"No. We are going to build a new settlement on a planet that has already been colonized. It will be independent in almost every way, but we will have infrastructure and some trade with existing colonies."

"Fascinating!" the younglings agreed.

The woman sitting closest to Torndale asked:

"You said they have strategic interests in these colonies. What does that mean?"

"They find people who are willing to move in and maintain the service ports they need for their spaceships. Those who populate the maintenance colony are then free to expand, to spread their settlements and thrive as an otherwise independent community."

"That is so exciting," said a young man. "The others who live there now . . . are they Danori?"

"No, they are humans like us. Not from here, of course, but from another planet."

"Humans like us?"

"Yes."

"It is just amazing that there can be humans on other planets. What are the odds?"

"Actually, from what I understand they are quite good," Torndale explained. "I mean, from a religious viewpoint . . . if you believe that God created all life, it would make sense, wouldn't it, that He also created life on other planets."

"So, this new planet, is it like ours?"

"Yes. All the worlds that the Danori colonize are much like our planet. But if you don't believe that God created us, there is also the evolutionary argument. The evolution of life follows pretty much the same pattern, from primitive life forms to more advanced ones. Think about it: all big mammals on our planet look pretty much the same in some ways. We have two eyes, a nose, a mouth and ears, all located on our head. We have a torso with four limbs. And so on. It is an efficient body for a higher life form."

"So, this new colony . . . " one of the young women said, "do we have to adopt the laws and the culture of the existing colony? Or do we write and make our own laws?"

Torndale smiled:

"You are a lawyer, aren't you?"

"Just finished law school," she smiled back.

"I was wondering about that, too," said the man sitting right next to her. "I can only imagine how different we must be. What do they think about . . . I don't know . . . violent crimes, or the formation of a family?"

"We will be granted self determination," Torndale explained. "We are free to set our own laws for our community, so long as we respect the sovereignty of other colonies, and we subscribe to and enforce three basic principles. The Danori call them The Constitutional Code."

He pulled out a small pamphlet from one of his pockets.

"You will all get one of these constitutional pamphlets as soon as you are onboard the spaceship," he said. "You will have ten days of travel . . . that is how long it will take to get to the planet where the colony is located . . . and we will use that time in part to study this constitution and to form our governing council. That sounds more dramatic than it is . . . but we need to get it done before the arrival at the colony. I got this copy of their constitution a while ago, so that I could better understand what we are all getting ourselves involved in."

He flipped through the first two pages.

"It is printed on paper," someone pointed out.

"They can print things like we do. Remember, they work with civilized societies all over our part of the galaxy, at different stages of evolution. They have to adjust their interaction to many different forms of communication. For our benefit, they print on paper. But it's different than the kind of paper we are used to. Here, feel it. It's different."

"Sturdy . . . almost hard."

"Yeah, like it would be hard to tear."

"The print is very good. Sharp."

Armo Torndale took the pamphlet back.

"Let me read the three principles to you," he said. "The three pillars of their Constitutional Code. One: life is sacrosanct. Two: every individual has an inalienable right to self determination. And three: the role of the state, of government, is solely to guarantee the rule of law, and independent arbitration of disputes."

"That's all?" asked one of the younglings. "That's all government does?"

"That's all," Torndale confirmed.

"So government does not provide for your needs?"

"No. You are free to do that yourself, as you see fit without violating anyone else."

"But is non-violation written into those three pillars?"

"Yes. It belongs under the first pillar, which says, simply, that life is sacrosanct. It comes with two sub-paragraphs, so to speak. The first one says 'Do no physical harm to any other individual'. They explain physical harm . . . you will get ample opportunity to read the explanatory notes later . . . but briefly, it is explained as not hurting another person and not interfering with him or her. That covers non-violence."

"Interfering," said one of the younglings, "as in . . . preventing them from going somewhere?"

"That is one example," Torndale agreed. "But it is broader than that. It means non-interference with anything a person does. It does not have to be physical harm. You could, for example, hinder someone from traveling down a road. That sort of interference. Or, in a more advanced meaning, if you have a contract with someone to, say, repair the roof on your house. By breaking the contract you are interfering with him."

"But what if he does not fulfill his part of the contract?" another youngling asked. "What if he is putting the wrong roof on it, or the job is of subpar quality?"

"Good point. That takes us to the third pillar, about the role of the state. It is the independent arbiter in disputes, such as the one you mention. The point with an independent arbiter is to avoid private attempts at settling disputes. But let's look at all aspects of the life pillar first. The other sub-paragraph says that you must not harm another person's property. This includes but is of course not limited to their land, their belongings, their home . . . tangible possessions. But it also includes the proceeds of your work. It means, plainly, that once a man gets paid for the work he has done, or a product he sells, he has the right to keep all the money he earned."

The younglings shared looks. One of them raised her eyebrows and turned to Torndale:

"That is a radical proposition," she said. "It means there cannot be any taxes, does it not?"

"Correct," Armo Torndale agreed. "The only exception is for the funding of government functions that are enumerated under the third pillar."

"But how do you provide for hospitals? Schools? The poor? What about inequalities?"

Armo Torndale thought for a moment. The young woman's eyes were inquisitive. Her questions were not merely rhetorical. She genuinely wanted answers.

"Tell me," he said. "Why did you join our journey?"

"You gave me and my fiancé . . ." and she reached out and touched the arm of the young man next to her, " . . . the permission to join. And we are very grateful and happy for that."

"Oh, I know you are, but that was not my question. You joined us for a moral or philosophical reason."

"Yes. We want to live in freedom."

"And you want to be free from . . . what exactly? I'm just asking because it sheds light on the good questions you just asked."

"We don't feel we have any freedom to live our lives," her fiancé said. "We are assigned housing, we are assigned jobs, we are given rations for food, clothes, everything . . . We have no say in how, or where we live our lives."

"We cannot even go see family without travel permits," the woman added. "And then you need coupons for government to get a train ticket."

"I mean," her fiancé said, "in practice you can travel if you have a permit and an automobile, but we can't even get on a waiting list for one."

"And even if you have a travel permit," said another youngling, "your coupons may not be enough for where you want to go. You can't choose when you want to travel. You are assigned travel times, on specific trains. You can't just buy a ticket whenever you want to."

"It wasn't like that under the federal republic," Torndale muttered.

"But you can't just drive your automobile as you please, either" the young fiancé pointed out. "There are fuel rations. You know how it works."

"I do indeed," Torndale agreed. "You need coupons for hotels, and for restaurant dinners. So you joined our freedom journey because you want to be free from the restrictions of a centrally planned economy."

All four younglings nodded emphatically.

"But why do we have a centrally planned economy in our country in the first place?" asked Torndale, with some enthusiasm in his voice.

The conversation was invigorating to him. And it helped him take the mind off the fact that he may not be able to join them at the new colony.

And that Naia Fernek would choose to stay behind with him, if he was not able to go. He loved her for her decision, and he was amazed at how much he meant to her. But he also wished for such a smart, ambitious, beautiful young woman to build a future for herself.

He was awoken from his thoughts about Naia by one of the younglings who answered his question:

"We have a planned economy because government says it needs to make sure our resources are allocated equally among the population. So that no one gets more than anyone else."

"And do you think that's fair?"

"No," all four answered.

"I work every day," said the fiancé. "I'm a carpenter. I can see the value I produce. And then . . . " he turned to his fiancée, "our neighbor . . . "

"A young couple," the fiancée filled in. "They both sit at home all day. They are loud and obnoxious."

"They get the same rations we do," her fiancé added in a bitter tone. "What incentive is there for me to work hard, then? Why would I want to spend more time away from my fiancée, and . . . when that day comes . . . our children . . . " and he shared a smile with his future wife, " . . . when we get nothing extra for it?"

"All we get is less time together," she agreed with him.

"But what about the distribution of the value?" Torndale asked. "That everyone gets the same food rations, the same housing rations, and so on?"

"It is the individual's responsibility to provide for himself and his loved ones," said another youngling.

They all agreed.

"Let me dial it up a notch, just for the sake of argument," Torndale said with a smile on his face. "Because I like how smart you young people are. As you know, our national value foundation says a lot of things. One of the things it says is that every individual has the same right to all the health care they need. We need health care to survive, don't we?"

They were quiet for a moment. Torndale wondered if he had taken the discussion a bit too far. Maybe they were getting tired? Or was he getting too professorial? He did not want to come across as if he was preaching to them.

Then again—some things required more than just a chat. Sometimes, you had to dig deeper to understand them.

"I read this article a while back," said one of younglings, "about what health care looked like under the federal republic. There were private insurance plans, where you bought a membership and the plan would cover your catastrophic health care needs. Like if you were in an accident, or you got a serious illness."

"But how did they set their membership fees?" another youngling asked.

He turned to Torndale.

"You remember that system, right?"

"I do," Torndale confirmed. "It worked. It wasn't perfect, but it was good."

He paused. He noticed that two of the younglings seemed to lose interest in the discussion. Maybe he should call it a day? But the man who had asked the question really wanted to know.

He decided to continue.

"You chose your insurance plan, you paid your monthly premium and you could go see almost any medical practitioner, anywhere. The insurance plans competed for you and your money. Same with health providers."

"But weren't there those who could not afford the health plan?" asked the young man.

The others were definitely losing interest in this discussion. Torndale decided to wrap it up as quickly as he could. But before he could say anything, the young man continued:

"Back in high school, we had a teacher who scolded that system and said that a lot of people died every year because they could not afford a health plan. Only the rich had a plan, she said. I asked her for some information on that."

"What did she say?" one of the other younglings asked. "I bet she didn't like it."

"She did not. She wrote me up and I had to go to the school supervisor. He asked me a lot of questions, like, if my parents opposed Grand Chancellor Sorto, or if I thought we should topple the government."

"And what did you say?" Torndale asked.

"I said no, of course. I didn't want to topple the government. That was a ridiculous question. I just wanted some information."

"So it's not true that people died under the old health care system?" asked the fiancé. "Is that a lie?"

"That system worked for almost everyone," Torndale replied. "There were special solutions for those who could not afford a plan. You had a lot of choices."

"You mean . . . ?"

"You could choose what doctor to see, and when. Today, you can't choose."

"That's different," the fiancé noted. "I had two coworkers who had to wait so long to see a doctor that it actually made their illness worse. One was denied care altogether. There weren't enough doctors or hospital beds."

"But why is that?" another youngling wanted to know. "Why is it that government can't provide what . . . under the federal republic . . . what private businesses could provide?"

They were interrupted by a camp watchman. He came up to Torndale, apologized for interrupting and leaned forward and whispered:

"We have spotted commandos at the foot of the mountain."

Armo Torndale did not react at first. Then he nodded, thanked the watchman and waited until he had left.

"I'm sorry," he said. "But they need my help with something. Let's continue this conversation later, shall we?"

❀ ❀ ❀

EDA STREBBER LEFT HOME EARLY on the holiday morning. She told her husband she was going to the gym and then had some work assignment to take care of. The first part was entirely true, the second part was not. She was going into her office because she was furious with the fact that Group Commander Torndale had chosen a petty little cadet to replace Olgar on his operations team—instead of her.

It was that simple. She did not care about Armo Torndale's explanation, which she did not believe anyway. It was probably just his way of getting back at her for having exposed Olgar's relationship with that little cadet.

But it still did not make sense. There had to be another reason why Torndale wanted Naia Fernek on his team, instead of any other adjutant of Olgar's rank. What interest could he possibly have in that young woman?

Was it personal? He hadn't even met Cadet Fernek, had he? Or was it Olgar's relationship with her that made Torndale interested? Did he want to see what it was Olgar saw in this young woman?

Maybe that was it. Or maybe it was political. Maybe Torndale shared the same interest in seditionism as Fernek did?

Whatever it was, Eda Strebber was certain that Torndale's decision was not based on professional judgment. If he had used his professional judgment, he would have known to put her on the team, not some snotty little cadet.

The whole situation made her restless. She had worked some of the stress out of her body at the gym, but she could not let go of the feeling of having been stepped over—twice! The first time was when Commander Torndale put together his operations team and chose Olgar over her. The second time was his choice to replace Olgar with Naia Fernek.

"Naia Fernek," she spit out as she sat down at her desk.

She turned on her computer terminal. It gave her access to the database of confidential information about all employees within State Security. Maybe there was something she could dig up on Torndale. Something she could use to get back at him.

It took a while to log in. The system was running on low power over the holiday in compliance with the energy conservation demands that the National Power Supply Combinate had issued. Residential areas had their power supply reduced by half or—in some areas—cut out entirely every workday from the daybreak bell to sunset. Workplaces were asked to cut power usage over holidays, but core government agencies, such as State Security, had been exempt—until recently.

Once Eda Strebber had logged on to the computer network, she ran into a problem. She could see the files of all officers of her rank and lower, but not those of higher-ranking officers. Torndale was Group Commander and she was just Adjutant. His file was out of reach to her.

She felt even more frustrated. The feeling crawled all over her like a cheap suit. She browsed around a little bit, trying randomly to come up with some other way to access information. She looked at Olgar's files but found nothing of interest in there. Except, of course, for the note that Commander Kolmov had put in regarding Olgar's affair with Naia Fernek. That was going to be a big liability for him, of course, and it certainly too him out of the competition for higher positions within State Security.

Eda Strebber could not make changes to his file—only a superior officer could do that—but she was amused to see that all of her comments had been added. And, she noted, the testimony from the officer who had been present at the cantina when she and Olgar had that revealing conversation.

Nevertheless, there was nothing in there that she could use in getting back at Torndale. Which was really what she was out to do.

"If only I had higher clearance," she muttered.

She was unsure what to do. She wanted to do something, but she seemed to have run into a dead end.

She went back to reading Olgar's file. Doctor Smersch had added a comment where he said that Olgar's teaching was "average". Eda Strebber smiled when she saw it. An "average" evaluation was bureaucratic language for "not very good". She knew it was not true: in reality, students liked Olgar's teaching. His evaluations were strong, and his students had told Eda Strebber that they appreciated Olgar as an instructor. But none of that really mattered. What mattered was what the head of instruction at the State Security academy had to say about Olgar.

That head of instruction was Doctor Smersch.

Eda Strebber suspected that Doctor Smersch had added the "average" comment because he thought Olgar might be ideologically compromised. There was no evidence yet that he actually had been compromised and become a seditionist. His relationship with Naia Fernek was certainly a source of serious concern—given of course that she was the seditionist Eda Strebber suspected that she was—but in order to open a formal internal investigation against someone, State Security required hard evidence.

There was no such hard evidence. Not yet. But Eda Strebber was determined to find it. If she could prove that Olgar was a seditionist, there would have to be a way to use that against his permanent commanding officer, Torndale.

At least for now, Olgar was in the freezer. The "average" comment by Doctor Smersch would probably put Olgar's career on hold for the time being. That would give Eda Strebber enough time to find real, solid evidence of his seditionist leanings.

Eda Strebber wished that Doctor Smersch had added a comment about Torndale. Of course, it made no sense for him to do so in Olgar's files, but still . . . She recalled the conversation between Doctor Smersch and Torndale, where it seemed like Torndale had something on Smersch that he had in some veiled way threatened to use against him.

Something about command structures.

If only Doctor Smersch was here.

Of course! She could call him. It would be easy to explain: she was trying to catch up on some class preparations, and in view of Olgar's and Cadet Fernek's relationship she wanted to hear his advice on how to handle Cadet Fernek in her class, going forward.

It sounded like a perfectly good excuse to call Doctor Smersch on a holiday.

He did not agree.

"This could have waited until tomorrow," he muttered.

His reaction made Eda Strebber nervous.

"I am sorry, sir, of course it could," she said quickly. "It was careless of me to not think about that."

"No, no . . . that's okay . . . You went in to get some work done anyway, when everyone else is home."

"Well, Commander Torndale was here earlier," she lied.

She had not seen him, but she assumed he had been in, since he was supposed to work this holiday.

"Oh, that's right," Doctor Smersch mumbled. "He's temporarily assigned to operations."

"Sir, I was wondering," Eda Strebber said, shifting to a more girlish voice, "I thought it was really unfair of him to make those comments about the command structure. You know, when we had our meeting about Adjutant Olgar."

"Oh, that. Yes . . . it was unfair. Thanks."

"What was that all about?"

"It's not important. It was something that happened a while back."

"Okay . . . I was just surprised that he would bring it up like that . . . "

"Yes."

" . . . I mean, it must have been something substantial if he could hold it over someone's head like that . . . "

"Like I said," Doctor Smersch repeated a bit more sternly. "It is not important."

Eda Strebber heard the tone in his voice and realized she had pushed it too far. She pondered for a second whether or not she should pursue this further, but she decided not to. It did not seem appropriate, given his reaction.

"I understand, sir. So, do you have any advice on how I should handle Cadet Fernek?"

"Do you still think she is a seditionist?"

"I suspect she is."

"Hmm. Well . . . in that case, we have reasons to suspect that Olgar is also a seditionist."

Eda Strebber could barely contain her joy over his comment.

"Yes, sir!" she replied forcefully. "And that would have implications for Commander Torndale, too, would it not?"

"Well, let's not go there, at least not for now," Doctor Smersch advised her.

"Yes, sir, of course . . . "

"But this is potentially a chain of disloyalty within the ranks of State Security. And it starts with Cadet Fernek. Well, you might as well take out the big gun. Make her fear you enough to give you more information about herself."

"Fear me? How?"

"You know the tactics we use on people we arrest. Give them a catastrophic option and tell them that their cooperation is the only way they can save themselves."

"Of course, sir. Find some way to make Cadet Fernek understand that she has no other option than to fully cooperate with me on everything I demand."

"That's right," Doctor Smersch confirmed. "Make sure you own her."

"Ah . . . " Eda Strebber giggled. "Make sure I own her."

For some reason, she almost got aroused by that thought.

"And whatever you find out from her," said Doctor Smersch, "we can use to put the squeeze on Olgar."

"Maybe Commander Torndale, too . . . "

"Hmm . . . "

"What, sir?"

"Nothing . . . "

"Sir, do you actually suspect that he is a seditionist?"

"Again, that would be dangerous. I don't want to go there. Not now, anyway. No, I just don't like him."

"Sir, if you don't mind . . . I share that feeling."

"You do? Well, who can blame you?"

"I was wondering . . . maybe I am stretching this too far . . . "

"No, go ahead."

"Well, sir, if Commander Torndale gets along with Cadet Fernek, could that be a sign that they share the same values? I was just curious about his explanation to why he wanted her on his team."

"Yes, he did seem to like the idea of having her on his team. Well, let's start with Cadet Fernek."

ARMO TORNDALE LAID DOWN on his stomach and crawled out to the edge of the cliff. He put his hand telescope to his eye and searched the foot of the mountain.

"Right by that open spot," the watchman whispered. "Where the creek makes a sharp turn."

Torndale scanned the area.

"I don't see . . . wait . . . okay . . . I got them."

He saw two men tucked in under the vegetation, camouflaged and lying still. He thought he spotted footprints near the creek, but it was hard to tell given the distance.

"There should be six of them," he whispered to the watchman. "They are very likely commandos from a special assignment unit. Military, for sure. Not State Security. Commandos usually operate in groups of six."

He folded in his telescope, put it away and slowly moved back from the cliff edge. He crawled backward a little bit to make sure he did not make any moves that would cause any rocks to fall from the cliff.

When he had turned around and sat down with the two watchmen who were assigned to that spot, he saw worry in their eyes.

"Not good," Torndale said. "This means that State Security has handed us over to the military, and that means that the ministry of domestic security has decided that we are a big enough threat to them, that they want to take us out. They have probably discovered that we stole all those documents from them, and they think we still have them here."

"What documents?" asked one of the watchmen.

"Some confidential information I handed over to the Danori. But the good news is that they don't travel at day, only at night, and if they want to be really careful . . . I served in special warfare when I was in the military a long time ago . . . if they do as their training tells them to do, they will climb slowly up the western side. The same way we came up. It will take them two nights to do it. So we still have time."

"But how do we defend ourselves against soldiers?"

"First of all, find out who among our watchmen has military experience. We need all the expertise we can muster. We can't fight them in a traditional way. But they won't be coming up any other way than the path down here. The other sides of the mountain require rock climbing gear, and soldiers don't do rock climbing. It makes them too vulnerable if they are discovered. And we can make their climb up the path here, a bit . . . difficult."

"How?"

Torndale smiled:

"Well, we have gravity on our side."

He glanced over toward the path.

"Let's organize a defense line right away," he suggested. "But quietly. So long as the soldiers think they are going to take us by surprise, we still have the upper hand."

The one person who could organize that defense was Naia Fernek. She and the group she had arrived with had climbed the path at night, and they had a more recent memory of it than Torndale did.

Naia was in the middle of the camp. She was with a mother with twins, holding one of the babies.

When she saw Armo Torndale she looked up and smiled from ear to ear.

"He is just four moons old" she said and hugged the baby like it was her own.

Torndale stopped for a second. He saw the boundless joy in Naia's face.

"I hope one day you will be a mother, too," he said.

She just smiled and hugged the baby.

"Armo," said the mother. "I don't mean to be intruding, but . . . do you know who will be evacuated next?"

"I was just getting to that. Families first. But I need a word with Naia first."

She reluctantly gave the baby back to his mother and came with him to the edge of the camp. He explained the situation to her and asked her to take a lead on constructing a defense line.

"You know how far they can advance in one night," he said as quietly as he could, "and where they are likely to stop for the day."

She nodded. She looked dead serious, almost a bit angry.

"It's nightfall soon," Torndale noted.

Naia glanced over her shoulder, back at the twin mother.

"I don't get it," she said. "They are coming here to kill us, so we can't leave."

She turned to Torndale.

"To kill babies. For what?"

"To protect their government from the embarrassment that people are trying to escape."

"Escape their value foundation," Naia almost spit out.

"And they have probably discovered that we stole those documents you brought here. They think we still have them, and they want them back."

Naia nodded.

"Okay. Who do I work with?"

"Your team, and two watchmen. I am going to organize the next evacuation group. But keep it quiet. We don't want the soldiers to know that we know they are here."

Naia gave him a hug.

"I would rather die than be captured," she whispered.

"Me, too," he said.

She went off to start the work. Torndale went to find Rhem Strebber.

"I was just looking for you," Strebber said. "There's been questions about the evacuation sequence. Who gets to go, and who has to wait. I have a suggestion, a priority list. It's based on the list of nutrition priorities that we made on our way here."

While he explained the criteria, Torndale looked out over the camp. He saw men, women and children who had no idea of the danger lurking at the foot of the mountain. Those commandos were incredibly well trained, and even though the refugees could make surprise traps for them, there was a substantial risk that the soldiers would overcome those traps and still reach the camp before the last evacuation flight had left.

"What do you think about my criteria?" Strebber asked.

"What? Uh . . . well, it's gotten a bit more complicated."

"What do you mean?"

Torndale took Strebber to the side and explained the situation with the soldiers.

"Oh, great," Strebber muttered. "Just what we needed."

"Exactly. We are going to need to be tougher in who we prioritize. We need to get as many kids out of here as we can, with their mothers. But we are going to need as many men as possible to stay behind and fight."

"But that means separating families from their fathers. I don't think they are going to accept that."

"We need at least ten men to stay and fight."

"Or women."

"Mothers go with their kids."

"There are women in the camp who don't have kids," Strebber pointed out. "You know, like Naia."

Torndale looked over at the camp, then at Strebber again.

"Of course," he smiled. "Stupid of me. Alright. Get a list of everyone who is not a parent. They should be no more than ten, at best, if I'm right. They can all go on the last flight. Then get the families with the most kids out first."

"Why?"

"Because if those soldiers get here and start slaughtering people, then we will have maximized the number of kids we actually evacuated. The kids are the future of our colony."

"Those are some hard priorities," Strebber noted.

"Are there any better ones?"

Strebber looked at Torndale. He looked over at the camp, then at Torndale again.

"No," he admitted. "But it is not going to be easy to convince some families that they have to wait longer than the others."

"It will be alright," Torndale reassured him. "So long as they don't know about the soldiers."

❉ ❉ ❉

ARMO TORNDALE AND HIS TEAM drove in silence from the detention center, where they had dropped off Mrs. Veesaus, to Garage Two. It was as if nobody moved, or even breathed. Even the com radio was silent.

The agent behind the wheel, Kelm, drove more slowly than normal. His movements were muted, as if he wanted to do as little as possible to bring the cage van back to the garage.

Torndale stared out the side window. The scenery of the city passed by at a mellow pace. Pedestrians walking down the street, bicyclists navigating narrow bike lanes, cars parked along the sidewalks.

His thoughts left the van and scattered in the wind. He tried to collect them, to stay focused, but something bothered him.

The sheet of paper in his inner pocket. It felt like it was made of iron.

But there was something else. Something stinging him in the neck.

He closed his eyes and tried to think it away. But it came back. That feeling in the back of his head just would not go away.

He opened his eyes again. He realized what it was.

Naia Fernek was looking at him from the back of the van. He glanced at one of the mirrors inside the van.

Yes. She was sitting as far back as possible, slouching a bit to the side, but her eyes were on Torndale. And there was no mistaking the expression in her face. A mixture of disappointment and doubt.

But there was something more in it, something that looked almost like grief. Or was it sorrow? Or was he reading too much into the expression on her face?

He looked outside again. He happened to see an old book store that had survived the cultural upheaval in the transition from the old to the new. Maybe he should go there tomorrow? Take an extra long lunch and go browse the shelves of that bookstore? Just for fun.

Then it hit him. Like a sting from a wasp.

The image of Mrs. Veesaus's library.

He shook his head, scratched his left temple, sighed and cleared his throat.

"Are you alright, sir?" Kelm asked.

"Me? Yeah . . . yes, I am fine."

He shared some administrative minutia with the crew and instructed them all to be extra careful about accounting for all equipment upon return to the garage. It was unnecessary, of course: the garage manager would be meticulous about it anyway. But it gave him something to talk about to break the awkward silence.

When the van was properly parked in the return lane at the garage, everyone disembarked slowly and quietly. All equipment, including two-hand firearms, were to be returned to the garage manager's gun vault. Torndale still had his personal service weapon in a holster inside his waistband.

He noted that Naia Fernek tried to get ahead of the rest of them, as if she wanted to get out of there as quickly as possible. He looked at her. She tried to avoid looking at him.

That letter was beginning to burn inside his jacket.

He made a snap decision.

"Cadet Fernek!" he said in as commanding a voice as he could without sounding intimidating.

She turned and looked at him. Her eyes were cold.

"Yes, sir," she said reluctantly.

"I'd like to do a short debriefing with you before you leave."

"When, sir?"

"Here and now. As soon as all equipment has been checked in."

She looked around.

"Just me, sir?"

"Yes. You have never done this before. It is only proper that you get a debriefing on the spot."

She bit her lip and nodded reluctantly.

"Yes, sir," she said in a hushed voice.

Torndale waited until they were alone and back in civilian clothes outside the garage manager's office. She stood a few feet away from him, her arms crossed, her eyes looking for nothing in particular on the ground. It was not a proper stance given that she was in the presence of a higher-ranking officer, but Torndale did not worry about formalities.

He walked over toward her. She tensed up, still looking away from him.

He looked at her for a second. What he was about to say would once and forever change his career with State Security.

"Come with me," he said in as friendly a tone as he could.

"Sir . . . ?" she said cautiously and looked at him.

"Come with me. I will explain. But not here."

He glanced over at the garage manager's office. She followed his eyes, frowned, looked at him again, and got the message.

"Okay, sir," she said, though she was still cautious and not too happy about having to do this.

He took her across the street. They walked in silence in on State Security's main property. They passed through a short tunnel and came out in one of the the large inner yards of the structure. They met one or two others, but for the most part the entire building was empty.

"Holiday" Torndale commented.

Naia did not say anything. She kept up with him but made no effort at engaging in conversation.

As they reached the entrance that led up to his office, he turned right instead of walking straight into the building.

"Sir . . . " Naia said. "Where are we going?"

"We are going down to Garage One."

"May I ask why, sir?"

He stopped, turned and looked her in the eyes. She looked cautious, a bit concerned and maybe even worried.

He got it. She was just a cadet, he a commander. Another officer had just betrayed her, both professionally and personally. She had probably pinned her hopes on decency and moral integrity on Torndale, wishing for him to restore her faith in her choice of career. Then she had seen his actions at Mrs. Veesaus's house, where he had decided not to look for exculpatory evidence.

It made sense that she would not trust him. And yet, there she was. A short, young woman with very intense eyes and some intangible sense of courage and integrity.

Torndale realized that he almost never saw that in cadets, not even in young officers. More and more of them just seemed to come into State Security for a nice, well paid and comfortable career.

Somewhere, he admired Naia. He was not sure why, but there was something about her that made him forget rank, form and institutional protocol.

He looked over to the side for a moment, then down at his shoes. When he looked up again, the expression on her face had mellowed a little bit.

"Naia," he said quietly. "I know you did not like what I did over at Mrs. Veesaus's house, with that letter and shutting down the search for evidence. But please trust me. There was a reason for it. And . . . "

He hesitated for a moment.

"I am not going to explain it now. But, please, come with me. I need your help."

He reached inside his jacket and pulled up the sheet of paper from Mrs. Veesaus's house. He showed her just a sliver of it.

When Naia saw it, her face changed on a dime. Torndale placed his index finger over his mouth. She looked at him in astonishment, then she nodded slightly.

"Come on," he whispered.

The garage manager was not happy about seeing someone on this fine holiday. She looked like she would rather sit in her little office and knit than to check out a vehicle for a group commander and whoever he had with him.

"Sign here," she said in a monotonous voice. "How long will you need the vehicle?"

"Not sure."

"I'll put in 'open return' then" said the garage manager. "But that means you'll get a call about it tomorrow. From my boss."

"I look forward to it," Torndale smiled.

"I bet you do," the garage manager yawned, put the check-out form in a cabinet and went back to her knitting.

They had barely gotten in the car before Naia said:

"Sir, I'm sorry for my attitude before . . . "

"Let's put titles aside," Torndale said. "Let's be Armo and Naia for a moment."

She glanced at him.

"Okay . . . "

"It makes the conversation so much easier," he explained.

He hauled out the letter he had taken from Mrs. Veesaus's library.

"Read this again."

Naia unfolded it, cleared her throat and read:

"Dear Mrs. Veesaus. On behalf of the Kowraami government, I wish to express my deepest gratitude for the generous charity that you and your husband have provided to our nation. We can directly link the survival of at least ten thousand ill and malnutritioned children to the aid you have provided. I am pleased to announce that you and your husband will be given honorary citizenship of Kowraam, with the certificates being presented by our president upon his visit to your capital next month."

She folded it and held it in her hand. They both sat in silence for a moment.

"Is this exculpatory evidence?" Naia asked eventually.

"Yes."

"So . . . do you want to go back and gather evidence for her trial?"

Torndale shook his head.

"No. There is no point in that."

"Then why are we going back to her house? Because that's where we are going, isn't it?"

"We are."

"So is it not our job . . . your job . . . to gather evidence for the trial of someone you have arrested?"

"In theory, yes."

"What do you mean 'in theory'?"

Torndale hesitated for a moment.

"The formal process," he said slowly, "for someone like Mrs. Veesaus is that she is arrested, booked and provided a counsel. The investigative division then has a limited period of time to gather evidence. Both incriminating and exculpatory. That evidence is then turned over to the prosecutor and to the counsel, and Mrs. Veesaus is then put on trial."

Naia nodded and waited. When nothing more came, she looked up at him:

"You said that that was the formal process," she noted.

"Yes. In reality . . . and I am telling you this although you are absolutely not supposed to know this . . . " and he gave her a pleading look, " . . . so please, do not talk to anyone about what I am about to tell you."

She nodded emphatically.

"I promise," she said.

"Thank you. The informal process," he said while turning into Old-town, "is that the person arrested is kept in the incarceration facility for a few days, then shipped on to one of the SICR camps."

"No trial?"

"No trial."

"What is SICR?"

"You haven't learned about them yet," Torndale nodded and turned into Mrs. Veesaus's street. "It's short for Seditionist and Insurrectionist Correction and Re-education."

"But why would she be sent off without a trial?" Naia asked as they pulled up to Mrs. Veesaus's house.

A group of people had gathered outside the house. Some of them were in the front yard. They were standing there, apprehensively looking around. When they saw Armo Torndale pull up, they paid very close attention to him.

"Just what you'd expect," he muttered and jumped out of the car.

Naia got out slowly and cautiously.

"State Security!" he declared in a commanding voice and showed them his ID.

He put the ID back and drew his gun. He pointed it to the ground but made sure it was visible to everyone. The crowd slowly pulled out of the front yard.

"This property is under the jurisdiction of State Security!" he declared. "Anyone who enters this property will be arrested under the Insurrection Act! Stand back and do not interfere with our investigation!"

The crowd withdrew and split up into smaller groups. Most of them disappeared into other houses. A few people hung out on the other side of the street but moved further away when Torndale gave them a stern look.

When they got inside the house, he was careful to lock the front door behind them.

"Neighbors, right?" Naia asked.

"Yes."

"And they are not here to show sympathy for Mrs. Veesaus."

"Right," Torndale replied and climbed the stairs. "Remember the ransacked apartment we went to first thing this morning?"

"Yes . . . they want to rob this house."

"Yes."

When they got to the top of the stairs, he took her to the large window at the top of the hallway. From there they could see several houses up and down the street.

"Look at those properties," he said. "Look carefully."

She did. She squinted, looked one way and then the other way.

"They . . . all look like they are rundown and in need of repair."

"Exactly," Armo Torndale nodded. "Paint falling off, windows crooked, some of the yards are full of trash."

"Yet this house is well maintained," Naia noted.

She looked up at him.

"I don't get it," she admitted.

"One of the charges against Mrs. Veesaus is that she refused to surrender her privilege," Armo Torndale reminded her as they slowly walked toward the library in the back of the house. "She is the only one on this street who hasn't done that. All the other homeowners have either surrendered their homes to the city government or turned them into multi-resident units, in compliance with the Equality Act."

"So that means all the other houses on the street are now under city housing board management?"

"Yes."

They entered the library.

"I guess that explains the different condition of those houses," she said. "But I still don't understand why those neighbors would loot her house. Government provides them with everything they need."

"No, government promises them everything they need," Torndale replied and started looking through the bookshelves. "That does not mean they get everything they actually need. These are people who live on standard rations of food, clothing, fuel, housing obviously. Most people do, these days, except for government employees. We get better rations, we have access to first-tier retail and we can even have a say in what housing we are assigned. But the people who live on this street, Naia, they are just like everyone else. There is not a single government employee on this street, or else these houses would not all be run down like this."

He stopped at a particularly interesting book.

"I have not seen a copy of this one in years," he smiled and flipped through the pages.

"So what you are saying," Naia noted, "is that they were coming here to loot because they believed that Mrs. Veesaus had more than they did."

"That's a nice way to put it. They wanted to help themselves to her privilege. In reality they aren't getting enough of anything from government rations and will be coming here at some point for an opportunity to fill in the holes."

"But it is the responsibility of the city . . . to redistribute her privilege once she has surrendered it."

Torndale put down the book and turned to her.

"That is the official story," he said. "Again, there is one official side to the story and one . . . shall we say unofficial side. The looters will take whatever they can before our investigators get here and, so to speak, collect evidence. And that's on purpose. The more the looters take, the less work it is for us. Once the looters, and we, have ransacked the house, the property is signed over to the city housing board. They assign tenants to it, according to their preferential lists and practices."

"What happens to whatever our agency takes from the house?"

"It is thrown in some garbage disposal somewhere," Torndale explained neutrally and turned to another book. "Look at this! She really has an impressive collection of literature!"

Naia looked around.

"Sir . . . I mean, Armo . . . "

"Yes," he replied absentmindedly, reading the first page in the new book he found.

"Why are we here?"

He closed the book, looked at her and turned serious.

"Can I trust you?" he asked bluntly.

She looked at him with a completely open face. Their eyes met.

"Yes," she promised.

He nodded and took a step toward her.

"I noticed your reaction when were here for the arrest," he said. "You did not appreciate the . . . moral double standard . . . or the dishonesty . . . Mrs. Veesaus being arrested for not surrendering her privilege, which means she committed an act of aggression toward those who are less privileged. Yet she was awarded honorary citizenship in Kowraam for helping to save the lives of thousands of children there."

Naia nodded.

"Yes," she admitted in a weak voice. "Yes, I did . . . I did not like that . . . "

Torndale smiled.

"This is not easy, is it?" he said in a hushed voice. "You doubt the very doctrine you have built your life on."

She nodded emphatically but did not say anything. Her lips were tightly closed. He saw in her eyes how difficult this was for her.

"I did not realize until today," Torndale said, "just how much I have come to doubt that doctrine . . . that value foundation . . . myself. If you had not been here with me, in this room, and found this letter from the Kowraami vice president, I probably would just have moved on. But . . . maybe you gave me the moral approval to recognize my doubts . . . "

They looked at one another for a moment. She smiled and whispered: "Thank you for validating me."

He nodded, put his hand on her shoulder and said:

"I'll tell you what we'll do. Let's pack our vehicle full with as much stuff as we can, from this library."

"Okay," she agreed.

He looked around and pointed to a corner.

"Let's start with those boxes over there."

"Just one question," Naia said. "What do we do with all that stuff when we leave?"

WHEN THE FIRST RAYS OF SUNSHINE reached the camp on the mountain top, Armo Torndale was already awake. He had woken up just before the daybreak bell.

He turned and saw Naia next to him. She was fast asleep. He removed his blanket and put over her. She nodded approvingly in her sleep.

He reached for his hygienic bag and was just getting up when one of the watchmen approached him. Torndale pointed to Naia. The watchman nodded and waived at Torndale to join him a little bit away from their sleeping spot.

"The night was uneventful," the watchman whispered. "The soldiers advanced to exactly where Naia predicted they would go. Same place where she and her group stopped to rest. Our trap is set to go off only a little bit above where they are."

"Thank you," Torndale said.

"And we have a military veteran among the watchmen."

He pointed to a dad sleeping next to his child.

"Oh, yes," Torndale whispered. "I'll talk to him. Now, go get some rest."

"I have a question," the watchman said. "I heard that we are evacuating families based on how many kids they have."

"Yes."

"We only have one kid, but if we can evacuate my wife and daughter early, I am willing to stay behind and guard the camp until the last flight."

Torndale was not sure how to reply to that. He had not told anyone, except Naia, about the fact that there were more of them than there were seats on the shuttle craft flights.

"Thank you," he said. "We may have to do that. Let's talk about it again when you have gotten some rest."

It was time to bring the next round of evacuees down to the landing site. Torndale knew the Danori would be there on time, but he was still filled with joy when he saw the shuttle craft approach over the treetops, stop, hover for a moment, inflate its landing gear and slowly touch down.

A chorus of wows rose among the twelve who were getting ready to board. The door opened, the short stairs folded out and the Danori woman stepped out.

The sight of her made some of the evacuees gasp.

"A real alien," someone whispered.

Torndale approached her. She greeted him and smiled:

"Your information box was received with gratitude," she said. "Our diplomats handling the talks with your government were pleased."

"I am glad to hear that," Torndale replied. "Here are your passengers for the day."

The first officer stepped out and began helping them board the craft. The Danori woman pulled Torndale to the side.

"Your information box convinced the diplomats that your government is hostile to your group," she said. "There were some in the delegation who had some doubts about you, but those doubts are gone. This will help me help you. I still cannot promise that we can evacuate you all, but . . . as you humans would put it . . . there is hope."

"I am happy to hear that we have been able to help you. You do so much for us. But we have another problem."

"The men on the far side of the mountain."

"Yes. You know about them?"

"We picked them up on our scans. Who are they?"

"A military unit sent out to kill us."

The Danori woman's face shifted. She did not look happy. She excused herself, walked over to the first officer and had a brief chat with him in their own language. Torndale listened as best he could. The language sounded difficult, and it seemed to consist of a lot of consonants, which made it even harder for a human to speak.

The first officer took out some sort of communications device and started talking to someone. The liaison woman came over to Torndale with a confident look on her face.

"We cannot engage that military unit directly," she said when she returned. "It would be illegal for us to do so. But . . . " and she glanced over to the first officer, who nodded to her, " . . . our shuttle craft is equipped with light arms for self protective purposes. Nothing prevents us from doing some target practice before we leave."

The first officer came over and greeted Torndale.

"Our captain has approved a round of target practice with our defensive weapons," he said. "Here is another bag with food rations. And a letter for you."

"A letter?"

"It is from two of the refugees from yesterday's flight" the Danori woman explained. "Same time tomorrow."

They embarked on the shuttle craft, took off and disappeared over the trees. Torndale did not notice that they flew in the direction of where the soldiers were. He was too busy reading the letter.

To all of you who are still waiting to be evacuated: we just wanted to greet you and tell you how happy we are to be onboard this refugee evacuation ship. It is called the Rohax Four. We have comfortable rooms, large enough for a family, with very nice hygiene facilities, and we are eating very well! There is basic medical supplies, too. We are all tired but happy. We look forward to having you all onboard so we can leave for our new home!

The note was signed by two of the women who left on the first flight. It was hand-written with a pencil that one of the women must have brought with her. Torndale had seen moms at the camp keeping their kids busy with drawing and writing exercises.

As he walked back up to the camp, he felt happier than he had in a long time. He thought about what the past few moons had been like. Their long, hard journey. The struggle, the strife . . . the deaths of two of their fellow freedom refugees.

He could have been retiring by now. He could have moved to the Riverlands where his brother and rest of his family lived. He could have been cooking old-style meals for them and spent his time on the porch reading old books.

Sure. Like that would have worked out. First of all, he would have needed to get a housing re-assignment permit, and how easy was that? His long service in government would have given him a good chance to get ahead in the line, but not even spotless service to the state was a guarantee anymore. And retirement rations had gotten stingier of late: food, clothes, travel coupons . . . he knew a couple of recent retirees who complained about how little they actually got.

He thought especially of his old friend from the early days in State Security, back during the federal republic. They had spent a lot of time together. They had shared a hobby—building model cities—that drove his friend's wife crazy . . . but they had abandoned it when supplies dried up under the centrally planned economy.

Torndale thought about all their conversations about everything and anything. That friend had just retired and was surprised at how little he got in retirement rations. He and his wife had moved in with their son and his family, in order to make it work.

When the new people's democratic union was first announced, he had been lukewarm to it. He had shown due enthusiasm at work, and he had diligently fulfilled his duties to his employer. He had loyally served State Security, investigated the Grand Chancellor's opponents—or seditionists as they were called—and even arrested them at times. He had never questioned the ever wider definitions of "sedition" that seemed to come from higher up in the hierarchy with eerily regular intervals.

He could have carried on dutifully, taken his retirement for what it was worth, and withdrawn into obscurity.

But he could not do that. Somewhere deep inside, ever since the People's Democratic Union was announced, he had always harbored a flame of doubt. A flame of dissent. He never embraced the new value foundation that the new union was founded on. He never protested it, either, and never spoke out against it—to do so would have been the end of his career. But deep down in his heart, he could never really accept that it was his job to go after people whose only supposed crime was to disagree with the government on some issue.

Disagreement was not an act of aggression toward the government. Dissent should not be a crime. If someone lived their own life, minded their own business, then what difference would it make to government that they happened to not like the way the health care system was organized?

Like Mrs. Veesaus.

That was his moral turning point.

When he was almost at the camp, Rhem Strebber and Naia came down to meet him. They both looked excited.

"You should have seen it!" Naia exclaimed. "It was fantastic!"

"What was fantastic?"

"The shuttlecraft!" Strebber chuckled. "It went after the soldiers!"

"It flew in right over them," Naia explained excitedly. "So close they could probably have touched its hull. Then they made a fast loop, out from the mountain, and created so much air turbulence that one of the soldiers was pulled up from the ground. He fell over the cliff edge."

"They really made sure to intimidate those soldiers," Strebber smiled.

"And then they turned around and started firing at them," Naia explained enthusiastically. "But it was like they didn't want to hit them, more like scare them."

"Yeah, they hit rocks and trees and boulders right around them."

"They actually destroyed part of the path up from where the soldiers are. It was so amazing!"

"Yeah, that's gonna slow them down alright" Strebber agreed.

"And we haven't touched our trap yet," Naia added.

Torndale smiled. He explained what the Danori woman had said, and how the Danori had gotten mad over the information over the deception in the contact negotiations.

"We will make it," Strebber cheered.

"Now the Danori have made our government aware that they aren't going to accept any interference with us," noted Torndale. "The question is what our government will do in response to that. If they realize that the contact negotiations with the Danori have broken down . . . and by now they know that the Danori got our little package . . . they might just send more military. Out of sheer vengeance."

Strebber and Naia both looked at him with disappointment in their eyes.

"Don't get me wrong," Torndale said, trying to sound cheerful. "I'm as happy as you guys are that they made life miserable for those soldiers."

"Sure," Naia said. "Really happy . . . "

Torndale chuckled and put his arm around her shoulders.

"Let's go have something to eat. We got more food rations here."

"I guess . . . " she muttered.

He let go of her and pulled out the letter.

"Here," he said.

Naia read the letter, smiled and handed it to Strebber.

"That's exciting," she said, seeming a bit more upbeat.

"Wow, awesome!" Strebber exclaimed. "Can I share this with everyone?"

"Of course," Torndale said.

Strebber dashed off into the camp. Torndale and Naia remained for a moment. She was smiling, but she also had tears in her eyes. He took her in his arms.

"It's all going to be alright in the end," he said.

"What if we don't make it up to that ship?" she whispered. "What if they don't have room for all of us?"

"They will," Torndale told her. "They will."

"I'm so tired," she whispered back, burying her face in his chest. "I'm really trying to hold it together, but this stress . . . these swings between hope and . . . "

"Despair?"

"Yes . . . and so little sleep . . . "

"I know. But we are so close to the end now."

She cried. He held her, gently stroking her back. He whispered again that "we are so close", but he was not sure if he was trying to convince Naia—or himself.

❀ ❀ ❀

TWO DAYS AFTER THEY HAD RETRIEVED BOOKS, journals and photos from Mrs. Veesaus's house, Armo Torndale decided to take the morning off from work. He had some investigative work to do, but there were no urgent cases on his desk. He called Commander Kolmov, the staff manager, and said he had some personal matters to attend to.

"You worked on the holiday," Commander Kolmov replied. "Take some personal time."

"Thank you, sir. I will be in after the midday bell."

He drove out to his favorite place in the city: Ocean Park. It was a stretch of land along the shore of the mighty Silver Sea. The park was old, with wide lawns, very tall trees, winding walkways and two tea houses.

The smell of ocean blended with the seasonal scents from the park itself. Here, on the brink of autumn, the air felt crisp, clear, cold and humid. Torndale enjoyed the air from the ocean the most. He often caught it along the walkway right at the waterfront. It was a real promenade, and it stretched the whole length of the park.

The promenade made a loop around a tongue of land that brought the park straight out into the water. That part was Torndale's favorite.

As he entered the park from the parking lot, he was met by the soothing ocean breeze and the refreshing sound of ocean waves breaking against the waterfront. The wind was not strong, but it still rattled the aging leaves on the tall trees. Soon, the leaves would be covering the well-kept lawns.

Since this was a normal workday, Torndale was almost alone strolling from the parking lot in among the trees and the wide lawns. He appreciated the solitude, but he also looked forward to meeting someone up at the first tea house.

The weather was typical for the season, with a slightly chilly wind sweeping in from the sea, clouds gathering on the horizon and the sun just barely warming his skin. He walked a bit faster to keep the colder ocean wind from slipping in under his coat.

As he turned a corner and spotted the tea house, he looked around but could not find the person he was meeting. He looked inside, then walked around the house to the porch where guests would dwell for hours in the summer.

He smiled.

"You made it," he said.

"As did you," his brother replied.

"How was the trip up?"

"Uneventful. Except for the usual checkpoints."

"You mean . . . the ID controls?"

"Yes. They have them at every provincial border crossing now."

"I did not know they had already implemented that. I saw a memo about it a few moons back."

"How is life at the big agency?"

"Come, brother, let's go for a walk."

"You think someone is listening to us here? You've grown too paranoid working for State Security."

"No, I just want to stay warm. We'll go home to me later and have some tea and sandwiches. But right now, I need the fresh ocean air."

"That will be good. I brought some food coupons."

"Oh, don't worry. I get extra coupons. You know, working for government . . . "

"Of course. You mentioned you wanted to talk to me about some personal issues."

"Yes . . . let's . . . let's walk this way."

"Armo, you do seem paranoid. Is everything alright?"

"Yes. Yes, it is . . . I just . . . I just prefer the privacy."

"Okay. Oh, I like the breeze. It's cool and fresh, but not cold like in the winter."

"Kirin, I want to ask you a question. It is abstract, of sorts, and perhaps a bit provocative. But there is a meaning behind it. A point."

"Oh, this sounds exciting."

"I am not sure you are being sincere with me."

"Yes, Armo, you are."

"Yes, I am . . . Anyway. You still own your home, right?"

"Yes, we do."

"Why do you own it?"

"Why? Because a long time ago, Ilena and I bought it and . . . "

"No, that's not what I'm getting at. You own it because you acquired it. But how did you acquire it?"

"Armo . . . you were always the philosophical one. The one who asked all these existential questions. And then . . . you went on to do things that . . . well, got you that scar on your hand . . . "

"Please, Kirin, stay with me. You own your house because you bought it."

"Yes, of course."

"And you have not surrendered it as privilege to the housing board."

"They have never asked for it. I don't think there is much demand for common housing down where we live."

But you also haven't been driven by an ideological urge to surrender it."

"Armo . . . what are you getting at here . . . ? You work for State Security."

"No, please, Kirin. This has nothing to do with that. I have . . . shall we say, existential issues that I am dealing with. I need my brother."

"Yes. And your brother is here. I'm sorry."

"No need."

"We have not surrendered our property as privilege. It is not a conscious decision. It just hasn't occurred to us to do that."

"And you consider the property to be rightfully yours. Because you purchased it, you paid for it and you have maintained your obligations as prescribed by law."

"Yes. Well, it is getting increasingly difficult to comply with the laws. They regulate more and more details of how you can maintain your house and your yard, what electrical power you can use, and so on. But yes, we do our very best."

"I know you do. But here is what I am getting at. You paid for your house with money that you earned working."

"Of course. We paid our installment loan according to plan . . . "

" . . . and if you had not worked to earn that money, you would not have had a moral right to that property."

"Or legal right, eventually, since I would not have kept up with the installment loan. But, Armo, let's stop for a second . . . why are you asking about this? You know everything about my home, you were even there when we bought it. Why are you really asking all this?"

"Okay . . . but Kirin, my brother . . . what I am about to tell you is in strict confidence . . . "

"I understand that."

"I know. I know I can trust you. You know me better than anyone. Well, since mother died, of course . . . "

"Yes . . . nobody will ever know us like mother did . . . "

"I was on secondment from investigations to operations for two days. They are short on staff. We did low-risk arrests, and one of the people we arrested was this old lady. She was charged because she did not surrender her house, which she owns, to the local housing board. They equated her house with privilege. She was also charged with sedition. She had criticized our health care system for not delivering as promised."

"In all honesty, Armo, the health care system is not doing a very good job."

"I won't argue with that. But regardless, I would probably not have had a problem with her being charged under the Equality Act . . . for not surrendering her privilege . . . if it wasn't for what I found out about this woman's background. You see, the charge under the Equality Act means that she is accused of an aggression toward those who are less privileged. She is accused of depriving them of something they have an entitlement to."

"How can she be depriving people of something they are entitled to by simply living in her house?"

"She has a larger living space than is considered acceptable for one person. A much larger living space, in fact."

"I see. The value foundation."

"Exactly. So here is this gentle old lady, who spends her days in her house reading old books and knitting for her grandchildren, who keeps up her front yard and bothers nobody. She is accused of aggression toward the less privileged, simply by virtue of living in a house that she and her husband acquired in the very same way as you and Ilena acquired your house."

"Armo, you just questioned the very value foundation of the government you work for."

"I found the whole situation unbearable."

"For the fact that she owns her own house and was told to surrender her privilege?"

"There is more to it. In the subsequent investigation I found out that she and her husband had done considerable charity work in Kowraam. They had helped build private health care clinics that, according to the Kowraami government, saved the lives of thousands of children."

"Oh. And this is the same woman that our government accused of aggression toward the unprivileged."

"Yes."

"That must have been difficult to process."

"Kirin, you see that man over there? On the bench. He is just a random man. We know nothing about his background. We don't know if he is a doctor or if he even works at all. We don't know if he treats his family well, or if he has a family at all. We know nothing of his way of interacting with other people, whether he is a helpful neighbor or if he will steal whenever given the opportunity. Suppose he came up to this old lady's house and demanded to live there. Does she have a moral obligation to provide for him?"

"Good question. According to our nation's value foundation, yes, she has an obligation to do so."

"Good answer. Let's play this rhetorical game. My next question, of course, would be: why? Why does she have an obligation to do so?"

"Because he is presumably less privileged than her."

"And she is committing an act of aggression toward him by refusing to let him in. And by reaching that conclusion, we morally nullify the good deeds she has done for others who are severely under-privileged."

"And your agency . . . State Security . . . knew of this woman's charity work?"

"The evidence doesn't matter. It is not considered. She is already listed for transportation to one of our . . . re-education camps . . . "

"Do they actually exist?"

"Kirin, for me to reveal to you that they do . . . "

"I understand completely."

"We didn't even bother to collect the exculpatory evidence. I did, personally, but there was no point in submitting it to the agency. We simply executed the arrest and the seizure of her property. The house has already been turned over to the local housing board. We formally arrested her on the sedition charge."

"And what was the act of sedition she committed? That she had criticized our health care system?"

"Yes."

"You know, my dear baby brother . . . it's getting a bit cold out here."

"It is. Let's go to my place and have some tea and sandwiches. But you do see my existential dilemma here?"

"I do. And I will see it even more clearly if you still have some of that that pine smoked tea left."

❄ ❄ ❄

WITH TWO GROUPS OF REFUGEES having been evacuated, the atmosphere in camp on the mountaintop had turned from strenuous on the brink of depressive, to casual, even upbeat. There was more space for those who were still waiting, and more food and hygiene products.

For the first time since they had left their well planned, confined existence under the People's Democratic Union of Ripoma, their lives as freedom refugees almost seemed tolerable. A few of the adults even went a bit outside the camp to work up a suntan. It did not go very well given the tall, leaf-rich trees that were the forest around them, but they did not mind—all that mattered was that they could rest, relax and reinvigorate themselves.

The young men and women who had asked Armo Torndale to tell them about the colony they were going to build, wanted to hear more. He promised them to continue their conversation after he had escorted the third group of evacuees to the shuttle craft.

The Danori woman did not look as formal as she normally did. She was wearing a more relaxed outfit, unlike the uniform she had worn before, and she approached Torndale with a muted smile.

"I am pleased to see our evacuation plan proceed smoothly," she said.

Torndale returned her smile:

"So am I. You have met Rhem Strebber before. He has been of great help to me ever since we left the city. He is coming with this group so he can help get us organized onboard your ship."

"Pleased to see you again," the Danori woman said to Strebber. "We had not been properly introduced."

"Ma'm . . . " Strebber replied, having a difficult time approaching her. "It's my leisure . . . I mean pleasure . . . "

The Danori woman looked a bit confused for a second.

"He's just nervous meeting beautiful women," Torndale rushed to explain.

"Is that a human compliment?" she asked.

"A big one," Torndale assured her.

She accepted Strebber's greetings. Strebber turned to Torndale:

"Good luck with the rest of the evacuation."

"Thank you, my friend. See you in a couple of days."

Strebber gave him a quick hug and stepped onboard the shuttlecraft. Armo Torndale again turned to the Danori woman.

"He is a good leader," he explained. "He will be of great help."

"How are people doing at the camp?" she asked.

"Much better, thank you. There is less stress, more optimism, and living conditions are better."

"That is good news," she nodded. "I, too, have good news. Our government was very pleased with the box of information you provided us with. We have been granted permission to make a sixth shuttle run."

Torndale smiled. He laughed, looked down on his shoes, out into the forest and at the Danori woman again. He wiped a tear from his eye.

"Thank you," he whispered.

She handed him a bag of supplies.

"Since there are fewer of you, this will do for the remainder of the evacuation plan," she explained.

"Thank you," Torndale repeated, nodding emphatically. "You know, with this group, we will have shipped out more than half of the camp. Thirty-six of . . . of sixty-four."

The Danori woman examined his face for a moment.

"You humans have curious ways of expressing yourselves" she said. "But I gather from the tone in your voice and the look on your face that having a majority evacuated is better than having a minority evacuated."

"Wouldn't you agree?"

"My measurement of success is that all of you are evacuated as per our original agreement."

"I agree," said Torndale. "But I was not referring to success. I was referring to progress."

He looked her in the eyes and gave away another smile. She tilted her head slightly to the side. Her large blue eyes, her tall nose and cheeks and her thin lips all broke out in what almost was a laughter.

"You outsmarted me," she said. "I appreciate that. I look forward to our next conversation."

When the shuttlecraft had taken off, Torndale returned to the camp and broke daybreak bread with Naia. She was thrilled to hear the news that they, too, were indeed going to be evacuated. She had a book next to her resting place.

"What is that?" Torndale asked.

Naia smiled:

"These are propaganda poems. I could not leave my room at the academy without it. I mean, it's not exactly world class poetry . . . "

Armo Torndale laughed:

"I remember those. I never had to read them, although every employee got a copy. They came out after the transition. They are meant to drum up your value foundation spirit."

"Wanna hear one?"

"Sure."

"Okay, but don't laugh."

"I promise," promised Torndale while trying not to laugh.

"You're laughing already!"

"So what? You didn't write the poems."

"True," Naia smiled. "Anyway. Here goes."

She cleared her throat and pretended to be dead serious:

"At daybreak our people rise to the day . . . and stand with our leader who shows us the way . . . Oh Sorto you give us a future so bright . . . for you and your values the people will fight . . . "

"That's a succinct one," Torndale noted.

"Or how about this one? 'We stood up one day; And broke the shackles of freedom; We stood up one day; And said: give us equality or give us death; We stood up one day; And Sorto gave us equality; All the old we threw away; And all the new we ushered in; All the old we threw away; And with it freedom, a woeful sin.'"

Naia's face turned serious.

"You know, when I came to the academy, I actually thought that one made sense."

"And they really wrote this and published it . . . " Torndale said. "Pathetic. Really laughably pathetic. But that's what happens when you do away with freedom of speech, when you silence your opponents. You don't have to work hard anymore to win."

"Who said freedom is a woeful sin?"

It was one of the young men Torndale had talked to before about their new colony.

"Can we continue our discussion about the pillars of the constitution we are going to live under?"

"The three pillars of the Constitutional Code of Danor," Torndale noted, nodding emphatically. "Yes, of course. Naia, you want to sit in?"

"Sure."

"I gather this won't be as fun as reading state propaganda poems, but . . . "

"We can always get back to the totalitarian fun when we are bored with freedom," Naia suggested.

"I remember this poem from when I was a kid," said Torndale. "I don't have the book with me, but you remember it, Naia. Goes something like this . . . Freedom is your birthright . . . Freedom is your quest . . . Under the skies of freedom . . . "

" . . . all of us shall rest," one of the younglings filled in.

Torndale turned to him.

"You read that one?"

"My grandfather used to recite it," the young man smiled.

There were two more in the audience this time. Torndale welcomed the newcomers.

"Last time we met we covered the first constitutional pillar," he explained. "The one about the sanctity of life."

"We drifted off into a discussion about health insurance," one of the younglings remembered. "I never got the point there."

"I don't think we quite got to make it," Torndale agreed. "I think the point was that if you can get your health insurance, and access health care, on private terms, government does not have to provide it and tax us to pay for it."

"But how is taxation related to the sacrosanctity of life?" Naia asked.

"The sanctity pillar is the 'do no harm' pillar," Armo Torndale explained. "You shall do no physical harm to anyone else. But there is a second meaning to 'do no harm', namely that you shall not violate a person's property. That no-harm principle is just as strong as the one about harm to the person. Just as you cannot force a person to do something against his will, you also cannot force him to surrender any of his property. A tax forces you to surrender part of your property, therefore taxation is prohibited under the Danori Constitutional Code. There is one exception, and that is a tax to fund the military, police and justice functions that protect the very constitution itself and the freedom it protects on behalf of the people."

A moment of silence followed. It was almost as if they wanted to let Torndale's words sink in.

"Does that mean you don't get paid with rations and coupons for your work?" one of the younglings asked eventually. "How does government pay you?"

"You don't get paid by government," another youngling explained. "You get paid by your workplace."

"Your employer," Torndale confirmed.

"And you get paid with money, right?" Naia asked.

"That's right."

"Fascinating," said one of the younglings. "But doesn't that mean that all the stores, all . . . all the bills you pay . . . everyone has to accept money as a means of payment?"

"It does."

The younglings considered the consequences:

"So then you can choose a lot easier what you want to buy."

"Or if you want to spend a little less today, you can save up and spend more tomorrow."

"But can anyone open a store, like a shoe store?"

"Yes. That's right, isn't it?"

Torndale nodded.

"Self determination means anyone can open a business," he pointed out. "Businesses compete for customers, like we talked about last time."

"Sounds like you have a lot more control over your own life," Naia noted.

"Indeed" Torndale agreed. "The second pillar of the Constitutional Code talks about that. It is the pillar of self determination. It is, I think the most fascinating one, because it explains how a constitutionally guaranteed freedom also becomes a responsibility."

"Isn't the first pillar also both a right and a responsibility?" Naia asked.

"How?" one of the other younglings wanted to know.

"Well, if you have an absolute right to the sanctity of . . . how did they put it? Your person and your property?"

"Right," Torndale confirmed.

"If you have that right," Naia continued, "and if it is absolute, well, then everyone else around you has an obligation to honor that sanctity. Isn't that how it works?"

"Yes," said a young man with a long, almost completely white beard.

The color of his beard would have made him look old, had it not been for his young face. He was young, indeed, but his very light skin complexion and the pale blue color of his eyes gave away that his family roots stretched back to one of the remote islands way up in the northern ocean.

He had just joined their little study group. Torndale knew him as a studied man.

"Then you might like this second constitutional pillar," he told the man. "The one about self determination."

"What exactly does that mean?" asked one of the younglings.

"That you have the right to chart your own course in life," the white beard replied without hesitation.

"Pinpoint accurate," Torndale noted. "In theory. But what does it mean in practice?"

The present company was quiet for a moment.

"This is the important question," Torndale continued. "You will now get an opportunity to turn this nice philosophical principle into actual use. You will get a chance to a new community, to put it to work in real life."

The white-bearded man suggested:

"It means that your ability to feed your family, to provide for those you are responsible for, depends on your own willingness to work."

"A bit more specific," Torndale said in an encouraging tone.

"I'm not sure how much more specific you can be."

"Well, can a man get up in the morning and do just any work? Can he paint paintings and expect that to provide for his family?"

A moment of silence.

"Only if his paintings are so good that he can sell them for good money," said Naia. "If not, he has to do something that brings home what his family needs."

"Right!" Torndale exclaimed. "On the one hand, nobody has the right to prevent you from providing for yourself and your loved ones. On the other hand, nobody else has an obligation to provide for your family. It is your responsibility to use that freedom in such a way that your family is taken care of. Because if your work does not feed them, let's say because you choose to write poetry that nobody wants to buy . . . "

"Like poetry about the People's Democratic Union of Ripoma," Naia suggested with a conspicuous smile.

"Oh, what makes you think nobody would possibly want to buy that poetry?" Torndale asked and returned her smile.

"So," said the white beard, "you cannot expect anyone else to fill in what you failed to provide."

"Right on the money," Torndale agreed. "Pardon the pun. I could not resist it."

Muted chuckle was followed by silence.

"It's kind of a harsh principle," one of the women noted. "I mean, what if someone does work hard and still cannot fully provide for his family? Or what if he falls ill and cannot work?"

"Very good questions," said Torndale. "Exactly the right questions to ask. Comments, anyone?"

"Isn't that where charity comes in?" the white beard asked.

Torndale nodded:

"In fact, that is the very next part of this self-determination pillar of the Constitutional Code. We have a moral obligation to make available the resources that our community needs for precisely these purposes. To fill in the gap for those who don't have enough."

"But wait a second," Naia jumped in. "Are you saying that we have a moral obligation . . . an equal moral obligation . . . to provide charity to both the person who writes worthless poetry . . . sorry to put it that way . . . "

"No, that's OK," Torndale reassured her. "If nobody wants to buy it, it is literally worthless."

"To the worthless poet, and to the person who falls ill and cannot work?"

Torndale turned to the group. They pondered the question.

"No," said one of them eventually. "There is a moral distinction between the two. The person who falls ill has done his best. The worthless poet hasn't. The ill person is morally entitled to charity. The worthless poet is not."

"I think the poet also deserves help," said another of the younglings. "Would that be banned under the Constitutional Code?"

"It wouldn't," said the white-bearded man. "If I understand this self determination principle correctly, you are free to give your property . . . including your money . . . to anyone. You just can't be forced to do it."

"Correct," Torndale confirmed. "The idea that something is banned because it is not mandatory comes from the ideological campaign that the People and Progress movement ran against the old federal republic. For example, under the federal republic there was no mandate to vote. It was voluntary. But just because there was no law that forced you to vote, did not mean that voting was illegal. It was a choice you made as a citizen. It works the same way with charity. If you want to give charity to a person who spends his day writing poetry, then you are perfectly free to do so. It is your money that you rightfully earned and have the property right to. It is up to you how you choose to spend that money. If you want to give it to the person who fell ill, or to the worthless poet, or both, or neither . . . well, that is entirely up to you."

A couple of the younglings smiled.

"I think I am beginning to grasp the concept of freedom," said one of them.

"There is more to it," Torndale promised.

Before he got to it, one of the camp watchmen came up to him and handed him a note. He read it with a neutral face, gave it back to the watchman and said:

"I'll be right there. Sorry, my friends, but I have to take care of some practical matters. Let's convene again later, shall we?"

He got up and glanced over toward the forest on the west side of the camp.

"Naia," he said. "Come with me. I'll need you on this one."

EDA STREBBER WAITED at the instructors' break room. She was determined to wait as long as she could. She had her sedition class to teach, but she wanted to catch Olgar before she went to the lecture hall.

He was elusive. She had tried to find him the whole day before, but somehow he managed to avoid her.

The break room was located in a part of the building where all classrooms, lecture halls and meeting rooms were. The hallway outside the break room was wide and had a tall ceiling. Its floor was the typical kind of granite that made for loud echoes but was easy to keep clean and never wore out. The walls were also of granite and the ceiling was vaulted. Altogether, the hallway was a perfect amplifier even of muted conversations.

Eda Strebber wondered if there was a thought behind that. After all, this building had been specially designed for State Security.

She saw a couple of other instructors and exchanged greetings with them, all while she kept an eye on the hallway to make sure Olgar did not slip by undetected.

There! At the end of the hallway, down in the direction of the lecture hall. She barely caught a glimpse of him before he snuck into the male hygiene area. But it was him, no doubt.

He took his time in there. Eda Strebber realized that she would be late for her class if she wanted to talk to him, but it was worth the while.

As if he had purposely waited for her class to start, Olgar emerged on the very spot when Eda Strebber was supposed to close the door to her lecture hall and start teaching sedition. He was startled to see her and almost walked back into the hygiene area.

"What are you doing here?" he asked, evasive and startled. "Aren't you supposed to teach now?"

"Yes," she said and gave him a cold business-like smile. "I just wanted to hear . . . how you are doing."

His eyes wandered in one direction, then in the other direction. He cleared his throat, smiled uncomfortably and then turned serious again.

"Oh yeah, I'm good, I'm fine," he said rapidly. "I'm doing well, thank you. How are you?"

"I got a note that Cadet Fernek dropped your class," she said, ignoring his courtesy question. "That's odd. Why would she do that?"

"Look, uh . . . " he mumbled. "I really have to rush. I have . . . a meeting with . . . I have to go."

He dashed off toward the break room.

"I bet you do," Eda Strebber said to herself and smirked.

She excused her late arrival at the lecture hall with some unexpected confidential meeting. The class was quiet, attentively awaiting her lecture.

She stopped at the lecture podium, placed her notes on the desk and looked around the classroom. She spotted Naia Fernek sitting far up in the back. She was almost hunkering down, like she did not want to be noticed.

Eda Strebber smiled. She folded up the first page of her lecture notes and glanced them over.

"Alright," she said, still looking over her notes. "Today . . . " and she raised her eyes and looked squarely at Naia. "Today we are going to talk about the difference between sedition and insurrection. And we are going to do so in the context of our national value foundation."

Naia Fernek winced. Eda Strebber drew a breath of fresh air, raised her head even higher and chose her words carefully:

"When you are done here at the academy, you will be assigned to the operations division. There, you will participate in the arrest of people who are accused of sedition. Sometimes they are accused of both sedition and insurrection."

Naia looked down at her notes. She tried her best to avoid being the focus of attention.

Eda Strebber was satisfied with her submissive attitude. She looked around the classroom to make sure all students were paying attention. When she noted that they all were, she went straight for the meat of the lecture:

"Our nation's value foundation states that every person in this country has the right to all his needs, regardless of who he or she is, where he or she came from, and what he or she has chosen to do in life. Those needs are listed in a supplement to the value foundation, and is accounted for in your textbook, appendix one. But our government cannot just guarantee those rights without having the resources necessary to provide for all out needs. Therefore, government must have the authority to secure those resources, wherever they are available."

She paused, left the podium and walked slowly out to the middle of the open space in front of the students.

"Anyone who withholds resources that government could use to provide for the needs of others . . . anyone who has more than what he or she needs . . . must therefore surrender that surplus to government. If a farmer harvests more than he needs for himself, the value foundation says that he has to give the surplus up to the local farming board. To make sure we never end up in a situation where farmers do withhold surplus, we have eliminated private farms. By the same token, a tailor who makes more clothes than the family needs, must give the surplus over to the local industry board."

She once again sought out and fixed her eyes on Naia.

"Anyone who has more living space than is appropriate for one person, must give up the surplus living space to the local housing board."

Naia stared down at her notes. She put her hand up against her forehead to shield her face from Eda Strebber's piercing eyes.

Eda Strebber was just about to continue when a student in the front row raised her hand.

"Yes?"

"Adjutant Strebber, may I ask . . . for clarification . . . a question about the practice of the value foundation?"

"Of course."

"My grandparents had a neighbor who was a tailor, and he refused to work more hours than it took to provide clothes for his own family. He told my grandfather that since he and his family got everything they needed from government anyway, he did not have to work more than to clothe himself, his wife and their children. But he was charged with insurrection as a result of that . . . and I am not questioning the charge . . . I just never understood why he would be charged with insurrection . . . for not putting in a full day's worth of work as a tailor. I just wanted to understand . . . "

Eda Strebber nodded to her.

"Yes, of course," she said. "Thank you, that is actually a very good question. It goes hand in hand with the point I was just making about the value foundation. I assume that your grandparents' neighbor worked less than ten bells per day."

"Yes. I think that, when he only made clothes for his own family, he never worked more than a bell or two every day."

"And that is very likely why he was charged with insurrection," Eda Strebber explained. "Again, let us go back to the point I made about government having the authority to summon the resources needed to provide for everyone's needs. If there is a shortage of something . . . say clothes . . . then of course government has the authority to request that our tailors produce the clothes needed. To not do so . . . to not comply with the government's request . . . is to commit an act of violence against those who need the clothes that you refuse to produce. You are charged under Chapter Three, Section One of the Equality Act."

She made sure the class was paying close attention. It was.

"An act of violence against another person is criminal. If it is a matter of physical assault, it is of course an act under the criminal code. If it is a matter of denying another person his needs, it is an act of insurrection. Therefore, anyone who does not work a full day's worth, in other words until the tenth bell has rung, is an insurrectionist."

Another student raised his hand.

"Yes?"

"Is an act of insurrection punished more harshly than a criminal act?"

"Sometimes. It depends on the severity of the insurrection. If you physically assault one person, you harm one person. If you deny to provide, say, clothes to five people, you harm five people. Five is more than one, therefore you should be punished five times harsher."

She looked out over the class.

"Any other questions on insurrection? No? Let's move on to . . . sedition."

After the class Eda Strebber waited for Cadet Fernek to descend from the row way up in the back. She watched as Cadet Fernek exchanged a few words with a fellow student and seemed to dwell up in the back of the classroom. She was probably waiting for Eda Strebber to leave, and when she didn't leave, Naia had no choice but to try to get out of the classroom as discretely as possible.

It did not work. Eda Strebber gave her no choice.

"Cadet Fernek."

"Yes, ma'm."

"How did you like the class?"

"It was good . . . informative . . . "

"I heard you dropped Adjutant Olgar's class."

Naia stared at the floor.

"Yes, ma'm."

Eda Strebber waited. She was pleased to see Cadet Fernek's level of discomfort escalate.

"That was probably not a good idea," she said slowly. "Career-wise."

"No, ma'm."

"Why did you do it?"

"I . . . had a pretty heavy load and . . . I had to deal with some personal matters . . . "

"What personal matters?"

Naia did not respond immediately. Eda Strebber waited.

"Well?"

"Ma'm . . . I'd rather not . . . "

Eda Strebber took a step closer.

"I am giving you direct order," she said in a hushed but very harsh voice. "Tell me why you dropped Adjutant Olgar's class."

Naia closed her eyes for a second. She took a deep breath to manage the anxiety.

"Because," she whispered. "Because . . . Adjutant Olgar . . . "

"Speak up, I can't hear you."

"Because Adjutant Olgar . . . made advances . . . "

Naia was still staring into the floor. Eda Strebber had not expected such a forthright answer, but she quickly realized the explosive nature of Cadet Fernek's statement. This could be useful.

"Made advances?" she asked in a slightly less authoritative tone. "How?"

Naia looked up, glanced at her instructor, then looked away again.

"You mean sexual advances?" Eda Strebber asked.

Naia nodded.

"And . . . how did you respond to those advances?"

Naia's lips were tight. She refused to look her instructor in the eyes, yet Eda Strebber could see a glimpse of a tear.

She was not going to let this one fly.

"Cadet Fernek," she said in a hushed but clear voice. "You have just accused a superior officer, your instructor at that, of serious misconduct. Either you clarify your statement, or you retract it and resume his class."

Naia broke out in tears. This was more than she could handle.

And it was exactly what Eda Strebber wanted.

"There now," she said, putting a fake compassionate arm around Naia. "There, there."

"I'm sorry," Naia whispered. "This is hard for me."

"Come, sit down," Eda Strebber said and offered Naia a chair right next to the instructor's desk. "Now . . . tell me what's going on."

❀ ❀ ❀

THE CAMP WATCHMEN who kept an eye on the soldiers had reported some activity that they did not know what to make of. The the military veteran had been watching the soldiers since daybreak.

"It looks like they are setting up some sort of outpost camp," he suggested. "They can't advance, and since they know we know they are here, the logical thing for them to do would be to abort the mission and withdraw. Instead, they have made a permanent camp about forty leaps below where the shuttle craft fired upon them. They have arranged it exactly as you would a longer-term outpost. And we spotted them making radio calls."

"They are not discrete at all," Armo Torndale noted.

"They don't have to be," said the veteran. "Now that they know that we know, and so on."

Torndale nodded.

"They are waiting for reinforcements," he suggested. "Why else would they simply not just leave?"

"Reinforcements that would have to come by air."

"By air?" one of the watchmen asked.

"It takes too long to get reinforcements here by road transportation," the veteran explained.

"Does that mean air strikes?"

"You mean by fighter planes?" Armo Torndale asked. "I doubt it. It would be overkill . . . if you pardon the expression . . . but it is not impossible."

The veteran agreed.

"It's more likely that they fly in reinforcement troops," he said. "Perhaps another commando unit. And they would come by helicopter."

"Because that way they can land them up on the open plain where the shuttlecraft lands," Naia suggested.

"Yes," confirmed the veteran. "But most likely two units, one on each side of the camp."

"How long do we have?" Naia asked.

"The nearest helicopter base is a full day's flight from here," the veteran recalled. "The helicopters will have to refuel before flying back home. And they would probably stop and refuel before they drop off the troops. Add the fueling time . . . plus, they have to get the ranger units to the helicopters before they even leave their base. Two days is my guess."

"Two days," Armo Torndale mumbled. "They will be here right as we ship out the last big group. Then we have only a small group that stays behind for the last pick-up. What would be a likely time of day for their assault?"

"Before daybreak," the veteran suggested. "Most likely halfway through the night."

"Naia," said Torndale. "You are very organized. Unlike me and most of everyone else here."

Everyone chuckled.

"Set up a schedule for the watchmen and the firearms we have. We don't have enough of them, so we need a system for getting the most firepower to the appropriate location, in as short a period of time as possible."

"I'll use the field operations manual from the agency," she said.

"Finally, that piece of junk will do us some good," Torndale smiled.

The watchmen reorganized their schedule. It was not easy: they had to take into account who was going to be evacuated when, and still not wear out the manpower that was left. They needed more eyes at night than during the day, but they also could not let the daytime go unguarded. Fortunately, Torndale's plan to evacuate families with children first had worked out to their advantage: of the 28 people left in the camp, 24 were men and women capable of doing watch and guard duty.

The third evacuation day went by, nightfall rolled in and with it another rainy night. The camp was in better shape than last time—the makeshift shelters left behind by the evacuated were being used for added protection by those who were still there—and this rain was not nearly as hard as the last one. But it made the watchmen's job harder.

Fortunately, nothing happened during the night. There were no sightings of helicopters or other aircraft.

When the fourth evacuation day broke and the shuttlecraft landed for another pick-up, Torndale was in for a surprise. Instead of the Danori woman, Rhem Strebber stepped out and greeted him.

His face was brimming with a smile.

"You look like you spent all day taking a bath," Torndale noted.

"That ship is fabulous," Strebber smiled. "What facilities they have. I mean, they tell us that the ship is an outdated space ferry, but it sure isn't outdated to me. It's fantastic."

The twelve evacuees who were ready to board heard his comments.

"What is it like?" they wanted to know.

"Please, hop onboard and I'll tell you!" Strebber suggested and turned to Torndale. "We get good food. Great food. I can't remember ever eating this well. The rooms are small, but very comfortable. The beds are infinitely adjustable, I don't know how they do that . . . but it's amazing. I haven't slept this well since I was a kid!"

"I'm glad to hear that," Torndale said and pulled Strebber to the side. "Listen . . . tell them we have a problem. The soldiers on the west side of the mountain have called in reinforcements, and we estimate they will be here probably during the next night. Hopefully after tomorrow's pick-up. But they are coming."

Strebber looked genuinely worried.

"More soldiers?"

"Yes."

"But how can they get here this fast?"

"We are pretty sure they will fly them in by helicopter."

"That's bad. Tomorrow, you said?"

"Any time between tonight and tomorrow night."

"What do you want the Danori to do?"

"Send us a detachment of their military."

Strebber looked at Armo Torndale in disbelief.

"I'm kidding," Torndale explained. "We are short on firearms. Do they happen to have something they could let us borrow?"

"I'll ask them."

❀ ❀ ❀

When Naia Fernek went home from the State Security academy, she did not walk with her usual light and determined feet. Her steps were slow, her head hanging, her eyes searching aimlessly for something on the ground in front of her.

Traffic was light, but there were a good many pedestrians on the sidewalk. She did not care too much to avoid them. She did not care too much about anything, in fact.

Eda Strebber had encouraged her to make a long statement about her relationship with Olgar. Naia had hesitated at first, but when Eda made clear that it was either her career that would be affected, or Olgar's, she had felt a level of anger rising within her, anger that she had not felt since— since when? Her childhood?

She had gotten angry with Olgar. Yes, she had been attracted to him, flattered by his interest in her, yearning for the closeness, the embracing love of a man's arms. She had lived for so long in emotional isolation. Her father, long dead and gone, had been polite and kind, but distant. Her mother, first busy with Naia's older brother, then with her own mother, was emotionally unavailable.

She had learned to take care of herself. She had learned that nobody else would be there for her, so she needed to be there for herself. But no woman could live like that forever, and certainly not at her young age.

Olgar's invite had been like the flame that melted the ice. She had thrown herself into his arms. She had felt a surge of joy, of happiness, of lust . . .

And yet—he had known all along that their relationship could not last. He had known that it would end the career for one of them.

When it came down to it, he had chosen himself over her.

As she turned a corner and headed north, a headwind caught her off guard. Suddenly, her eyes were filled with tears. She was not sure if it was the wind or her heart grieving her loneliness, but she stopped at a park, sat down for a moment and let her tears flood down her cheeks.

Eda Strebber had taken her statement and assured her that justice would be served. She had been cordial, professional and courteous.

And cold. Her mouth had smiled but her eyes told a different story. Naia could not let go of the feeling that Eda Strebber was using her. She could not see how she was being used, but the feeling was real.

Then she had been sent to the course administrator to formally resign from Olgar's class. The course administrator had asked her for the reason.

"It just doesn't fit my schedule," Naia had told her.

The middle-aged lady had looked down her nose at Naia. She had examined the young woman's face . . . and body . . . and said, with a smile filled with contempt:

"You sure know how to use your assets, don't you?"

In her other classes, it was almost like the other students withdrew from her. Maybe she was just imagining it; maybe she was stressed out and paranoid. But even her two best friends from the student dorm kept unusual distance to her.

Or so it felt. Maybe it was just her yearning for a friend, someone to cry with, someone who would be there for her, hug her and let her pour out her sorrow.

For some reason, Armo Torndale's face appeared in her head. She smiled and wondered what he was doing on an evening like this. He seemed lonely, like someone who did not have a family.

She went home, had a meal in peace and quiet and listened to a radio show about mountain wildlife. She knew nothing about the mountains, and very little about wildlife in general. But it took her mind off the stressful day.

It felt better after dinner. The rations were not great, but nutrition was always good. The radio show shifted to music, with a couple of musicians from up north.

Which reminded her of her mother. She still had a couple of phone call coupons left for this moon.

"Hello?"

"Hi, mom, it's me."

"Hi, Naia! How are you, sweetie?"

"I'm . . . I'm okay . . . how are you?"

"I'm good. We baked some dark thin bread today. You remember that?"

"Yes. Grandma always made it when we came visiting."

"Yes! How is college?"

"Uh . . . the academy . . . it's alright, I guess . . . "

"You sound tired."

"Yeah . . . it's a lot going on . . . "

"Well, you get some rest and you'll be fine tomorrow."

"I guess . . . I just had this thing happen . . . with one of the instructors . . . "

"Uh huh . . . "

"And . . . it's kind of complicated, but . . . so, I was taking his class, and one day he wanted to talk to me in private . . . and . . . "

"Hang on, dear, let me check on grandma . . . just a moment."

"Sure."

"I think she needs some help with that. Can I call you right back?"

"Sure."

"Love you, sweetie!"

"Love you, too . . . "

The instant Naia hung up, she wanted to throw the phone across the room into the wall. Never in her life had she felt more lonely, more abandoned, more deserted. Never before had the desire for company—that simple human touch—been stronger inside her. And never before had it felt so distant, so far away.

Literally. Her mother was halfway across the country, up in a small town on the northern shore. The only way to reach it was on a three-day trip, either by automobile or bus, or by train. There was no air service, and besides, traveling by air had become so rationed that very few people could do it anymore.

Not to mention how her mother always had something else to do when Naia wanted some attention.

She got up, went to the window and looked out. The sun had set, the first night bell had rung and the stars were lighting in the sky.

Should she go out for a walk before curfew? Or maybe go to the academy sports club? Whatever she did, staying inside was not an option. The loneliness of the room was becoming unbearable.

She looked down at her desk. Textbooks, class notes, a couple of pencils . . . and Armo Torndale's name scribbled on the side of some class notes.

Armo Torndale.

She felt a sting in her belly. She saw the old commander in front of her. His quirky face frowning at some of the books they had found at Ms. Veesaus's house. His eyes looking both confused and inspired while trying to explain some principle behind State Security operations.

She smiled, but she also bit her tongue to hold back the urge to call him.

Besides, she didn't have his number, so why bother?

Before she knew it, she picked up the phone and called the State Security on-call service.

"I need to get in touch with Group Commander Armo Torndale."

"He is not in his office at this time."

"I know. I just need to convey a message to him."

"I cannot give you his home number."

"Can you call him for me and leave my name and number? He can call me back if he has time."

"I can do that."

Naia hung up. What had she done? Had she once again gotten into something with a superior officer, someone she should not communicate with outside the office?

No, she had not. She did not have that kind of feelings for Torndale. She just wanted to tell him about today's experience with Eda Strebber. That was perfectly legitimate.

Then, on the other hand . . . she did not mind his company. He was like a father figure, that old kind of guy she could feel safe and comfortable with. Someone who would not be overwhelmed by emotions or upset over something she did. Someone who . . .

"Yes, this is Naia Fernek."

"I heard what Eda Strebber did."

His voice was soothing. She could not hold back her tears.

"Are you alright?" he asked.

She sobbed.

"No, you're not," he noted. "Do you need some company?"

"Yes . . . " she whispered.

"I have a spare couch you can sleep on. I'll pick you up at next bell."

"That's not necessary . . . "

"Yes, it is," he said in a warm voice. "Meet me in front of your building at next bell."

"Is that appropriate?"

"You mean, you sleeping over at my house? Of course. I'll explain when I pick you up."

"Thank you . . . " she cried uncontrollably.

❈ ❈ ❈

There were no children left in the camp. Only sixteen people remained, most of whom were camp watchmen. With so few people, it made it both easier and more difficult to defend themselves. they could not keep watch as they had before, but they could also regroup and hide more easily.

Which was exactly what they did. They packed up most of the camp and regrouped into the woods. Half of them had moved into the woods north of the camp site, which placed them closer to the steep slope down toward where the soldiers were. The other half had set up camp in the woods between the camp site and the shuttlecraft landing spot.

It was better to be split up, in the event they were attacked.

They spent their time rotating rest, food service and watch duty. The sky was cloudy, and the temperature had clearly shifted for the colder. One of the older watchmen, who had grown up in this part of the country, suggested that winter could come any time now.

The day went by quietly. Armo Torndale was adamant that the watchmen search the skies for any signs of helicopters. There were two spots on the mountain where they had excellent far-away view of the sky, one looking west and one looking east and southeast.

As the sunset bell drew close, nothing had been reported.

"Hopefully we will all be out of here before they attack," said one watchman.

"Hopefully," Torndale mumbled.

"You don't seem too optimistic."

"The soldiers could have made their call for reinforcement days ago."

He had barely spoken those words before another watchman came jogging up from the site where they had made a trap for the soldiers.

"The soldiers are moving away," he said. "Down the mountain."

"Victory," exclaimed the first watchman.

"Where are they heading?" Torndale asked.

"Home again, I assume," said the second watchman.

"Doesn't make sense," Torndale mumbled. "Keep a very close eye on them."

When the sunset bell rang, Torndale took the watch over on the east side, just beyond the shuttlecraft landing spot. Naia joined him. They did not talk much, mostly just sat at the watch spot together. Torndale swept the skies with his portable telescope, while she occasionally looked down at the steep slope of their mountain to see if there was any activity on the ground, deep below them.

They shared some water and some berries they had picked in the forest north of the landing site. Some of the berries were sweet, but most of them had a bitter aftertaste to them.

"The bitter ones are the best," Torndale noted. "Very nutritious."

"Of course," Naia sighed. "What's good for you never comes easy."

"I love your humor," he smiled.

"Thanks."

A rock hound howled on a nearby mountain. It seemed to come from south of them.

"I'm glad we don't have them here on our top" said Naia.

"They are shy. They stay away from us. I guess we smell bad to them."

"Especially after this much time with very little hygiene."

Another rock hound joined the first.

"That's unusual," Armo Torndale noted. "Those are not mate calls. Sound more like territorial calls. I wonder if the soldiers moved over to that mountain."

"So they can keep an eye on us," Naia suggested.

"Exactly. To help the helicopters."

He got up and moved closer to the southern edge of their mountain top. Dense vegetation prevented him from reaching the edge, but he found a fallen tree to stand on and a narrow angle between the trees that gave him a telescope view of the next mountain top.

But it was too dark.

He got back to Naia just when a watchman emerged from the woods and crossed the landing site.

"The soldiers are up on the southern mountain top," he reported.

"You were right," said Naia. "That's why the rock hounds were howling."

"The helicopters aren't far away, then, are they?" asked the watchman.

"Right," Torndale noted. "A night assault. Makes sense. The only question is which way they will be coming."

It was not until two bells after sunset that they could see the helicopters. They were coming from two sides, one from the southeast, one from the west. The military veteran studied them carefully in a night vision telescope.

"Troop carriers used by special warfare units," he said. "They are purpose built to drop off a unit and fly off, and have it done in very short time. They will need a big clearing. One will probably land over at the shuttlecraft spot, and the other will drop off its unit at our former camp site."

"Don't they know we will be firing upon them?" asked another watchman.

"They are equipped with machine guns. They will make sure we aren't interfering with them."

"Our only choice, then, is to withdraw into the woods and try to hold out to the morning," said Naia.

"There is one thing we can do," Torndale suggested. "How long before they get here?"

"Halfway to next bell," the military veteran estimated.

"Then we have no time to lose."

Torndale brought six of them with him up to the camp site.

"What are we going to do here?" asked the veteran.

"They can't land if there is no clearing," Torndale explained, picked up an axe and tossed another one to the biggest guy in the group. "Find a medium-sized tree."

The veteran smiled.

"I see what you are getting at," he said.

They picked a few younger trees, with trunks that were still soft enough to allow for a quick chop-down. With Herculean efforts they managed to cut down four of them and make them fall in a criss-cross pattern across the camp site. Two of them were so tall that they fell into the trees on the opposite side, forming angled barriers to any helicopter trying to land.

Moments later, the first helicopter swept in. It flew above the tree line, hovered for a moment right above the clearing and angled itself as if it was going to dive, nose first. Then it leveled out again, circled for a moment.

And opened fire.

It was not a long series of shots, only five or six of them, but the gun was of a caliber large enough to penetrate structures. The bullets slammed into the ground and into the fallen trees. The helicopter turned and flew over to the slope on the east side of the mountain, where it dropped off a group of six soldiers, just below where the other group had been camping out.

"We fended them off," Naia cheered. "Good job, everyone."

"We won the first round," Torndale chuckled.

His joy was short lived. Another series of shots rang out from down east. They rapidly moved in the direction of the landing site. It was a short run, but it felt like an eternity as they heard more shots from the other helicopter.

The watchmen at the landing site had hunkered down a safe distance from the clearing. They hid among the trees, with guns aimed at the clearing where the landing site was, but no helicopter had landed. Not yet.

"It's circling above us," said one watchman. "Probably trying to see how many of us . . . "

He was interrupted by more gunfire from the helicopter. The bullets ripped through the branches at the top of the trees.

"They don't seem to be aiming directly for us," Torndale noted.

"Scare tactics," the veteran suggested. "They can't fire at us directly because of the trees, so they want to intimidate us so they can unload their unit."

Moments later the helicopter sat down and dropped off its commando unit.

"Well," Torndale said in a fateful voice. "This is it. Under the skies of freedom . . . "

❁ ❁ ❁

ARMO TORNDALE HAD MADE NAIA the biggest cup of pine smoked tea he could find in his kitchen cabinets. She was sitting on his couch, legs pulled up to her chest, a thick blanket wrapped around her. She slowly sipped the tea, as if to savor every mouthful.

"This is very good," she said. "Where did you get it?"

"It's from a small tea grower up by Three Lakes."

"Can you grow tea up there?"

"They have a greenhouse, so they don't grow a whole lot. But they don't sell it through the stores. You have to know the owner, or someone who does."

The storm was gaining force. They could hear it against the windows. A forceful wind made its way through one of the ventilation openings in Torndale's apartment.

"Sounds like a big one," said Naia.

"It's that time of the year. But this one is not from the ocean. It's coming from the mountains."

He was right. The wind was sweeping down from the Coldrange mountains. It blew life into the vast forest outside the city, forcing the trees to dance with the animals that called the forest home.

The wind pushed on, reaching the outskirts of the city where homes were small and streets were wide. As it worked its way in through the city, the wind caught power lines in its grip, rattled them and played with them, as if deciding on the move if it should rip them down or not. It pulled trash out of trash cans, forcing the discarded remains of daily life into a whirlwind game of catch-me, then dropped the garbage in the street and moved on.

Not many people were out this late. The standing curfew order went into effect at two bells from midnight, and only those who had a permit to be out after that time would be out in the streets. But the wind did not need a permit to sweep through the city. It rattled the trees in the park, drummed against windows and howled around corners.

"Thank you for picking me up," Naia said.

Torndale was sitting in one of the armchairs. He was slouching, sipping his own small cup of tea.

"You needed some company," he noted.

She nodded, smiled briefly, then turned serious.

"It was a rough day," she admitted.

"You didn't tell me much on the drive over here."

"I didn't want to talk about it."

"Sometimes, talking about it helps."

She nodded.

"You're right," she said and put down the tea glass.

She told him about the conversation with Eda Strebber, and about Olgar's and her brief relationship. She hinted at how she felt betrayed by him, but also guilty over how she had put the entire blame for the affair on Olgar when she talked to Eda Strebber. Torndale reassured her that she had no reason to feel guilty, that it was a natural reaction in a situation like hers, but that Olgar was the one who should have known better. Naia nodded, cried a little bit, wiped her tears and giggled at herself.

"I'm such a wreck," she said. "I shouldn't even be at the academy."

"Why not?"

"They keep telling us we have to be strong, to not be emotional. We do those drills . . . didn't you do them when you were at the academy?"

"You mean the drills to teach you how to bury your emotions?"

"Yes."

"No. We never did those. I joined State Security way back. During the federal republic."

"What was it like back then?"

The academy?"

"No, the country."

"Oh . . . well, to tell you the truth . . . it wasn't bad at all. Sure, it had its flaws, but . . . "

He dropped the rest of the sentence and smiled at Naia.

"You know, just having this conversation is enough to get us both booted out of State Security."

"But why?" Naia wanted to know. "Why can't you talk about the . . . the federal republic and . . . why does it always have to be so one-sided?"

Torndale looked down at his tea glass and nodded.

"Yes," he said. "There is no room for nuances."

He pondered for a moment whether or not he should tell her about the conversation with Commander Kolmov and Doctor Smersch, about their suspicions that Naia was a seditionist. It would be a serious breach of protocol, far worse than any conversation they would have about generic facts from the federal republic.

He decided to take a less obvious route.

"There are some controversies within State Security that you probably haven't really seen yet," he said. "It's an ideological struggle between those who want us to be tougher, and those who believe that if you tighten our enforcement further, we will eventually cause a lot of resentment among people in general."

"But we are only going after seditionists. Why would people object to that?"

"The government . . . that is, Grand Chancellor Sorto, keeps expanding the definition of sedition. More and more of normal conversations that people have become thought crimes. We are at a point now where a lot of people object to the very existence of a sedition law. Today, the mere fact that you disagree with government is an act of sedition. Generally, the public still believes that you should be allowed to express your opinion without being called a criminal by government, and regardless of what the law says, you just cannot incarcerate half the population."

Naia made big eyes.

"That many are seditionists?" she asked.

"By the strict, legal definition that we apply today, I would say probably more than that."

"I honestly had no idea."

"They don't tell you this at work," Torndale said. "But we have internal data that show this. We have developed methods for keeping track of the general sentiment among people."

He chuckled.

"It's ironic, really. We have made it illegal to disagree with government. Our laws declare that disagreement is the same as a desire to overthrow government. Yet we are obsessed with finding out what people really think. If we hadn't made it illegal to disagree with government . . . if we allowed freedom of speech . . . we could easily keep track of public opinion. Now we have to work with costly, convoluted and inefficient methods instead."

He shook his head, finished his tea and put the glass on the floor next to his armchair.

"But doesn't this mean that our government is unpopular?" Naia asked. "Why is that?"

"Do you remember when Sorto was first elected president?"

"Not really."

"He was young, charismatic and looked good on television. He was eloquent, and he carefully crafted his message to young people. He talked about ushering in a new era where we would all care for each other and where you would be free to do whatever you wanted. You would not have to worry about housing, feeding and clothing yourself. All that would be provided for you."

"Isn't that what the national value foundation says?"

"Yes, it is. Sorto proposed that already when he was running for president the first time. And he became very popular for it. He won the votes of the young almost unanimously. But there were many others who voted for him. I remember my aunt, a wealthy woman. She said that it was a shame that so much wealth was concentrated into the hands of so few. It was about time that we spread the wealth around, she said. And she voted for Sorto. He raised taxes, quite a bit, too, especially on people as wealthy as her."

"Was she happy about it?"

"No," Torndale chuckled. "She said she'd rather decide herself who to give money to, and for what purpose. My brother pointed out to her that she could have voted for Cormer, the guy Sorto defeated, and . . . well . . . she did not talk to him for a while after that."

Naia thought for a moment. She looked out the window at the raging storm.

"So Sorto promised that everyone would have everything they needed," she said, "and people voted for him. We get everything we need now. But it comes in rations. Food, clothes, housing, transit coupons . . . And they just seem to be getting smaller. When you run out of your rations, you can't get more until the next month's coupons arrive."

She turned to Torndale.

"Did people ever feel they didn't have enough under the federal republic?"

"Oh yes. Most people, in fact. But it was a different kind of want, if you will. I suppose you can think of it as wants, not needs. Almost everyone had food, shelter, clothes, transportation . . . when they said they didn't have enough, it was because they wanted more and better. They worked hard to make enough to move to a bigger house, or a better house, or buy a better automobile, or . . . "

"People bought automobiles? What do you mean?"

"If you had the money, you could walk into a dealership and buy an auto of your own."

"People did that?"

"Almost everyone had an automobile. Some families had more than one."

"So that meant other families couldn't buy one because some families had two."

"No, that's not how it worked at all. If more people bought more automobiles, the auto manufacturers just produced more of them."

"I'm confused . . . " Naia admitted. "I guess I haven't studied economic theory . . . "

"What's confusing you?"

"Who made the decisions to produce more automobiles?"

"The manufacturers. The businesses made those decisions."

"On their own? Weren't they issued government quotas?"

"No. They responded to the ups and downs in demand for whatever they produced."

"Was it the same with other things . . . clothes, or television sets . . . ?"

"Everything. Homes or haircuts, it worked the same way."

Naia took a deep breath.

"This is overwhelming for me," she said. "Do you think life was better under the federal republic?"

Torndale looked at her. For a split second, he remembered Eda Strebber's and Doctor Smersch's suspicions that Naia actually was a seditionist. Then he swung to the other end of the spectrum and spent a moment pondering the possibility that she had become Eda Strebber's agent. She could be trying to compromise him . . . to give Doctor Smersch the upper hand against him . . . to let Vigo Smersch, the weasel, get compromising information on Armo Torndale so Armo Torndale could no longer hold Smersch's own missteps over his head . . .

No. It did not make sense. Naia's eyes were as honest as any pair of eyes he had ever seen. Her voice was relaxed, sincere. Her entire body language signaled openness, comfort and trust. All his training in interrogation tactics told him that she was what she came across as: an honest young woman asking questions because she was curious.

"For me personally?" he said. "A bit, but not too much. Well, I haven't seen my retirement yet . . . But I get generous rations of practically everything. It comes with the job."

"What about people in general? You mentioned those internal opinion polls . . . "

"Yes. They show that most people are unhappy. Very unhappy, in fact, and not only with our sedition laws. Most people feel that life is . . . how do they put it . . . static. There is no forward progress. It doesn't matter what you do, how hard you work, or if you work at all, you still can't improve your life. If anything, as you mentioned, the rations are getting smaller. And I get it. I can see why people don't work as hard anymore, because it doesn't do much for them anyway. And as you saw when we visited Ms. Veesaus's house, there are people who don't work at all. They just cash in their rations. That share of the population is growing."

"So why are our rations getting smaller?"

"There's your answer," Torndale explained. "More and more people choose not to work, or don't put in much effort at work. They are entitled to their rations anyway. But they can't get all their rations because producers can't put out everything that people need. In the latest study we did . . . and this is highly confidential . . . "

"I understand."

"Nobody can know I told you this . . . "

"Of course. I appreciate you sharing this with me."

"In the latest study we did, the biggest complaints were about health care. People see longer and longer waiting lists for all sorts of medical issues, but especially when they need surgery or other complicated treatment. We see the same complaints when it comes to food, clothes, even transit services in some cities."

"Is that because more people choose not to work?"

"Yes, it's a good part of it. And I understand why. Take a physician, for example, a surgeon who is specialized in something. He or she has been training for a long time. You are responsible for other people's lives. One mistake and someone dies. If a factory worker makes a mistake, let's say doesn't mount the screen properly on a television set, well . . . all that happens is that there is a deficient television set somewhere. But the surgeon and the factory worker get the same rations of everything. At some point, it makes sense that you can't motivate that many people to become surgeons."

Naia looked down at her hands. She nodded quietly for herself. Torndale waited.

"So this whole value foundation," she said slowly, "is it just a . . . what do you call it . . . a losing proposition?"

Torndale glanced at the window. The storm was subsiding, but it was still sending waves of rain up against the glass.

"That's what it looks like," he said eventually.

He looked her in the eyes:

"Which . . . " he said slowly, "raises the question . . . what are we doing working for State Security in the first place?"

IT TURNED OUT THAT Armo Torndale was wrong. It did not happen very often—or so he thought himself—but he was wrong about the commando unit that disembarked from the helicopter on the landing site. Instead of rapidly launching an attack on them into the woods, it withdrew to a smaller, wooded area on the far side of the landing site. The helicopter remained on the ground, with its guns pointed right at Torndale and his group.

The soldiers moved rapidly, cautiously watching the side of the landing site where Armo Torndale and the watchmen lay hidden in the vegetation. As soon as they had disappeared in among the trees, the helicopter took off and went back the same way it came.

"What are they doing?" asked one of the watchmen.

"They were planning a two-front attack," the veteran explained. "Now they have to wait and see if the other unit can get up here."

He was right. Shortly after the second unit had moved into the wooded area beyond the landing site, the first unit started climbing up on the west side of the mountain. They advanced rapidly.

"They are going to attack us," whispered one of the watchmen at the trap they had set just a little bit higher up the steep slope.

He was the younger of the two.

"Get ready," the older watchman whispered.

"What if it doesn't work?"

"It will."

"When do we . . . "

"My count."

The slope between the soldiers and the watchmen was steep, but anyone who was physically very fit could climb it outside of the path. There were no tall trees there—the trees began forming again right where the watchmen waited. The slope down to where the soldiers were, was covered with tall shrubbery, small mountain trees that never grew past a man's shoulders, small rocks and lots of poisonous and slippery little mushrooms. It was a stretch of terrain that required attention, caution and agility.

The soldiers moved upward with confidence, and in almost complete silence. They passed the small flat part where the other commando unit had camped out. They stopped for a moment to assess the damage to the terrain done by the shuttlecraft.

"Now?" whispered the younger watchmen.

"Wait until they reach the designated point," whispered the older.

They waited. The soldiers moved up on a broad front. The side of the mountain where they could climb was narrow enough that the six soldiers could almost hold hands as they climbed. It was difficult to get past the damaged part, but with the patience and determination of elite warriors they gradually worked their way past it.

The two watchmen at the trap waited silently. They watched the soldiers as best they could through their hand telescopes.

The older watchman held up his hand. He held up all his five fingers. He folded them slowly, one by one.

Five . . . Four . . . Three . . .

The commando leader was climbing the path. He stopped, hunkered down and pointed his weapon up hill. The others continued to climb.

Two . . .

The leader made a hand signal. The others stopped.

158

The watchmen waited.

A forest cat jumped up from its hiding place just a few steps from the unit leader. It dashed upward, jumped up on a piece of rock and disappeared on its far side.

The leader made another hand signal. They all started climbing again. One . . .

They reached the point.

"Now," whispered the older watchman.

The second he whispered, all the soldiers stopped. Their attention was immediately focused on the spot from where the whisper came.

They had no time to wonder who was whispering. A tidal wave of boulders, rocks and tree trunks came tumbling down the hill. They made a formidable noise, and they tore down all the vegetation in their way. It took only a couple of seconds for the first pieces of rock and wood to come flying down on the soldiers. They all threw themselves to the ground and tried to take cover as best they could.

The watchmen unleashed a second wave with larger rocks and tree branches that had been cut into rock-size pieces and tied to the larger boulders. They came loose as the rocks were tumbling down, multiplying the number of projectiles that flew down the steep hill. Two big tree trunks got hooked together and formed a massive object with formidable force. It hit three of the soldiers and forced them to fall uncontrollably down the mountainside. A large boulder rolled down the path, giving the unit leader no other option but to throw himself toward the edge of the cliff. He slipped on a cluster of mushrooms, lost his footing and fell over the edge.

A fifth soldier tried to hide behind some bushes but was hit over the head by a heavy tree branch. He passed out in an unnatural position.

Only one soldier survived. When the material from the trap had passed and he realized that his group had almost been wiped out, he stood up and fired his weapon in the direction of where he had heard the whisper. He fired in a targeted way, a few rounds at a time, trying to hit as many spots as he could.

When he ceased fire, he hunkered down again, listened and tried to determine if he had hit anything. He thought he heard the distant sound of someone running away from him, breathing heavily, but it was difficult to tell.

He moved closer to where his buddies should be. He found only the one who had passed out.

No life signs. And no signs of the other four.

He kneeled, touched his buddy's face, thanked him for his comradeship, bid him farewell and promised to come back and bring him home. He took his rifle and all the supplies he could carry, then slowly moved on upward.

The perpetrators up on the mountain were enemies of the state. They were terrorists who had gathered there to plot the assassination of Grand Chancellor Sorto. It was his job to kill them.

And kill them he would.

❀ ❀ ❀

THE DAY AFTER NAIA FERNEK had slept on Armo Torndale's couch, Grand Chancellor Sorto was giving a major speech in the national parliament. The assembly hall was filled to the brim. Every member of the parliament wanted to be there, not just the 72 percent of them that represented the People and Progress party.

All senior parliamentary staffers were there, sitting in a special section on the balcony. Invited guests had their privileged seating assignments: provincial party leaders, members of the extended Sorto family and the nearest family members of his three most prominent cabinet members. They were served drinks and hors d'oeuvres and even given foot massage by specially hired servants.

The seven members of the nation's highest court were seated in a side section down on the parliament floor. Opposite them, on the other side of the chamber, was a section for the top military brass and a dozen officials from State Security. There was the high commissioner who was the chief of the agency and his four deputy commissioners. There were also the commanding officers of the four divisions within the agency: investigations, operations, instruction and administration.

Four high-ranking officers had also been invited, including Storm Commander Kolmov. However, he had fallen ill the night before, been taken to the hospital and was undergoing surgery. The director of investigations had to quickly fill his seat.

"This is Commander Torndale."

"Please stand by for a call from Director Hemmig."

"Armo?"

"Director! What can I do for you?"

"Get over to the national parliament on the double. Kolmov is sick and we need to fill his spot for the Grand Chancellor's speech."

"Yes, sir, I will be honored to attend."

That was a big lie, of course. Armo Torndale wanted no part of Sorto's annual speech to the parliament. Even if he had liked the Grand Chancellor—and God knew he didn't—it would have been a complete waste of time. Sorto would not speak about anything of any consequence to anyone. He would share platitudes and party talking points. Sometimes he dropped hints of news, such as last year when he suggested that 'we must all work harder for our people's democratic union to make sure everyone is fed, clothed and housed properly'. That was the convoluted message that people's rations of everything essential were going to be tightened.

Which they were.

But Armo Torndale could not refuse the invite. He knew the pecking order and how hard some people worked to get on that invite list. He knew that by being invited, he would step on a few toes around the agency—even if he did not mean to.

One of those toes belonged to Doctor Smersch. Torndale ran into him on his way out the door.

"You're in a hurry today," Doctor Smersch noted.

Torndale smiled and could not resist the opportunity:

"I'm attending the Grand Chancellor's annual speech."

Doctor Smersch tried not to frown, but it did not work very well.

"How did you get on the list?" he whispered.

"Hard work, Vigo," Torndale smiled, patted him on the upper arm and dashed off to his car.

He used emergency lights and sirens to get through traffic. It wasn't really necessary: the streets were almost never congested these days. It was not like under the federal republic, when the city had been bustling with automobiles, taxi cabs, delivery trucks, and limousines and buses hired by private companies to get employees to work.

Back then, the streets could often get very crowded, especially during rush hour. Nowadays, those who had been able to obtain a permit to have a vehicle were careful with where they drove, when and for what reason.

After having rushed past other motorists at high speed and driven through several traffic lights, sirens blaring, Torndale reached the national parliament just in time to park, clear security, dash through the corridors and take his seat in the assembly hall. Director Hemmig turned, looked at him and nodded approvingly.

The ceremony to introduce the Grand Chancellor got more complicated with each year. This year it consisted of six steps. First, the speaker of the national assembly explained what a privilege it was for them all to be there. Then the ceremonial master of the national assembly called up a choir of school children who sang a long song of praise to the people's democratic union. After them, it was time for each of the leaders of the opposition parties to give brief speeches where they praised the Grand Chancellor and promised with all their hearts that they were his most loyal and approving opposition. After them, the chairman of the nation's highest court gave an account of all the cases her court had reviewed, and all the opinions they have issued, that followed the lead of the Grand Chancellor.

After the chair of the highest court had spoken, the First Marshall of the military pledged the unwavering loyalty of the armed forces to the Grand Chancellor "and the value foundation upon which he has built our people's democratic union".

In the past, the preamble to the Grand Chancellor had ended there, but this year there was one last item on the agenda: the People's Anthem.

The ceremonial master of the national assembly went up to the speaker's podium and asked everyone to stand up for the anthem.

"After the anthem, remain standing" he said plainly.

The People's Anthem went on for five minutes. Armo Torndale had not yet learned the words perfectly, and he noted that almost nobody around him sang with any enthusiasm. No harm done, then, stumbling with the lyrics. But he made a mental note of studying up on the lyrics in case he was invited next year; the singing of the anthem was an opportunity for everyone to show their loyalty, and the Grand Chancellor's staff took careful note of how people performed during such expressions of loyalty. Anyone caught not singing could expect a phone call from someone representing government.

Or maybe even a knock on the door from State Security.

Torndale wondered for a second if it would be considered an act of sedition not to sing the People's Anthem. But before he could elaborate on that thought, the anthem was over and the ceremonial master signed to them all to stand in quiet.

Nothing happened for several minutes. Torndale was glad he had taken good care of himself; a man of his age in poorer condition may not have been able to stand for this long.

His thoughts went out to Commander Kolmov. He was going to stop by the hospital after this was all over.

Eventually, the main doors to the assembly opened. Eight members of the Grand Chancellor's own guard entered, in full uniform and fully armed. They marched perfectly, stopped in pairs with a few feet in between, and stepped to the side of the walkway from the entrance to the speaker's podium. They turned and faced each other.

Two more guards marched in: the commander and deputy commander of the chancellor's guard. They marched all the way up to the podium, stopped in front of it and turned around.

One more person entered the assembly. It was the sergeant at arms of the national assembly. He walked up to the podium, stopped in front of the two guard commanders and turned around. In a loud, clear and trembling voice he declared:

"Members of the People's National Assembly! It is an outstanding honor to introduce to you: the leader of the People's Democratic Union of Ripoma! Grand Chancellor Magnor Sorto!"

Everyone applauded. The chancellor guardsmen saluted. The sergeant at arms stepped aside so everyone would see that the guard commanders also saluted.

The applauds intensified and were accompanied by cheers when the Grand Chancellor entered the assembly. He was a relatively tall man with grey hair. He wore a uniform with a long range of medals and markings representing distinctive service. Torndale wondered when the Grand Chancellor had been able to squeeze in such brave, frontline military assignments into his busy chancellor's schedule.

On the shoulders the Grand Chancellor had two swords, made of pure gold. Torndale had read somewhere that the sword now symbolized the highest rank a military officer could achieve.

He had also heard somewhere that the Grand Chancellor had put on quite a bit of weight recently. It turned out that those rumors were correct. Torndale was disturbed by how big of a waistband the Grand Chancellor had acquired—whenever he was shown on television, he always looked fit. But then again, they never showed his full figure.

The Grand Chancellor's guard had its own intelligence unit, which was always on the lookout for threats against his life. They also kept a close eye on how people reacted to the Grand Chancellor, especially in formal settings like this one. Torndale knew very well how it worked: they looked for even the slightest signs of disloyalty. He had gotten a few reports from the guard's intelligence unit on suspicious behavior. Sometimes it was obvious, as when a student held up a sign saying "Sorto Sucks" when the Grand Chancellor visited his university. That student had been arrested, charged with sedition, found guilty, and disappeared into some SICR camp.

Sometimes, though, the grounds for the guard intelligence's reporting were highly questionable. A few moons back, Torndale had outright rejected a report on an individual who had simply walked out of a room where the Grand Chancellor was going to speak, just before he took the stage. The guard intelligence agent who reported that woman claimed that "leaving the room instead of hearing the Grand Chancellor is an act meant to incite active opposition". In other words: sedition.

Torndale had written back and explained that "if this is sedition, going to the hygiene area will be classified as sedition". He had not heard back.

Grand Chancellor Sorto stopped in front of the podium, turned and waived. Applauds and appreciating cheers almost lifted the ceiling. He stood tall, nodded and smiled for a couple of minutes, before going around the podium and taking position behind the microphones.

While the applauds continued with unrelenting intensity, the eight guards that had lined the walkway marched up and formed a line in front of the podium, facing the assembly members. Four on each side of the Grand Chancellor and hands on their rifles, they monitored the assembly with menacing looks on their faces.

There was no mistaking their purpose.

The Grand Chancellor assumed a statesman-like posture. As he looked out over the room, his smile gave way to a serious face.

He allowed the applauds to continue for yet another minute. When he finally raised his hands and signaled to them to stop applauding and to sit down, Torndale was actually grateful. Applauding was getting tedious.

As they sat down, Grand Chancellor Sorto looked down at the podium.

"He does not have a written speech," someone whispered behind Torndale.

"There is a computer screen in the podium," someone else whispered.

Torndale did not know that, but he also did not care too much. He would rather be almost anywhere else than where he was, with or without a computer screen in the speaker's podium.

Grand Chancellor Sorto looked up. He took a deep breath and was just about to speak when an assemblyman stood up. It was a young woman from a remote province.

She knew she only had a few seconds. And she used them well.

❄ ❄ ❄

THE UNLEASHING OF THE TRAP had not only killed five of the six soldiers on the west side of the mountain, but it had also sent a message to the commando unit on the far side of the landing site. They had been told that they were sent out to eliminate a group of violent seditionists, but they had not been told that those seditionists were that sophisticated. The unit on the other mountain had tried to warn their commanders that the terrorists were smarter than they had been told, and that they had support from an alien spaceship. But none of that had apparently affected their planning of the attack on those terrorists.

When the unit on the west side had almost been wiped out, the unit on the other side of the landing site decided to wait. They could not approach the wooded area where the terrorists were located without crossing the open field. They needed a two-front attack, and they could do it once the third group, on the southern mountain, had moved to reinforce the lone surviving soldier on the west side. But it would be daylight before they got there.

Torndale took no chances. They were sixteen refugees remaining, and every single one of them was on guard or camp watch all night.

Nothing happened, except that one of the watchmen thought he saw the commando unit on the southern mountain start moving.

"It's hard to tell given the darkness," he said.

"It would make sense, though," the military veteran said. "From what we could tell, the trap on the west side did what it was supposed to do."

"Any survivors there?" Torndale asked.

"None that we could see, but I left two men there with our best rifles, just in case."

They laid still, waiting. The daybreak bell would soon ring, and with it the Danori shuttlecraft would return. Twelve of them would leave.

And four would remain for another day.

It was a losing proposition. The soldiers would never dare to attack so long as the Danori ship was present, but they would also see twelve men leave. They would know that only a few remained.

And they would not wait for the shuttlecraft to come back for one last evacuation.

He looked over to his right side. Naia was sitting behind a tree, leaning against it, doing maintenance on a handgun. He smiled: only a little while ago, this young woman had been an academically minded student, living in a student dorm at the State Security academy, studying history, political theory, law . . . And here she was, a full-fledged freedom fighter. Ready to fight for the freedom of others.

As if she heard his thoughts, she turned and looked at him. She smiled.

"How are you doing?" she asked.

"Good. It's almost daybreak."

She nodded, smiled even more. And then lost her smile.

He knew what she was thinking. They were staying behind, and she knew the odds.

Naia put the gun back together and crept over toward Torndale. She did not say anything, just laid down next to him. She looked him straight in the eyes.

"They will never take me alive," she whispered. "I'd rather die on my feet . . . "

" . . . than live on my knees," Torndale nodded. "Did I ever tell you what happened to that young woman in the parliament?"

"The one who stood up when Sorto was going to speak?"

"Yes."

"What happened to her?"

Armo Torndale was just going to tell her when they heard a familiar, humming sound. The shuttlecraft came in over the treetops, made a turn around the wooded area on the far side of the landing site and hovered for a moment. It was almost as if the pilot considered firing upon the soldiers.

When it set down, Torndale was the first out of the woods to greet them. The Danori woman was back again. She did not look very happy.

"I see the military has brought in reinforcements," she said. "Strebber told me of your predicament. I regret that I have no weapons to offer you. Our laws and regulations are quite clear."

"I understand," Torndale nodded. "We will manage."

The woman looked like she was actually worried about him.

"There will only be four of you left," she said. "From what we can tell, these are well trained military personnel."

"We call them commandos. They are better than regular infantry soldiers. Trained in special warfare tactics. Better equipped, and so on."

While the twelve passengers for this evacuation flight boarded, the Danori woman took Torndale to the side.

"Strebber is doing a fine job organizing your group on the ship," she explained. "They have already set up a council, they have begun formulating a legal framework for their colony and they have brought me and one other person in for consultations to facilitate the process."

"I am glad to hear that," Torndale replied and tried to sound happy.

"You have done a very good job, Armo. Very good. I have been to two other worlds, on a total of four missions to evacuate freedom refugees, and your group is the best organized I have seen."

"Thank you," Torndale said and nodded, but had a hard times showing enthusiasm.

He knew the odds were he would not make it off this mountain.

The Danori woman came closer. She put her hands on his shoulders. He was startled by it at first, but when he looked into her big, blue eyes he saw nothing but warmth, compassion, respect and—he almost could not believe it—a touch of love.

"We will be back same time tomorrow," she promised. "But with the odds you face, I want you to know how much I respect and appreciate your work."

Torndale felt tears in his eyes.

"Thank you," he whispered. "That means a lot to me."

She smiled and brought him back to the shuttlecraft. They stopped at the open door. She put one foot on the stairs and grabbed the railing.

"It's a big galaxy," she said. "I want to show it to you some day."

Naia came up to Torndale just in time to see the Danori woman board the shuttlecraft. The woman exchanged a greeting with Naia just as the hatch closed.

"Why can't they break their rules and wipe out those soldiers?" Naia asked.

"Because if they do that, their government will never allow them to resettle refugees ever again."

"No one would know, would they?"

"Maybe. But in a free society, you self enforce laws, regardless of what you might get away with."

He paused.

"It's the difference between the rule of law and the rule of men," he added.

The shuttlecraft lifted off, hovered for a moment, then slowly made another loop around the wooded area where the soldiers were hiding. Torndale and Naia walked back their way.

"Can you fight for freedom with the rule of law?" Naia asked.

"What do you mean?"

"When tyrants break the rules all the time, how can you win against them if you never break the rules?"

The shuttlecraft climbed a little bit and made a loop over to the south side of the mountain.

"We broke the rules to get here," Armo Torndale pointed out.

"Is it enough?"

The shuttlecraft climbed a little bit more, returned to the small, wooded area by the landing site and stopped for a moment.

"What are they doing?" Naia asked.

"Trying to give us a little bit more time," Torndale guessed. "I don't know if it is enough. But it's the best chance we'll get. And we have evacuated sixty freedom refugees who can build a new life in liberty."

They walked deeper into the forest, back toward the old camp site.

"Maybe we'll make it," Naia said.

"Maybe," Torndale agreed.

"What happened to that woman?"

"The one from Sorto's speech in the national assembly?"

"Yes."

❋ ❋ ❋

Armo Torndale knew the procedure very well. He had been in Room 703 many times. It was the place where all sensitive investigations by State Security began. It had no windows, it could seat forty people and it was sound proof, bullet proof and—Torndale liked to point out—dumb proof. You needed special clearance to participate in meetings in that room.

The High Commissioner of State Security was sitting at the short end of the table. To his right he had the commanding officer of the Grand

Chancellor's guard. To his left was Director Hemmig, head of the investigative division of State Security.

There were ten other people in the room, four from the guard and six from State Security.

Torndale had been asked to sit right next to Director Hemmig.

The atmosphere in the room was tense. The High Commissioner looked at the men and women present, rolled a pencil back and forth between his index finger and his thumb and seemed to weigh his words carefully before he spoke.

He put the pencil down, took a deep breath and leaned forward on his elbows.

"I cannot emphasize enough," he said slowly, "how exceptionally important it is that we get to the bottom of this case."

He looked down at some notes in front of him.

"This must never happen again," he continued. "Never."

He turned to the guard commander.

"It goes without saying," the guard commander agreed. "It is intolerable. We protected the Grand Chancellor today, and we will do it again, wherever it is necessary. But the Grand Chancellor has made clear that it is unacceptable that a case of sedition like this one, can slip through the cracks and make it all the way into the national assembly."

The State Security Commissioner nodded emphatically.

"Absolutely intolerable," he said firmly. "This must never happen again. Therefore, we have put together a joint task force to get to the bottom of this. We are going to pursue every lead, dig up every piece of information we need, in order to make sure that our beloved Grand Chancellor is never exposed to this type of sedition . . . this . . . this terrorism . . . ever again."

He was visibly upset. The guard commander looked at the Commissioner. He was clearly satisfied with the Commissioner's reaction.

"Thank you for your support in protecting Grand Chancellor Sorto," the guard commander said. "I look forward to working with you on this."

"As do I," the Commissioner confirmed.

He turned to Director Hemmig.

"This falls on your shoulders," the Commissioner said.

"Yes, sir."

"You need to put your very best people on it."

"Absolutely, sir. Group Commander Torndale here is already assigned to the case."

The Commissioner looked at Torndale as if he was examining him.

"Yes," he said. "I know you. You are an experienced investigator."

"Thank you, sir," Torndale said.

"You were there, at the assembly, when this happened."

"Yes, sir. I was asked to give the group a recap of the events there."

"Good. But before you give us your presentation, let me emphasize again that this is a joint investigation between State Security and the Guard of the Grand Chancellor. Everything pertaining to this case will be shared between State Security and the GGC. When we get to arresting people, we will do so with joint task forces. Custody of arrestees will be joint, as will interrogations and prosecutions."

Armo Torndale wanted to ask how that was going to work in practice, but the atmosphere in the room was such that any questions of that nature would be ripped to shreds. As would probably whoever asked them.

"Commander Torndale," the Commissioner continued. "You will be working with senior officer Ghehor from the guard."

A young man, probably half Torndale's age, nodded and looked confidently at him.

"I suggest the two of you get to know one another after this meeting," the Commissioner advised. "Now, Commander Torndale, give us your recap of what happened at the national assembly."

He tried to keep his recap free of emotions. It was not entirely easy for him, given his own growing doubts about his job, his employer, his government . . . but he summoned his professionalism and did his job.

The assembly member, Epai Sekkes, was a young woman from the Kaukano province, far away on the western side of the country. She was tall, slender, with long, dark hair and clothes in matching colors. She was a graduate of a local college that was known for still harboring independent-minded faculty and had been elected to the national assembly for one of the remaining opposition parties.

Like every other assembly member, she had signed a pledge of allegiance to the Grand Chancellor—nobody could be seated in the assembly unless they first signed the pledge—but apparently it had not deterred her from doing what she did as the Grand Chancellor was about to speak.

She stood up, raised her arms up in the air to show that she was unarmed, and shouted:

"Dissent is not a crime! Free the spoken word! Dissent is not a . . . "

Two bullets ripped through her body. The nearest officer of the GGC had shot her in the abdomen and the shoulder. While she collapsed to the floor, other guard officers whisked the Grand Chancellor out of the chamber. Orders were shouted, people were screaming, weapons were drawn and medics were summoned.

"We were seated near her," Torndale explained. "I rushed in to secure her, as did several others. She was conscious the whole time, but she did not say anything more, at least not as far as I could hear. She was taken to the Westview Medical Center, where she remains and should be undergoing surgery as we speak. She is in our custody and we will . . . "

"No," the guard commander interrupted him. "She is in our custody."

Torndale was a bit surprised to hear that.

"I'm sorry, commander," he said. "I was under the impression that we had her booked on sedition charges."

"Yes," the guard commander agreed.

"Investigations of sedition fall under our jurisdiction," Torndale explained, looking to the State Security Commissioner for support.

"Yes, Commander Torndale, you are correct," the Commissioner replied. "But this is more serious. This was an attempt on the Grand Chancellor's life."

Torndale frowned.

"Please excuse my confusion, Commissioner," he said. "But . . . I thought she was unarmed."

"She was challenging the Grand Chancellor in person," the guard commander replied. "She has to face the stiffest charges possible."

"I agree," said the Commissioner.

At that point, it would be almost career suicide for Torndale to argue the facts.

"Yes, sir," he said. "I understand, sir. I will proceed with the investigation along your guidelines. My next step . . . our next step . . . I suggest, would be to interrogate her."

"Officer Ghehor will head the interrogation," said the guard commander and looked at his officer, sitting further down the table.

"Yes, sir," officer Ghehor replied. "Commander Torndale, you are welcome to attend the interrogation."

When the meeting in Room 703 was over, Torndale grabbed his lunch sandwich and went to find Director Hemmig. He was in his office.

"May I join you, sir?"

"Sure," said Director Hemmig. "Close the door."

That was exactly what Torndale had hoped to hear.

"Have a seat," said the director while taking a bite out of his own lunch sandwich. "I figured you'd come over here. It's about Assemblywoman Sekkes, right?"

"Yes, sir."

"I talked to the Commissioner about it. He is as frustrated as I am. And you are. We all wanted this to be our matter, but orders are coming from higher up . . . "

"You mean the Grand Chancellor?"

"Basically. His office, anyway. It's very simple. The Commissioner has to accept that this is run by the GGC, or it's his job."

"Run by? I thought it was a joint investigation. I don't even like that, sir. They have almost no investigative experience. But are you saying this is actually run by the GGC?"

"We're only participating because they need our help to crack down on the circle of seditionists that Sekkes belongs to."

"But we don't even know if . . . "

"I know," the director said. "I know, Armo. But your job on this one is not to uncover the truth. This is not a normal seditionist investigation. This is a matter of making a big political point. It's about telling people, everyone, that you don't even think about disrupting the Grand Chancellor, ever."

"I see."

"So your job is to find seditionists, the more the better. You might want to make sure you can get a flight to Kaukano in the next couple of days."

Torndale nodded.

"I will do that, sir. But first . . . I have to attend the interrogation of Assemblywoman Sekkes. She should be out of surgery and waking up by this afternoon. I should probably get over to the hospital right away."

He got up and went to the door.

"She won't be at the hospital," Director Hemmig informed him.

Torndale was startled.

"What do you mean, sir? She just got out of surgery."

"The GGC is transferring her to an undisclosed location. They will give you the address if you call them."

"But she just underwent surgery!"

Director Hemmig looked at Torndale. It was a look that Torndale had not seen before. He realized what it meant.

"I'm sorry, sir," he said. "I apologize. I just . . . It's my experience that if you want to interrogate someone . . . and I have done a lot of that over the years . . ."

"Yes, I know. You are a good agent, Armo."

"Thank you, sir."

"I don't want to lose you," Director Hemmig said sternly.

There was no mistaking the tone in his voice.

"No, sir, of course not, sir," Torndale quickly replied. "I've just learned that . . . it is usually easier to get people to talk if they are comfortable in some way . . . like in a hospital bed instead of . . . a detention facility."

The director relaxed.

"I see," he said and nodded. "You are just being professional. I appreciate that. Unfortunately, this one is not in our hands. Give GGC a call and be on your way."

The address where Assemblywoman Sekkes was being held was not even a detention facility. It was an abandoned garage on the far south side of the city. The building did not have any distinctive markings on the outside that even hinted of the building belonging to the GGC. The only clue was one of their vehicles, parked on the street by a broken driveway.

As Armo Torndale pulled up he was approached by two heavily armed officers.

"This is GGC property, no outsiders allowed," said one of them.

He was barely old enough to be of legal adult age.

Torndale showed him his State Security ID.

"I'm investigating the case of Assemblywoman Sekkes," he said.

The young officer looked at his ID and shook his head.

"This is GGC property, no outsiders allowed," he repeated.

The other officer nodded.

"Move along," he added.

Torndale looked at them both for a moment. They tried to look authoritative, but did not do a very good job of it.

"Alright, guys," he said. "You know I am a group commander with State Security. I am going to walk into that building right now. If you shoot me, you will be committing a crime that falls under State Security jurisdiction. Do you guys know what we do to people who harm one of our agents?

Do you know anyone who has been picked up at two bells after midnight by one of our special operations teams?"

The two GGC officers lost some of their resolve.

"And do you know what we do to our detainees when we . . . want them to give us information? No? Well, I guarantee that you will both find that out pretty quickly."

The officers exchanged a look.

"Alright," said one of them.

Torndale didn't even look at them. He was getting pretty irritated as it was. He did not need a couple of young punks with uniforms and wet ears to get in his way.

He went straight up to the building and knocked on the first door he found.

Officer Ghehor opened.

"Welcome," he said. "I was just wondering . . . "

"Your two errand boys down there didn't want to let me in."

Officer Ghehor glanced at the two young officers.

"I will have a talk with them," he promised. "Come with me."

THE OLD REFUGEE CAMP SITE on the top of the mountain was partly covered by tree branches and other debris. It still offered some protection and there were still a couple of shelters that Armo Torndale, Naia, the military veteran and the fourth man in their group could use. They organized it so that they could rest while also keeping a watchful eye out for the soldiers.

They had done everything they could to make the forest as impenetrable as possible. They had put wires up between trees, hard enough that anyone who did not pay attention would trip on them. They had chopped down smaller trees, broken off branches and thrown them around as best they could. They had tossed garbage around in the hopes that some of the soldiers would step on it and make noise.

The veteran had suggested they fill whatever containers they had with whatever combustible liquids they had left. Those containers were placed out through the forest. Hopefully, when the soldiers came the refugees could fire a bullet into them, make them explode or at least catch fire.

"We can't stop the soldiers entirely," the veteran said. "But we can slow them down."

"We have one thing going for us," Torndale noted. "We have almost all ammunition left. We should be able to hold out for a while."

The camp site was located close to the edge of the mountain. When the soldiers moved in, they would only be able to mount an attack from two sides of the camp: northwest and east. If anyone of them tried to sneak around, they would be easily spotted and stopped.

It would still be a while before they attacked. The commando unit from the southern mountain first had to make it up the west side. But there was no doubt they would be there well before the sunset bell.

All they could do was wait.

❋ ❋ ❋

THE OLD GARAGE BUILDING was poorly lit. It still smelled of oil spill and tire rubber. Daylight seeped in through dirty windows far up on the tall walls.

In the middle of what once was the hall where mechanics worked on vehicles, stood a gurney. On it was Assemblywoman Sekkes, handcuffed to the railings on the side. She had been propped up by pillows to where her upper body was in a thirty degree angle to her legs. A couple of blankets covered her body up to her shoulders.

She looked barely conscious. The gurney was surrounded by half a dozen GGC officers, all of them as young as the ones Armo Torndale had encountered on his way in.

"There she is," said Officer Ghehor with a smile. "You are just in time for the interrogation to start."

Torndale swallowed hard. The poor woman on the gurney was weak, her face almost drained of life and her eyes looked hollow.

"Why couldn't you have done this at the hospital?" he whispered.

"This is more efficient," officer Ghehor replied. "All we need is some information. Then we can leave her to die."

So that was the plan. Raw and cynical, with not even a pretense of the rule of law.

Torndale approached her slowly. The young GGC officers backed off a little bit. Assemblywoman Sekkes turned and tried to focus on Armo Torndale.

"I am Commander Torndale of State Security," he introduced himself. She nodded.

"I saw you at the . . . " she whispered.

"We'd like some information from you," he said in as lenient a voice as he could without losing his authority.

"I want freedom for all Ripomans," she whispered.

Torndale took a step closer. He stood so close he could have reached out and touched her face.

"Who are your accomplices?" he asked matter-of-factly.

She shook her head.

"Just me," she said weakly.

Officer Ghehor came up on her other side.

"That is a lie," he said aggressively. "Come clean, and we will let you go back to the hospital. If you don't come clean, however, we will leave you here to die."

"Just me," she repeated.

Officer Ghehor slapped her over the face. Torndale looked at him with stunned eyes. Ghehor ignored him.

"Speak now!" Ghehor ordered her. "Name your accomplices!"

"I have no acc'lices," she whispered.

Ghehor raised his hand again. Torndale held up his.

"Just one moment," he said. "Assemblywoman Sekkes, as you can see, we have methods for finding things out. However, we don't want to have to leave you here to die. We just want some information. If you give us that information, we will take you back to the hospital and make sure you get all the treatment you need to live."

She shook her head.

"I'm alone . . . just me . . . please let me . . . go back . . . "

Ghehor grabbed her by the throat. He was just about to choke off her air supply when Torndale put his hand on his shoulder.

"Can I speak with you alone?"

Ghehor glanced at him, hesitated for a moment, then let go of the woman's throat.

"Very well," he said and walked over to a corner, far away enough that the assemblywoman could not hear them.

"Listen," Torndale said in a quiet voice but with a very firm tone. "I have been doing investigations of state security matters for thirty years. I have interrogated thousands of people. If you let me handle this, we can find out if she really has accomplices, or if she actually acted alone."

Ghehor looked at him with a cold, neutral face.

"If there is one thing I've learned," Torndale continued, "it's that the use of force often leads to false confessions, and false confessions, I can assure you, make investigations a lot more difficult. You end up chasing phantoms instead of actual enemies of the state."

Ghehor did not even flinch. He waited until Torndale was done, then glanced over at Assemblywoman Sekkes and looked at Torndale in the eyes again.

"She is under GGC jurisdiction," he said. "We will do this our way. We don't need her. She is expendable. But we are going to use her to set an example that others can learn from."

He turned to walk away, then stopped and looked at Torndale again.

"Fear is a powerful weapon," he said, as if talking to someone younger and less intelligent. "You guys at State Security should think about that. If it wasn't for your weakness, that woman over there would never have dared to do what she did in the first place."

He walked back to the gurney and signaled to the other officers to close in.

What followed was an episode of raw, unhinged, brutal savagery, one that Armo Torndale knew he would never forget for as long as he lived.

❊ ❊ ❊

They could hear the soldiers closing in. And see them. Although trained to move around without being noticed, the soldiers did not make much of an effort to conceal their advance. And why should they? There was no escape from the old camp site. There was no other way to go—except over the edge into the valley below.

The military veteran and the camp watchman had taken position to confront the soldiers who came up on the west side of the mountain. Armo Torndale and Naia hunkered down at the camp site where they had ammunition and weapons to keep fighting for a while.

Hopefully . . . hopefully long enough until the shuttlecraft returned.

There was gunfire exchange from the west side. One of the bottles they had placed out exploded. More gunfire. Then silence.

Eerie silence.

Torndale and Naia had crawled up to the edge of the camp site. They tried to see the soldiers. And their friends.

Nothing.

"Think our friends are still there?" Naia whispered.

"Probably," Torndale whispered back. "If not, the soldiers would be advancing."

He was right. Suddenly, another makeshift bomb exploded, more gunfire, someone shouting, a brief moment of silence and the one single shot.

Very soon, they could see the soldiers advancing from the west. Soon, they would reach the point where they were just north of the camp site.

The other commando unit also began moving forward. Slowly, cautiously and always with a maximum of cover.

Torndale fired off a couple of rounds in both directions. Naia did the same. The soldiers took cover. But they did not fire back.

More silence.

"This is unnerving," Naia whispered. "I'd prefer they tried to kill us."

"It's psychology. They are trying to wear us down so we will give up. Lower risk to them. They've lost a few men already. They don't want to lose more."

"You mean they want us to surrender?"

"Yes."

"I am not going to jail."

"They won't take us to jail. Once we surrender, we'll be executed."

They looked at one another. Torndale saw a bright flame of freedom in her eyes.

"Never," she whispered and took his hand. "They will never take us alive."

"Never," he promised.

THE FIRST SNOWFALL always made Armo Torndale excited. The old man he was, he still retained memories from the rare occasions during his childhood when he had seen snow. After he had served in the army and moved north, he could enjoy snowy winters every year.

He still got excited by the first snowfall.

But not this time.

The skies over Ocean Park were grey. The clouds shifted from pale to dark. The ocean reflected the same ominous colors. There was not much wind, only a faint, cold, humid breeze, but the temperatures were below freezing and the humidity bit him in the cheek. The trees had almost all lost their leaves, and the park workers were busy clearing the lawns of them. Torndale never understood why: the leaves were good fertilizers for the grass. But appearance was probably more important than functionality.

He walked slowly into the park.

Appearance was more important than functionality.

Torndale had not reported the brutal killing of Assemblywoman Sekkes. He had simply told Director Hemmig that he had attended the interrogation and gotten the information he expected.

"Then I left the interrogation room," he lied.

"Well, so long as we show some effort, it's all fine and good," the director had replied.

Then he had asked Torndale when he was flying out to Kaukano.

"I am planning on doing that tomorrow," Torndale had let him know.

He really had no interest in flying over to the far side of the country, especially not for a case over which he had no jurisdiction, or even influence. But the director wanted him to fly out there anyway.

"It's important we show some effort," he repeated.

Because if they did not show effort, the Commissioner of State Security would not look as strong and ruthless as the commander of the Guard of the Grand Chancellor.

Armo Torndale walked over some frozen water from last night's rainfall. It made that familiar cracking sound under his shoes. He glanced over at one of the tea houses and thought about how warm and refreshing it would be to have a cup of tea, but he also did not want to be among people right now.

He aimed for the outer section of the park. There were not many people in the park generally, but the outer section was almost always empty. He did not understand why—he loved the sound of the ocean waves out there on a windy day—but he was grateful that he could be guaranteed to be alone somewhere, without having to lock himself inside his apartment.

Last time he was out here, he had talked to his brother about his emerging feelings of doubt regarding his work. This time, there were no doubts anymore.

Armo Torndale was not an ideologue. He did not have any strong feelings for Grand Chancellor Sorto's value foundation, but his opposition to it was based mostly on practical experience. He could see that government was unable to keep its promises—rations of food and other necessities were slowly shrinking and the waiting times for health care were getting too long—but if there was a way to fix those problems, surely someone would do it, right?

Or maybe they were a systemic problem. Maybe the fact that government regulated everything, taxed everything and micro-managed almost everything . . . maybe that was actually the problem?

Either way, no problem could be fixed if people weren't allowed to speak up. If there was a better way to do things, then why not let the best argument win? Maybe, at the end of the day, government was right, but if so—why would government be afraid of criticism?

For some time, Torndale had not wanted to admit to himself what the answer was, but with the hypocrisy of the charges against Mrs. Veesaus, and certainly after the GGC's brutal killing of Assemblywoman Sekkes, he could not self-deny anymore.

Officer Ghehor's words . . .

"Fear is a powerful weapon"

. . . echoed in his head. The Sorto-led government was not driven by benevolence. If it were, Epai Sekkes would not have felt it necessary to sacrifice herself like she did, for the freedom of the spoken word. She knew that her career would be over. Maybe she thought she would just be sentenced and sent to a re-education camp, but given how tough those camps had become, it would still have shortened her life quite a bit.

"Dissent is not a crime," Armo Torndale said to himself as he walked along the railings by the waterfront. "Free the spoken word."

The water was almost still. The snowfall had tapered off, but the sky was covered with heavy clouds in the moodiest of winter colors. The trees out here on the edge of the park were wind-battered and a bit crooked.

He sat down on a bench and looked at nothing in particular. He was absolutely alone out here. All that reminded him of the city was its distant, muted noise.

"I can't do this anymore," he said to himself. "I can't."

He had once read a book by a political thinker, from back when the federal republic was founded. He could not remember the man's name off the top of his head, but he distinctly remembered how he defended that the constitution of the republic should protect the spoken word at any cost.

"Where words are banned . . . some day, people will be banned as well," Torndale remembered.

Assemblywoman Sekkes's words had already been banned. Now she had been banned as well. Banned from existence. Banned from life.

Torndale had to get out. But where would he go?

He started slowly walking back toward the center of the park. The wind had picked up a bit. Fortunately, it came from behind and did not really bother him. He looked around and still did not see anyone else.

An airplane flew over his head. It was a government plane, probably carrying supplies for government employees to some other province in the country.

"If only I could fly away. And take Naia with me . . . "

He smiled at the thought of her. She was such a unique person. He had no kids of his own. Was she like a daughter to him?

It didn't matter, really. He enjoyed her company. He liked her humor, and he really appreciated her wit, her thoughtfulness and her dynamic intellect.

"Fly away," he said again. "Kaukano . . . no, not far enough."

He saw the other tea house and once again was tempted by the warmth of fresh-brewed tea. But he had to get back to work, so the tea would have to wait.

The problem was that there was no other country to go to. Every one of the 63 nations in the world had one way or the other created the same type of government as the Ripomans had under Sorto.

"There is nowhere else to go," Torndale thought out loud. "Except . . . "

He stopped dead in his tracks. He stared at the horizon and the Coldrange Mountains. The airplane he had looked at continued to rise and disappeared into the clouds over the range.

"Nowhere else to go . . . " Armo Torndale said. "Except . . . Project Candor!"

❀ ❀ ❀

THE SUN ROSE TO MIDDAY over the mountain-top camp site. It traveled slowly over the sky as the bells went by.

Armo Torndale and Naia waited. So did the soldiers.

Naia brought them some food rations. They ate quietly, cautiously.

"What are they waiting for?" she asked.

"That we run out of stamina, so they can take us without gunfire. No more casualties on their end."

She nodded.

"That's right. You told me."

He looked at her.

"When was the last time you ate?"

"Don't remember."

"They are trained for this. They can go on for days on end, just sitting there."

"We don't have to wait days," Naia whispered. "Tomorrow morning . . . "

"Hopefully."

"You never told me how you came in contact with the Danori."

"I didn't?"

She looked at him.

"When was the last time you ate?"

He smiled.

"I don't remember."

"Was it through work?"

"What?"

"The Danori."

"Oh . . . Right. In the first year after Sorto became Grand Chancellor, I was on secondment to something called Project Candor. It was run by the military, but they were purging officers that refused to swear loyalty to Sorto. Many of them said that their loyalty was to the country, not its leader. So they were short on experienced people with a high-level security clearance. We were the only agency that also had a lot of people with high security clearance, so they brought in some of us to work on the project. I was one of them."

"What's Project Candor?"

"The biggest secret in government history."

He was interrupted by muted sounds from the forest to the east of the camp site. The soldiers had started advancing again. And they did not do it clandestinely.

Torndale raised his rifle.

"Mr. Torndale!" a voice cried out. "Mr. Torndale! We know you are there! Can you hear me?"

Torndale looked at Naia. She looked worried, but she nodded.

"Yes, I'm here!" Torndale shouted back.

"Lay down your weapons! You are outnumbered! There is no point in fighting!"

"Why? Are you afraid of us?"

A brief pause. Naia thought she heard laughter from the forest.

"If you lay down your weapons," the soldier shouted, "no one more will be killed!"

"Except Naia and me!" Torndale shouted back. "You will execute us!"

Brief pause again, but no laughter.

Naia nodded.

"You were right," she whispered.

"Mr. Torndale! We have your brother! And his whole family! And we have Ms. Fernek's mother! If both of you give yourself up they won't be sent to camps!"

Naia stared at Torndale. She started breathing fast, trying strenuously to control her anger. He put his hand on her shoulder.

"They will go to camp anyway," he whispered. "At this point . . . we've lost them . . . "

"I know," Naia said and fought to hold back her tears. "I just . . . "

"Wait," he whispered to her and shouted to the soldiers: "A government that takes hostage! Is that a government you want to serve?!"

"Give up, or they go to camps!" the soldier shouted back.

Torndale looked at Naia. She wiped the tears from her eyes.

"This is it," he said.

She nodded.

"I'm ready," she said.

"Me, too."

They looked at one another. They smiled. He kissed her on the forehead.

"I'm so proud of you," he said.

"I love you," she whispered back.

He glanced over at the soldiers.

"Let's fight one last fight."

"Alright."

"Remember that poem?" he asked.

"What poem?"

"Freedom is your birthright . . . "

She smiled.

"You read it to me the night we decided to leave State Security."

"Let's recite it . . . as we go . . . "

She grabbed her rifle. He grabbed his.

"Freedom is your birthright . . . "

They slowly rose from the campground.

" . . . freedom is your quest . . . "

They approached the edge and the rock they had called the podium.

" . . . under the skies of freedom . . . "

They aimed their rifles at the forest where the soldiers were.

" . . . all of us shall rest . . . "

They opened fire.

❈ ❈ ❈

HE TOOK THE BULLETS. He struggled, staggered, tried to protect her.

He knew she did not want him to protect her. It was just his instinct.

Another bullet hit him in the chest. He fell, face down.

She threw herself down with him. She did not want to . . . it was just her instinct. As if she knew.

She kneeled, put her hand on his body.

Her heart broke.

"Goodbye my hero" she cried. "Thank you. I love you forever."

She could hear the soldiers closing in. There was nowhere else to go now. Nowhere else to turn. This was it.

She closed her eyes for a second, but the tears kept pouring down her cheeks. Her heart pounding, she jumped up, raised her rifle.

As the bullets hit her, she stumbled and fell to her knees. She was not sure where she was hit, but she knew the end was near.

She laid down next to him, reached for his hand.

She found it, held it. As the light of eternity unfolded its umbrella over her, she whispered:

"Under the skies of freedom . . . all of us shall rest . . . "

www.ingramcontent.com/pod-product-compliance
Lightning Source LLC
Chambersburg PA
CBHW050403030726
47503CB00006B/1992